White House Usher

"Who Killed the President?"

Christopher Beauregard Emery

BookLocker

Saint Petersburg, Florida

Print ISBN: 978-1-64719-761-2
Ebook ISBN: 978-1-64719-762-9

Christopher Beauregard Emery
Manns Choice, PA
WhiteHouseUsher@gmail.com
www.WhiteHouseUsher.com

Ordering Information:
Quantity sales: Special discounts are available on quantity purchases by corporations, associations, and others. For details, contact the publisher at the address above.

Orders by US trade bookstores and wholesalers. Please visit:
www.WhiteHouseUsher.com.

Printed on acid-free paper.

Publisher's Cataloging-in-Publication data
Emery, Christopher Beauregard
White House Usher: "Who Killed the President?"/Christopher Beauregard Emery
p. cm.
1. The main category of the book—Fiction F0000.A0 A00 2010
299.000 00–dc22 2010999999
Library of Congress Control Number: 2021915141

First Edition

Dedicated to:

Katie
Waverly
Parker

And

Isabelle

Acknowledgments

This is my second book and my first work of fiction. My efforts could never have been possible without my partner, Isabelle, who provided constant interest, encouragement, and enthusiastic support. I am forever grateful for the inspiration she provides.

There are not enough words to sufficiently recognize the efforts of my sister Ariane Emery and her husband, Steve Moorhouse. They spent endless hours reviewing my writing, discussing it, and offering their help on everything from Russian weaponry to the cause and effects of various medication interactions, etc. This dynamic duo was beyond fabulous. If there are any successes to be realized from this effort, I owe it to them.

I also wish to extend my gratitude to:

Dr. Alexandra Goldman, MD, for her subject matter expertise, but more importantly, for being my fabulous niece and always supportive of my efforts!

Scott Saras, Secret Service (retired). Scott is a great guy and one of my former motorcycle riding buds. He offered helpful subject matter expertise on specifics regarding law enforcement processes and procedures.

Scott Jessee, FBI senior executive (retired). A brilliant man with great knowledge and experience who, among the many other things I have learned of, is a constitutional scholar. His advice on the FBI and the warrant process, etc., were invaluable.

David Aretha and Andrea VanRyken provided phenomenal editing; they were really great to work with.

Angela Hoy, my publisher at Booklocker; simply put, she continues to be beyond stellar!

Thank you to Victor Marcos, my Manila-based graphic designer, for his superb book cover.

Some of the members of my first book's Sanity-Checkers—the team that provided endless support and have helped me multiple times—as well as the following individuals: Christina Beltramini, Brent Brookhart, Chris Fahey, Edwin Huizinga, Ian Komorowski, Suzanne Cheavens, Philippe Hauswald, Johann Hauswald, Sogoal Salari Hauswald, Brian Lisle, Scott Paton, Al Salas, and Tam Stephanadis. All these wonderful individuals offered friendship, advice, encouragement, and discussion whenever needed.

And finally, I dedicate this book to the individuals who inspire me endlessly: my daughter, Katie, and my grandchildren, Waverly and Parker. This book is for you and the future generations who follow.

White House Usher
"Who Killed the President?"
By
Christopher Beauregard Emery

Introduction

Author Christopher Beauregard Emery published his first book, *White House Usher: Stories from the Inside*, in 2017, a memoir detailing his time managing the White House for Presidents Ronald Reagan, George H. W. Bush, and Bill Clinton.

This book, a mystery novel, takes place in one of the more unique settings in existence: the White House executive residence, home of the first family. Murder, romance, deceit, and a suspenseful struggle all ensue as the main character struggles to solve the case. Emery uses his in-depth knowledge of White House history and the inner workings of the private residence to create a thrilling murder mystery from an insider's perspective.

Plot

The world is rocked by the sudden death of the president of the United States. Almost as shocking, details soon emerge implicating a member of the White

House Ushers Office. The evidence seems overwhelming, and the case is soon considered as open and shut. If only the rest of the world knew how much more was going on behind the scenes. Read how Chief Usher Bartholomew Winston, a fifty-year veteran of the White House, works with investigators to uncover the truth, even if that means diving headfirst into dangerous political waters to find it.

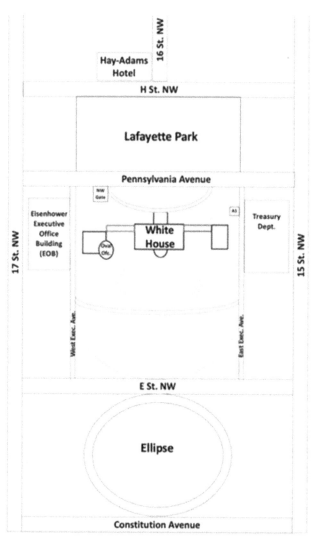

White House complex and surrounding area

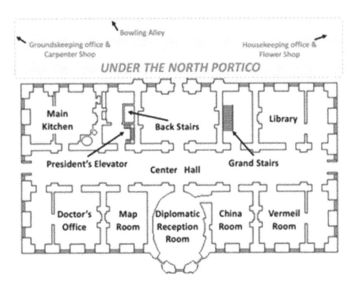

White House: GROUND FLOOR

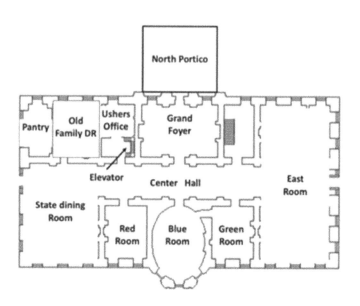

White House: STATE FLOOR

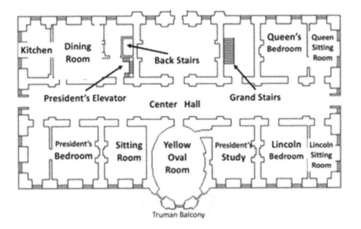

White House: PRIVATE RESIDENCE

Chapter 1
Washington, DC

Two years into the current administration

5 a.m., Monday, March 2: The White House

White House Chief Usher Bartholomew Winston sat alone in the ushers office just off the state floor. He was absolutely numb, mind empty as if caught in a trance. On his lap sat the latest edition of *The Washington Post*, front page screaming out the headline: .

"PRESIDENT BLAKE DIES
WHITE HOUSE ASSISTANT USHER IN CUSTODY"

On the office TV, CNN's nonstop *Breaking News* segment repeated ad nauseam that President Blake had been reported "dead on arrival" at George Washington Hospital at 8:19 p.m. yesterday.

The chief usher's eyes moved just barely across the broad, ornately decorated room, settling on the balding seasoned anchor, every blemish of his face shown in vivid detail thanks to the merciless definition offered by the screen mounted on the beige-colored wall. The man's lips seemed to move almost faster than the words that flew out of his mouth and filled the room:

"Cause of death has not been officially released, although an unnamed White House source is saying the president died suddenly after dinner. Earlier this morning, President Blake's body was taken from George Washington Hospital to Walter Reed National Military Medical Center in Bethesda for autopsy, and we are expecting the official cause of death to be released shortly.

"Meanwhile, we have received confirmation that the first lady, who was in China, is en route back to Washington on a military aircraft. Vice President Elizabeth Gentry was sworn in as the nation's forty-sixth president shortly after 9 p.m. yesterday. She becomes the first woman president and the youngest to have ever served. CNN can now report that there is a person of interest in custody, an assistant usher named Brenton Augustus Williams. He was taken into custody yesterday afternoon from the White House and is now being questioned by the FBI at a secure location."

The ushers office, hidden behind its double mahogany doors just off the northwest corner of the grand foyer on the state floor, had been the management office for all White House serving presidents for the past one hundred and seventy years.

This early in the morning, with its chandeliers and wall sconces at their lowest setting, the White House appeared cavernous, a maze of long shadows and dark corners. Inside the ushers office, the only light came from the dim chandelier hanging from the center of the thirteen-foot ceiling. The small lamps atop the two desks were off; the only other light came from the wall-mounted television. The staff would start to arrive within the hour.

Bartholomew Winston remained seated, his posture perfect, his dark eyes glazed over, no longer watching but continuing to listen to the TV. He was a man quite dignified in style and appearance, tall and thin, with an uncanny resemblance to actor Morgan Freeman. Winston, as everyone called him, wore a perfectly tailored, medium-gray Armani suit, a starched white shirt, a light blue Hermes tie, presidential cufflinks, light gray socks that perfectly matched the color of his suit, and black wingtips. He conveyed class and sophistication and exuded confidence. But right at that moment, he was in shock. Footsteps thumped up the back stairs, and he was suddenly aware that others were present. He turned toward the sound and watched as four men walked into his office.

One of the four stepped forward, a tall black man with a grim look on his face. He removed the badge from his jacket and flashed it before stating in a monotone voice, "Mr. Winston, we're from the FBI. I'm Agent Clayton, the lead for the investigation. We would like you to come with us for questioning."

Bartholomew Winston placed the newspaper on the desk and slowly stood while explaining to the gentlemen that he had already answered questions for several hours late last night and into the morning. The FBI men did not appear to have much patience, nor did they seem to feel any need to explain themselves. They insisted that he follow them, so down the back stairs they went.

Chapter 2
5:10 a.m., Monday, March 2: The White House Map Room

The White House map room on the ground floor of the executive mansion had been President Roosevelt's Situation Room during World War II; it was there that the D-Day invasion was planned and monitored. These days, the room remained secure, rarely visible to the public, often used for private meetings, it was appropriately furnished in the style of English cabinetmaker Thomas Chippendale—though rather sparsely so, facilitating easy conversion when setting up the room as a studio for television interviews and tapings.

The FBI led the chief usher into the room, where several other agents were already waiting. It was still dark outside, so the two south-facing windows did not offer any light, and the antique lamps and ceiling light were not particularly bright. A dozen chairs had been arranged behind a row of folding tables that sat over the large, antique Persian Farahan rug. Agent Clayton, the senior-most agent, motioned for Bartholomew Winston to have a seat at the single lone chair facing the agents ten feet away. Winston was impressed that they had bothered to include a tray table with a glass and pitcher of water next to his chair. Off to his right, a lone video camera on a tripod was being operated by a short, stout female agent. Along the north wall of the room, a temporary table had been set up, where four staff members sat with various laptops and electronic equipment.

Ten FBI agents took their seats facing him. Agent Clayton, seated in the middle, nodded to the camera operator, and a red light at the top of the camera illuminated, indicating the recording had begun. Clayton then started the session.

"Mr. Winston, allow me to start by stating the obvious. We are dealing with traumatic events of historic proportion and need your help. My sincere apologies for our abruptness moments ago when we barged into your office. We're all under tremendous pressure. The bureau thanks you for being here. Please know your outstanding reputation, excellent judgment, and well-documented, exemplary job performance are not in question here. You have served many presidents during a distinguished career that has been noted favorably by world leaders, historians, and scholars.

"I wish we were meeting under different circumstances, but I must now get to the matter at hand. We have a series of questions, and I cannot emphasize enough that this is a matter of national security and utmost urgency. Given these current events, you are not entitled nor are you permitted to have legal counsel. Also, for the record, this session is being recorded for use of the Federal Bureau of Investigation and the ODNI [Office of the Director of National Intelligence]."

Winston acknowledged all this with a nod as he crossed his legs.

"This will be sworn testimony, Mr. Winston," said Clayton. "Please raise your right hand. Do you, Bartholomew Winston, solemnly affirm that the evidence that you are about to give shall be the truth, the whole truth, and nothing but the truth?"

Winston, speaking with a hint of a Southern drawl, responded: "I do."

"Thank you, Mr. Winston. Members of my team will now ask you a series of questions for the record."

Agent 1, a fit older man looking like an agent from the 1960s with his graying military haircut, dark suit, and dark, thin tie, leaned forward in his chair, elbows on the table, looking down at his legal pad: "Mr. Winston, please state your full name, age, date of birth, and job title."

"Bartholomew Roosevelt Winston, White House chief usher. Oh, and I was born August 1st, 1945. I am seventy-five."

Agent 1: "Place of birth?"

"Salisbury, North Carolina."

Agent 1: "What is your current address?"

"12301 Imperial Drive, Bethesda, Maryland."

Agent 1: "How long have you lived at Imperial Drive?"

"Forty-two years." Winston's anxiety increased as he dreaded with anticipation the next questions, which he knew would be about his wife, who had died in a tragic accident.

Agent 1: "Are you married, Mr. Winston?"

"I'm widowed. My wife passed away eighteen months ago. We had been married for forty-six years." It was still so painful for Winston to admit that his life's soulmate was no longer.

Agent 1: "We're sorry for your loss, Mr. Winston." Winston nodded slowly in acknowledgment. "What was your wife's name?"

"Connie."

Agent 1: "Any children?"

"I have a forty-year-old son, Bartholomew Roosevelt Winston, Jr. He's a cardiologist in San Diego."

Agent 1: "Are the two of you close?"

"Very. We talk often. Since his mother passed, I'd say we're in contact via text or phone daily."

Agent 1: "Grandchildren?"

Winston smiled. "Not yet. And I ask him about it daily!"

Several of the agents smiled.

Agent 2, a young African American man in a gray suit and dark red tie: "How long have you worked in the White House?"

"Fifty years."

Agent 2: "Mr. Winston, did you attend college?"

"Yes. Winston-Salem State College, and I graduated in 1966 with a bachelor's of arts degree in history."

Agent 2: "Are you a military veteran, Mr. Winston?"

"Yes, I was in the Marine Corps from 1966 to 1970. I served two tours in Vietnam and retired with the rank of captain."

"Did you receive any awards for your service?"

"Silver Star, Bronze Star, Purple Heart, Combat Action Ribbon, and the Presidential Service Badge."

Agent 2: "Tell us how you got to the White House."

"After Vietnam, I became a military aide for then-President Nixon. This was a temporary post, and not long thereafter, with the war effort starting to draw down, I retired from the Marine Corps. At that time, President Nixon arranged for me to become a member of the White House ushers office."

Agent 1: "Please describe for us the history, purpose, and function of the ushers office."

Winston began with the description he had used to answer variations of that question a thousand times:

"For more than two hundred years, a small office has operated on the state floor of the White House executive residence. Since the 1850s, it has been known as the ushers office and has functioned very much the same as it has for its entire history. Our job primarily is to accommodate the personal needs of the first family and make the White House feel like a home rather than a museum or office."

The agents were all taking notes, and Winston could hear the other staff from the rear table as they typed on their laptops.

"We develop and administer the annual budget for the executive residence to cover our operation, maintenance, and utilities. We provide the oversight and management for the eighty-nine staff members who work here, and we also take care of the surrounding eighteen acres of grounds."

Winston looked back and forth at the entire row of agents. A few were taking notes, one was looking at his iPhone, and the rest were staring back at him. "We work very closely with the first family, senior staff, social office, press office, Secret Service, and military to carry out all White House functions, which include luncheons, dinners, teas, receptions, meetings, conferences, and more. We maintain the entire 132-room mansion, and of course, help preserve the fine arts collection. By the way, the White House became an accredited museum in 1961. We take care of setting up the house for the 1.2 million tourists who come through the White House each year."

Winston paused and quickly removed a handkerchief from his left suit pocket just in time to sneeze into it. He apologized, blaming it on dust, then folded the handkerchief and placed it back into his pocket. He continued, "We also field a variety of mail inquiries ranging from White House history and the fine arts collection to job opportunities. We are on hand for the arrival and departure of all first family members and guests. The assistant ushers and I have more access to the president than most members of the president's family and are responsible for taking care of the first family's most secluded area—their home. Because the first family's privacy is paramount, it is by design that little is known about the office or the ushers who work here."

Agent 1: "Describe the organizational structure of the office."

"Absolutely. There is one chief usher and three assistant ushers who manage the ninety or so staff members, who consist of butlers, carpenters, grounds personnel, electricians, painters, plumbers, florists, maids, housemen, cooks, chefs, storekeepers, curators, calligraphers, doormen, and administrative support."

Agent 1: "Are you appointed by the president?"

"The executive residence staff are a special type of presidential appointment: Schedule A, meaning we serve at the pleasure of the president, and typically, the staff serve for a lifetime."

Agent 2: "You say, typically. Have there been exceptions?"

Winston: "Yes. In 1887, President Cleveland fired some of the staff, and in the mid-1990s, Mrs. Clinton fired one of the ushers, but other than that, you'll find the executive residence staff remain until they either retire or die."

Agent Clayton then nodded to a petite Asian female agent with chin-length, dark hair who was sitting at the far end of the row. She quickly glanced down at her paperwork that lay on the gray table in front of her, then looked up to meet Winston's gaze. She raised her chin a bit, cleared her throat, and was ready to take over her portion of the interrogation. She would be the third agent under Clayton's watch to speak. Winston, not knowing her name, thought of her simply as Agent 3. "Thank you, Mr. Winston. Very helpful information. We are now going to focus on the events of yesterday, Sunday evening, March 1st. Let's start by having you describe to us in full detail your whereabouts and knowledge specific to when you learned about the circumstances involving President Blake."

"I was in the ushers office when we heard all sorts of commotion. Someone was running down the back stairs from the second floor of the private residence, and they were yelling."

Agent 3: "What time was this?"

"It was just before 8:00 p.m."

Agent 3: "Was there anyone else in the ushers office?"

"Yes, Assistant Usher Brent Williams was seated at his desk, and Secret Service Agent Greg Leidner was standing in the doorway.

13

Agent 3: "What happened next?"

"Our conversation stopped because we heard the yelling. It was Sous Patrick Chef Sullivan. He was running down the back stairs yelling the president had collapsed. Patrick was out of control with grief as he entered the office. The Secret Service agent who had been on post in the stairwell adjacent to the private quarters must have radioed for backup because suddenly several agents ran up the back stairs. I grabbed the chef's arm and told him to come with me. We followed the agents up the steps, although we weren't as fast."

The grief was beginning to show on Winston's face. He paused to gather himself and fought to focus on hiding his emotions. He took a deep breath and continued. "When we got to the second floor, we walked into the west sitting hall and followed all the noise coming from the family dining room. When we entered, I saw President Blake sprawled out on the floor with several agents attempting to administer CPR."

Agent 3: "Who else was in the room?"

"Chef Sullivan and the two butlers that were on duty. And I should mention, one of the butlers was kneeling next to the president assisting with CPR."

Agent 3: "Where was Assistant Usher Brenton Williams during all this?"

Winston paused and thought for a few seconds, then responded, "He wasn't there. He must have remained in the office." Winston, with a steady hand, poured a glass of water from the pitcher that was next to him and took a drink.

Agent 3: "Please continue."

"It was mass bedlam. Everyone was frantic and yelling. I saw Chef Sullivan standing in the far corner sobbing. Suddenly, staff from the White House medical unit rushed in with two nurses and a physician's assistant. They brought a stretcher and resuscitation equipment and immediately took over the CPR activities. It all seemed so futile because there was absolutely no response from the president. I kept thinking; this can't be happening. President Blake was such a vibrant man. And poor Mrs. Blake—this is going to be a terrible a shock."

Winston again paused and took a sip of water to steady himself. Agent Clayton unconsciously drummed his fingers on the table, looked at his watch, and observed Winston drink. He pressed his thin lips together, and with his impatience quickly mounting he reminded everyone of the criticality of the interview and encouraged Winston to continue.

Winston went on. "The medical unit continued with their attempts, and moments later, the president's physician, Dr. Jenkins, came running into the room, followed by the chief of staff. By then, the president had been placed on the stretcher. Dr. Jenkins frantically searched for a pulse, then yelled that they needed to get the president to the hospital. I held the elevator doors as they boarded. Dr. Jenkins barked out orders, telling others to take the stairs and not crowd the elevator. When we got to the ground floor, the stretcher was quickly wheeled out to the south portico, where an ambulance was waiting. The Secret Service loaded the president into the ambulance, and Dr. Jenkins jumped in, followed by two agents. Everyone else rushed to the other vehicles, and a small motorcade, a lead sedan, the ambulance, and a follow-up SUV sped out the southwest gate toward the hospital."

Agent 3: "What did you do then?"

"I headed back to the ushers office. I encountered several White House residence staff in the hallway. They all wanted to know what was happening, and so I simply told them the president is on his way to the hospital and we'd know more soon. I then walked back to the ushers office and encountered Vice President Gentry with several of her staff. They were all pressing me for details.

"I think every phone line in the ushers office was lit up, some in use by the VP and her staff, and others flooded by incoming calls. I wondered why my assistant Brent was not there. I needed his help! I stepped into the hallway, pulled out my cell phone, and saw that Brent had tried to call me several times. I immediately tried calling him back but could not get a signal. I then ran up to my private office on the mezzanine level directly above the ushers office so that I could use a landline. But I could not get a dial tone. I went back down to the ushers office just as the VP and her staff were hurriedly leaving.

"On the office TV, CNN was breaking the news about the president being rushed to the hospital. All the phone lines in the ushers office kept blinking with incoming calls. I started picking up calls from the press and staff. I took a call from the Secret Service that I could not comprehend. It just didn't make any sense. They told me that my assistant Brent Williams was being detained at the east gate because he had concealed a controlled substance."

Agent 3: "Mr. Winston, do you now know the specifics on why Brent Williams was detained?"

"I only know what the Secret Service told me and what I saw this morning on CNN."

Agent Clayton rejoined the conversation. "Mr. Winston, let me remind you—and also to ensure that it is part of the record—you, all the ushers, and everyone in this room have a top-secret clearance, known as 'Yankee White.' This designation is among the highest in existence. I am herby reading you into Special Compartmentalized Information, which is United

States classified information concerning or derived from sensitive intelligence sources, methods, and/or analytical processes. Do you understand?"

Winston with a raised eyebrow, "Uh, of course. Please go on."

Agent Clayton handed a document to one of the staffers, who then handed it to Winston. "I need you to sign this nondisclosure agreement. This is to officially 'read you in' to the material you are about to have access to. This document will be recorded in our official access register. Once it is determined that you no longer require clearance for this information, we will terminate your access, and you will sign a second disclosure document. Do you have any questions?"

Winston shook his head and signed the document.

"For the record, Mr. Winston did not have any questions and has signed the NDA," declared Clayton.

Agent 4, an overweight, middle-aged man wearing a brown suit: "As soon as the president became incapacitated, the director of the Secret Service invoked Emergency Directive 501, the lockdown procedures for the White House complex. This to prevent anyone from leaving. Assistant Usher Brenton Williams was stopped after exiting Post A1, the east entrance gate to the White House, at approximately 8:07 p.m. Assistant Usher Williams consented to a search, which revealed he had in his possession two vials of a substance. Tests have since revealed that Brenton Williams was concealing botulinum toxin, which in microscopic amounts can cause paralysis and immediate death through respiratory failure. Furthermore, and let me emphasize this information is strictly confidential and will not be released to the press, initial toxin reports from George Washington Hospital, and now just confirmed by Walter Reed Medical Center, indicate President Blake died from ingesting botulinum type H. The FBI has since received intelligence that your assistant usher had searched the dark web in order to obtain botulinum toxin. Mr. Winston, Brenton Williams is being held as not only a person of interest but as the prime suspect in the murder of the president."

Bartholomew Winston was speechless; he could not move.

Chapter 3
7:00 a.m., Monday, March 2: The White House, Second Floor, Private Residence

Winston escorted the FBI, Secret Service, and DC Metropolitan Police detectives to the second floor. Now that the Secret Service had the preliminary toxicology reports, they had officially designated the second-floor private residence of the White House a crime scene.

The chief of the Secret Service presidential protection detail pulled Winston aside. "Winston, it's going to be a bit chaotic up here for the next several hours. We will have a lot of personnel coming and going."

Winston had known Chief Dan Livingston for years. "Dan, the first lady is due back at 11 a.m. I will need everyone off the floor and everything back to the way it was. I know that is a challenge. I really appreciate your help."

"Agreed," said Dan. "And I just checked. She is now due back at 11:15. Our goal is to be done in less than four hours. And by the way, we're going to need to interview everyone that was on duty yesterday, so please provide me with a list of all staff and ensure they are available this morning."

"Of course. I'll have the list for you in fifteen minutes."

"Thank you."

Winston stood just outside of the doorway to the family dining room and observed the coordinated activities. Two men were taking photos from every possible angle of the family kitchen, dining room, and west sitting hall. Another man was videotaping all the activities, and a fourth man used a hand-held laser device to take measurements and plot the floorplan.

The area in immediate proximity to where the president had been seated and the location of where he had been on the floor were now cordoned off with yellow police tape. Inside this isolated section, three men wearing sterile white jumpsuits, gloves, goggles/face masks, hairnets, and booties were delicately using brushes, tweezers, and other small tools to gather fibers and collect various microscopic materials. The president's dinner dishes were still in place, as was the small table next to his seat, which contained the leather pouch he used for his insulin. The general public was not aware that President Blake was a type 1 diabetic and self-administered his insulin injections each morning and at dinnertime each evening.

Chapter 4
7 a.m., Monday, March 2: Interrogation Facility, Undisclosed Location

White House Assistant Usher Brent Williams sat in the dark on a cold, concrete floor. He was completely nude and had no concept of time or the duration of his stay in that room; it was so dark, he wondered if he had gone blind.

A competitive distance runner, at five-foot-eleven and 155 pounds he was always an example of good health, Brent was a good-looking man with a youthful face. He now felt weak and out of shape. His body ached and he could not get warm. He wondered what became of his eyeglasses. At some point earlier, he had spent what seemed like endless hours under very harsh florescent lights answering the questions of people he could not see. He had no idea what botulinum was or why they kept asking him about it. Yes, he was well aware that the president had gone to the hospital, but what did that have to do with him? Brent had many friends in the administration and even more in the Secret Service. He thought it could not be too much longer before someone cleared him from this nightmare.

Suddenly, the bright lights came back on. Brent quickly looked around, his pale blue eyes squinting as he was having difficulty adjusting to the light. The room was maybe ten feet by ten feet square. The concrete block walls were unpainted, the floor gritty and bare. He could not see the ceiling, as the lights were so bright it hurt to look up. He faced a wall with a large mirror—probably one-way glass, he thought—where there must have been people on the other side watching him.

A voice from above began asking him new questions and repeating the old ones: "Why were you trying to leave the White House? Why did you go on to the dark web to seek deadly toxins? Did you have an accomplice in the attack of the president? How long had you planned the assassination of the president? Your stepfather was from Pakistan. We know you went to Pakistan twelve years ago. What was the purpose of your trip? Were you secretly converted to Islam? Are you an extremist?"

Brent stared straight ahead and protested, saying he'd already answered all their questions. He then thought of a way to show his cooperation, so he offered his iPhone, Mac Pro, and iCloud passwords, but the interrogators responded that they already had them. Their questioning continued.

Interrogator: "Tell us again why you were trying to leave the White House?"

Brent shifted his position. He felt humiliated as he tried his best to conceal his privates. He looked toward the mirror and said, "Could I please have a blanket, a robe, clothes…*or anything*?"

Interrogator: "*Just answer the question!*"

"As I have told you, I was in the ushers office about to go up to the private quarters to see how I could be of help. The phone rang. It was the president's physician, Dr. Jenkins. He told me he had received an emergency call from the White House admin operator, and he asked me how bad was it. I told him all I knew was that the president had collapsed and that Winston and others were upstairs. Dr. Jenkins told me he was driving from the Dubliner near Union Station and would arrive on the east side of the White House complex and would park on East Executive Avenue. The doctor was very specific, shouting, '*I don't want the press to see me enter the White House!*' and he asked me to meet him at A1, the east appointments gate, so that I could take him directly inside the White House via the east wing service tunnel, where he would not be seen."

Interrogator: "Who knew you were meeting the president's physician?"

Brent thought for a second. "Uh, I don't know. Oh, wait—Wendy Wolf."

Interrogator: "Who is Wendy?"

"Wendy Wolf, the vice president's chief of staff. She's always with the VP."

Interrogator: "You stated in an earlier interview that the vice president was in the ushers office?"

Before he could respond, Brent could hear the interrogators mumble amongst themselves, wondering in hushed voices whether to refer to Gentry as the vice president or president.

"Has the president died?" exclaimed Brent as he began to realize the enormity of the situation.

Interrogator: "*We'll ask the questions*! Was Elizabeth Gentry in your office?"

"Uh, yeah. She was there with several of her staff. She—no, Wendy—told me that I needed to go to A1. I'm not sure why she suggested it. I don't believe she had talked to the president's physician."

Interrogator: "So, what did you do next?"

"I took off running out of the office and across the grand foyer, then I flew down the grand stairs and through the east wing colonnade. I passed by a couple of Secret Service uniform officers. I could hear over their radios that an ambulance was being maneuvered into place outside of the south portico. I dashed out the doors to exit the east wing and covered the remaining fifty yards to make it to A1."

Interrogator: "What happened once you got to A1?"

"I walked into the guard house and said hello. I knew all the Secret Service officers except for one, a captain that I did not recognize. All the officers looked very tense. They were facing the captain, who was telling them something about a directive locking down the White House. I quickly tapped my ID card onto the reader so I could exit. The door unlocked, and I immediately walked out and onto East Exec to await Dr. Jenkins. Before I knew it, I was surrounded by several Secret Service counterassault team members. They were pointing their guns at me! I know all these guys. I'm looking at them, and I say, 'What the hell?!' The CAT sergeant yelled, '*Brent! Raise your hands and do not move!*' Next thing I knew, I was on the ground, and they were tying nylon cable-ties around my wrists. Everything happened in a flash." Brent blinked hard and shook his head. "I was totally bewildered!"

Interrogator: "Were you not aware of the Secret Service Directive 502 lockdown policy?"

"What? No. Well, I may have been aware of it, but I have never experienced anything like this. How or why would I know about that?"

Interrogator: "Did the Secret Service ask if they could search you?"

"I don't remember them asking, but I would never have any issue with that."

Interrogator: "Mr. Williams, the search revealed that in your suit jacket, you had two small vials of a controlled substance. How do you explain that?"

Brent, now beyond exasperated, exhaled and replied, "Just like I answered when you first brought me here, I have no clue. I saw them hold up something, and then I watched the captain place it into a zip-lock bag and rush off. Whatever it was, it wasn't mine! This is all so beyond insane! I don't do drugs! I have a clearance! I'm drug-tested! Look up my record. See my reports!"

The lights went out as suddenly as they had come on. All was quiet, and Brent shivered.

Chapter 5
8 a.m., Monday, March 2: The White House

Winston sat gathering his thoughts in his private office, which was on the mezzanine level directly above the main ushers office. He needed to talk to his assistant ushers. With Brent gone, the burden would fall to his remaining two assistants, Loretta and Jim. Winston got up, trotted down the stairs, and then walked into the ushers office, where Loretta sat at her desk watching the TV.

The ushers office was a small room just off the state floor. The room had been designated as the stewards lodge in the first White House floors plans of 1792. It officially became known as the ushers office in the 1850s during the Franklin Pierce administration. The office décor at present was of the Victorian era and housed two wooden desks with chairs and two guest chairs. Various historic artwork hung on the walls. The room had a large window bordered by heavy gold-colored curtains with dark-red sashes. The view out the window was magnificent, overlooking the north grounds, Pennsylvania Avenue, and in the distance, Lafayette Park. When facing the White House from Lafayette Park, the ushers office window was the first to the right of the north portico.

The ushers office's wall-mounted television was as Winston had left it two hours earlier, tuned to CNN's nonstop *Breaking News* segment.

Loretta was focused on the television and looked startled as Winston walked in. She turned and gave Winston her undivided attention.

"Loretta, please schedule a staff meeting for 9 a.m. Make sure everyone knows attendance is mandatory. And we need to get Jim on the phone so the three of us can caucus."

Loretta said in a voice barely above a whisper, "Winston, I…I just don't know what to say."

"I'm not sure either. For now, let's get this meeting scheduled. The first lady is due back at 11:15, and I will need to spend time with her."

Loretta swiveled her chair back toward her computer and began typing an email to all staff.

Over the past twenty-four years, Winston had relied on Loretta for some of his more delicate and critical tasks. Loretta Fitzgerald was forty-seven, never married, attractive, thin, and of medium height. Her dark hair was always pulled back into a tight chignon. Combine all that with her dark-framed reading glasses that were perpetually halfway down her nose, and she looked like a librarian. Made sense since she had graduated cum laude from Vassar with a degree in library sciences. Loretta handled more of Winston's administrative duties, such as dealing with payroll and human resources, than the other two assistants. She worked White House events and other activities, as all ushers do, but being highly cerebral and very focused, she had provided outstanding work in support of the curatorial duties required by the ushers office to maintain the White House museum accreditations.

Winston's other assistant, Jim Allen, had been an usher for the past seventeen years, and prior to joining the ushers office, had been a member of the Secret Service. Jim was forty-three and married with no children. Tall, distinguished, and very charismatic, he garnered a lot of attention from many of the single women in the west wing, but he played it off well and remained steadfastly loyal to his wife. Jim had such a positive and endearing demeanor, the staff and first families loved him. There was no one who knew the history of the White House better than Jim. His in-depth knowledge of White House furnishings, artwork, and even the rugs and drapes was tapped often. Winston relied on Jim for the more public types of tasks such as providing guided tours to special groups. First families often requested that Jim attend their parties so that he could share his great stories of the White House.

"Okay, I've got Jim on speaker," Loretta announced.

Winston slid his chair to be closer to the speakerphone and was now close to Loretta. "Jim, I almost started to say good morning, but perhaps I should just leave it at 'morning.'

"I'm in total agreement with your sentiments," Jim said in an uncharacteristic somber tone.

"With Brent out, I'm going to have to rely on the two of you much more. Later today, I'll work up a schedule so that we can maintain proper coverage. I can't tell you yet how long we'll have to be under the new schedule, but my sense is, it could be a while. If you have any leave planned anytime during the next few months, that will need to be canceled. As for me, I will be putting in as many hours as humanly possible."

"Oh, so you're cutting back hours, are you?" Jim mused, his tone a little lighter.

All three of them chuckled.

"That's the first laugh I've had in a while," admitted Winston.

"Happy to oblige, but seriously, Winston, as always, I hope you know you can count on me for anything needed…and then some."

"That goes for me too," Loretta chimed in.

"Thank you both," said Winston, staring at Loretta's computer screen as Loretta leaned back to provide a clear view. "Jim, Loretta has just sent out an email announcing that we're having a mandatory meeting at nine. We will conference you in."

"Okay. I'll be on at nine," assured Jim. "Hear from you then."

"Good. All right, guys, I need to end our call and handle some things. Thanks again to the two of you." Winston stood, moved his chair back in to place, nodded to Loretta, and headed up to his office.

***

At 9:01 a.m., Winston walked into the helps' kitchen, a room fitted with round tables and chairs on the basement mezzanine level, which served as the staff's meal room. The entire residence staff of ninety sat at the available chairs while two dozen others stood against the walls in the back. The room was completely silent. No one uttered a word as they stared at Winston, who was standing at the front of the room.

Winston glanced to his right, where Loretta sat primly, her eyes wide with anticipation as they met his. "Do we have Jim on the speakerphone?"

She looked down toward the phone, which sat on a small table in front of her. Seeing the red light, she nodded yes.

Winston looked out over the staff, took a deep breath, then began. "Team, this will be brief as I need to prepare for Mrs. Blake's return at 11:15 a.m. All I can say at this point is that you probably know as much as I do from the various news reports. This is a very tragic time, especially for Mrs. Blake, the entire country, and all of us in this room. I ask that no one jump to any conclusions until we know all of the facts. I will share pertinent information as it becomes available. I expect each and every one of us to continue to focus on our mission: to provide outstanding, dedicated service in taking care of the first family and the executive residence. I also ask that all of us continue our practice of not talking to anyone on the outside. If you are approached, direct them to me. Thank you."

***

Winston sat in the ushers office preparing for the return of Mrs. Blake, as the TV was playing a piece about the Blakes. "John and Beverly Blake, both in their seventies, the pair had been married for forty-six years and have one daughter. A senator for fifty years, John Blake had made a name for himself as a strong anti-communist stalwart. While chair of the Senate Select Committee on Intelligence, he had led unprecedented public hearings exposing the numerous incidents of Russian attempts at espionage within the United States. He followed that with taking on and exposing the atrocities and corruption of Russian leadership. *The New York Times* attempted to diminish him by labeling him as the new Joe McCarthy, but their efforts were to no avail, and Blake's work only helped build his reputation as a strong leader and defender of American values, a stance that bolstered his popularity and helped win him the presidential election by one of the greatest landslides in history.

"Now dead, the country mourns, and some worry that the first female and youngest ever to be president, Elizabeth Gentry, may not be able to continue at the same level of success as the man she replaced."

***

At 11:15 a.m., right on schedule, Mrs. Blake, the first lady, arrived back at the White House from her trip to Beijing. After being briefed by the Secret Service, she told them she wanted a private meeting with the chief usher.

Winston stood at the south portico and watched as the first lady's limo entered the south grounds. The sun shone brilliantly, but the frigid wind reminded him that winter was far from over. The two-car motorcade came to a stop just beyond the south portico canopy. Winston stood back to allow the Secret Service agent who had hopped out of the front passenger seat to quickly release the lock and open the rear door for Mrs. Blake to get out.

Winston observed that even with the burden of the tragedy, Mrs. Blake still appeared striking in her stylish, full-length Bergdorf Goodman winter coat. However, once he got a closer look he could see the tension on her thin face, her red lipstick providing a stark contrast to her pale skin. She hesitated to look up, finally revealing a sense of comfort when she saw Winston.

Winston stepped forward and offered his hand, which the first lady grasped tightly, her gloved fingers curling around his bare hand as she gracefully levered her body out of the limo. She took one step toward Winston, and the two embraced one another almost simultaneously. She whispered in his ear, "Please get me inside. I don't want to see anyone."

The first lady kept ahold of Winston's hand as they walked in through the diplomatic reception room, crossed the center hall, and entered the president's elevator. Winston used his special usher's key to bypass the automatic security stop on the first floor, and the elevator moved smoothly up to the second floor.

Winston helped with her coat, and as he draped it over a nearby chair he asked if she needed time to herself. She shook her head. "Let's sit in the west sitting hall," she suggested quietly.

They sat next to each other on the sofa; behind them, the large, half-moon window provided a view of the west wing and the executive office building in the distance.

Mrs. Blake looked tired; her eyes were red and her voice weak. "Secret Service filled me in on the basics." She began to cry. "But I want to hear it from you, Winston. I have all these questions." She sounded robot-like as she rattled off her questions. "What happened? Where was he? Who found him? Did he suffer? He was absolutely fine when I left. I should have never agreed to do this trip—I hated being so far from John. He seemed fine. I never had any idea anything was wrong." She stopped, took a short breath, covered her face with her hands, and sobbed.

Winston edged closer to her and placed his hand on her upper arm while handing her his handkerchief. She lowered her hands, tears streaming down her face. She gratefully accepted the handkerchief, thanking Winston and then blowing her nose. "He had just finished his dinner in the family dining room," Winston began quietly, replaying the sequence of events in his head. "It happened suddenly. He just slipped from his chair onto the floor, unconscious. Patrick rushed to the ushers office. The Secret Service was there immediately and could not resuscitate him, so they began to administer CPR. Dr. Jenkins was there almost immediately and took over."

Mrs. Blake stared at Winston, her tears making it difficult for her to see. "Did my husband ever regain consciousness? Did he suffer?"

Winston paused. He turned to face her and took both her hands in his. "He never woke. I don't believe he suffered at all."

Mrs. Blake closed her eyes and took a deep breath. "Thank you, Winston. I could not bear the thought of him suffering. I just don't understand what they told me about the taxology report. They made it sound like John had been poisoned. How is that even possible?"

"Mrs. Blake, I don't think we know enough yet. I do know they have the best experts in the world working on this. I'm sure we'll get clarity very soon."

Mrs. Blake sighed, closed her eyes for a few seconds, and began to reminisce. "I'll never forget the day I met him. I had just completed my junior year at the University of Chicago, and instead of coming back to Philadelphia, I stayed in town because my dance instructor arranged for me to audition with the Joffrey Ballet. I knew I wasn't good enough, but figured what the heck, it'll be a great experience. The audition lasted three days, or rather I survived until the end of the third day when they told me I had great potential and with proper training I should come back in a year and try again. I wasn't totally surprised, although having made it to day three, I was beginning to believe I had a chance."

Mrs. Blake, looking straight ahead, began to smile as she continued. "My friends picked me up and took me downtown to cheer me up. We got to Grant Park where we saw this handsome young guy giving a speech. I liked what he had to say, and I also felt a little bad for him because there were less than twenty people listening. When his speech ended, the small crowd disbursed and the young candidate was busy packing up his materials, so I approached him and introduced myself. He told me he had just turned 25, which was the minimum requirement age to run for Senate. He had such a warm smile; he took my hand to shake and held it with both of his. It truly was love at first sight, and we've been together ever since, until now." Mrs. Blake's smile quickly faded, and she began to cry again.

They spent the next two hours together, sharing their sorrow and then discussing the viewing and funeral arrangements. They talked about how much she and her husband loved the White House and the residence staff. Winston was impressed with how steady she now appeared. She even thought to comfort him regarding the allegations about Brent. She was confident that the assistant usher would come out of this just fine and went on to say that there had to be an explanation for everything. She then asked Winston to share with her office in the east wing that they had met and she was in full agreement with him on all the arrangements. They hugged, and then Winston left.

Winston got back to the ushers office and found Jim there.

"Oh, good," Winston said. "You came in early."

Jim nodded. "Of course. I figured you would need all hands on deck."

"Much appreciated, although we need to pace ourselves over the next several weeks. I don't want you or Loretta to burn out. By the way, where is she?"

"Once I got here, she decided to take a break and go for a walk," Jim told him.

"Excellent. Good for her. When she gets back, let's all meet with the curator's staff. Please schedule it for 2:30. Thanks."

***

Winter fought to keep its grip; the air felt damp and cold. It was breezy, and a cloud moved in front of the sun, making it a struggle to stay warm. Being early March, with at least five weeks until the cherry blossoms, Washington was spared the throngs of tourists that would soon be arriving.

Loretta wore her recent purchase from Saks, a full-length Totême Alpaca Wrap coat with a stylish white cashmere ski hat pulled down over her head. She remained comfortably warm, while Chef Patrick Sullivan in his well-worn, vintage brown leather jacket with a plain black ski cap toughed it out. He had to be freezing, Loretta thought as they walked arm and arm at a leisurely pace, Loretta leaning into Patrick as they strolled in solitude past the Lincoln Memorial reflecting pool. The only sound was the crunch of the pea gravel beneath their feet and the occasional jets flying into Reagan National.

"I have to say," began Patrick, "I'm not surprised at all about Brent being taken into custody. He always seemed too smooth. I think there was a lot going on with him none of us had a clue about."

"It's a shock," agreed Loretta. "I thought I knew him well. None of this makes any sense. But I don't want us to waste this time together consumed by all that. So, have you thought about when you're gonna tell Winston about your offer from the Four Seasons Hotel?"

"Well, I was planning to this week, but with the death of President Blake, I think I need to wait at least a week. I spoke with the Four Seasons this morning, and while they want me there ASAP, they are being very understanding, given the current events."

"I am so proud of you," Loretta smiled. "Executive Chef Patrick Sullivan sounds incredible, and the Four Seasons... Such an amazing place!"

"I'm so excited. I think the timing is perfect. As I mentioned, I wasn't thrilled with the Blakes. I mean, they're nice and all, but I think it's time I moved on from the White House. And based on what I've been hearing about Elizabeth Gentry... Oh, my... All I can say is good luck!"

They walked toward the Lincoln Memorial. Through the tree branches bordering their route, they slowly watched the memorial grow larger. To their right was the path that led to the Vietnam Memorial. They stopped speaking as an older couple bundled up in their winter coats walked by them going in the opposite direction.

"I think you might be right," admitted Loretta. "From what we've learned so far, the Gentry White House may be a challenging place to work. But beyond all that, you and I haven't really had much chance to talk lately. Let's face it, our sex was always great, but even that hasn't happened in quite a while." Loretta, feeling a bit melancholy, continued. "There's so much more we could have, but with our time constraints, we never even get the chance to just talk."

They walked in silence for a bit, then Patrick spoke. "I haven't been fair to you. I haven't been open and completely honest."

Loretta suddenly felt cold. She stared straight ahead, took a jagged breath inward, and said, "You've been seeing someone else. I know that, Patrick. A woman always knows."

"Well, we really haven't talked during the past several months. I was going to tell you but never got the chance."

"You could have made the chance," Loretta said. She was feeling distraught. She had been wondering if Patrick had been seeing someone—there were always persistent rumors in the Executive Residence. The gossip was that Patrick was a player, but hearing this confirmation from him upset her.

"I met someone. It's over. It only lasted three weeks. She doesn't mean anything to me. The whole experience made me realize what you and I had, or what I believe and hope we can have that could be so much better. I also realized I need a friend. I don't have anyone I can trust. You're the only one I ever talked to about things."

Loretta was surprised at how hurt she felt, but she didn't want Patrick to stop talking so she tried not to show any emotion, but she was becoming angry. Patrick showed no real emotion. It wasn't personal at all; it was as if he were describing a scene in a movie.

They were now in front of the Lincoln Memorial. They sat down on the steps. The sun popped out, and the little bit of warmth it offered made the cold wind bearable.

"So, tell me about her," requested Loretta.

"She is Polish, in her thirties. Young, athletic, but not overly attractive. Just average."

"Where did you meet?"

"We met on the Ellipse. I had just left work and was going to my car. She was out for a run and slipped on the ice right in front of me. She landed hard. I helped her. We talked, she was pleasant, and we agreed to meet for coffee the next morning. It evolved rather quickly."

"What did you like about her?"

"She was interesting," Patrick recalled. "She works at the Polish Embassy, had traveled the world… She knew a lot about Washington politics—had some rather interesting things to say about President Blake. She didn't like him much, but curiously, she had a favorable impression of Gentry. Like I said, she was interesting."

"So why did it end?"

"I dunno. It was weird. It didn't even last three weeks. I helped her out with something, then we both sort of lost interest, and it was over, just like that."

"Do you miss her?" Loretta asked.

"Not at all."

"How'd you help her out?"

"She asked me to deliver a gift for the president."

"What?! Tell me you didn't…"

"No, wait! Don't overreact. It was totally harmless," Patrick reassured. "I could plainly see it. It wasn't even gift-wrapped, just a small package containing a Polish sausage that's the current rage in Europe."

"Tell me you had the Secret Service scan it."

"Absolutely. I brought it in through the northwest gate and asked Sargent Bamberger to scan it, and no, I didn't tell him it was for the president."

"Patrick, you do know that the proper procedure would've been to turn in any gifts for the president to the gift unit, where it would be examined, documented, and inventoried with the other nine million gifts in there, and since it was a food item, they would have disposed of it properly. So, what did you do with it?"

"Don't worry. I didn't give it to the president. I'm not that stupid. Sheesh, give me a break! I examined it. It was a very high-quality sausage. I gave it to the storeroom and told them to place it in the freezer for the first family."

Loretta made a mental note to retrieve it from the storeroom and throw it away at her first opportunity.

They stood and began their walk back to the White House.

"Sorry, but I hope you can understand that once I'm at the Four Seasons, my focus will be totally on my career," Patrick told her.

Loretta was becoming annoyed with Patrick's attitude. Her blood pressure rose and her face reddened. She was hurt and now wanted to be vindictive. "Well, now that we're being completely honest with one another, you should know, I've met someone else, and I need to explore that relationship to see where it goes."

Patrick, rolling his eyes and shaking his head, unhooked his arm from Loretta and took a sideways step away from her. Then with a steely stare said, "Wow. What the fuck?!"

Loretta, with an exasperated look, replied, "Why are you reacting like that? You're not fair. I was only trying to be open with you and share the things I had learned and my feelings about them."

"What the hell does all that mean?"

"It means, I think I'll be able to give you the time you need to focus on your new job."

Patrick shouted, "Just like that?! How long has this been going on?"

Loretta looked around to ensure no one was in earshot before responding. "It's been going on for a while. But wait a minute, Patrick. Think about it. It's not like we ever made any type of commitment to one another. I mean, you only seemed to enjoy the sex. There never was much else in our so-called relationship."

"Maybe that's because you made such a big deal all the time about keeping everything a secret!" retorted Patrick.

"That was best for us, and you know it!"

"You know what? Fine! This just makes my decision that much easier. I'll leave the White House. That way, maybe you can get in bed with the next sous chef!" Patrick was dazed by the strength of Loretta's slap. Even with her gloved hand, it stung. He touched his face where it hurt the most.

"Go to hell, you jerk!" She stomped away, leaving Patrick standing at the foot of the reflecting pool. On her way back to the White House, she checked her phone, noticing that she had a 2:30 meeting with Winston and the curators. She then reached into her purse for her personal cell phone and sent a text: *All done, when can I see you?*

Seconds later, she received a response: *Seven p.m. Our usual spot.*

Chapter 6
2 p.m., Monday, March 2: Interrogation Facility, Undisclosed Location

Not only was Brent freezing, thirsty, and hungry, but like President Blake, Brent was a level 1 diabetic and had missed his morning insulin shot. He was beginning to feel poorly, and even though he was freezing, sweat had formed on his forehead. How many hours had he been detained? He now understood that the president was dead, which meant that Beth was now the president. He thought about that for a moment.

He liked her; they had worked together a lot over the past two years. He always had a feeling that things between them may have evolved into something a lot closer, but he always quickly dismissed the idea and attributed his thoughts to wishful fantasy. Back to reality. Surely, she would inquire about him, and soon he would be cleared.

He also thought about his best friend, Greg Leidner. A few years younger than Brent, they were like brothers. At six-foot-four and muscular, Greg was an imposing figure. The only hair on his head was a bit on the sides, and his mustache. He was what his friends would say follicly challenged for his young age. Still, he took the ribbing well. Popular, witty, and gregarious, Greg had risen through the ranks quickly and become a Secret Service special agent. Years ago, he had saved the prior first family's dog from being run over by a presidential motorcade and, as a result, gained favor with the former first lady, with whom he still maintained contact. Greg was now the special agent in charge. If anyone could quickly clear Brent, Greg would be the guy.

Brent forced himself to focus; how could this be happening? Why in hell was he in this hell? Thinking back to the day before, Brent had been working a double-shift, which allowed for the other assistant usher to have the entire day off. Everything seemed perfectly normal; being a Sunday, it was quiet. With the First Lady out of town, it was always quiet. The president was so easygoing and unassuming, never demanding. Brent had guessed the president wouldn't bother with church and smiled when the president called him right at 7:00 a.m.

"Brent, good morning. I'm going to skip church this morning. Is the chef in? I'm in the mood for a big breakfast."

The first lady was very strict about his diet. Brent knew that was why the president didn't mind so much that she was traveling. "Yes, sir, Mr. President," Brent had responded. "Patrick is here. I will let him know."

"Good, and ask the butlers to bring me coffee."

"Right away, sir. Have a great morning."

"Thanks, Brent."

Brent immediately sent a text to the butlers who were on standby in the private family kitchen on the second floor of the executive residence. He then headed down to the main kitchen on the ground floor to find Patrick Sullivan, the tall, thin, dark-haired, thirty-nine-year-old sous chef. Patrick had been working in the White House for the past four years, having been highly recommended by his previous boss at the Biltmore Hotel. As the right hand, but always in the background of the executive chef, Patrick often struggled for recognition. He was somewhat of a loner, not always seeming comfortable working with others. His main duties involved preparing the daily meals for the first family—primarily dinner for the president and first lady.

"Good morning, Patrick," Brent greeted. "The president just called and said he wanted a big breakfast."

Patrick smiled. "Perfect, I'll make him bacon, eggs, biscuits, and sausage just like I did the last time the first lady was away."

Brent gave him a thumbs-up and headed back to the office.

Absolutely nothing on the schedule. Ah, it's going to be a nice, relaxing day, Brent thought. The phone rang. It was Chief Usher Bartholomew Winston.

"Brent, how are things?"

"Hi, Winston. Happy Sunday. All's quiet here. Nothing on the schedule—a great day! Oh, your son called. He said he'd catch up with you later." Winston thanked him and said he was going to go for a bike ride, then would be on his way in to work on the budget. Ever since Winston's wife had passed away a year and a half earlier, Winston had been coming in on the weekends and was also spending more and more nights at the White House. The man never seemed to take a day off, but it kept him sharp.

"Great. See you when you get in," Brent said and hung up the phone.

Brent loved Bartholomew Winston. He was the best boss he had ever had and was so good for the White House. Winston, as everyone called him, was a decorated Vietnam war vet, a stickler for form and protocol but unfailingly calm and gentile. Winston, with his strong resemblance to Morgan Freeman, always proved fun during White House events. Guests often believed Winston was the famous actor.

Brent used the remote to turn on the TV behind him. He would start with CNN and then eventually flip to

Meet the Press, *Face the Nation*, and *This Week*. He liked to watch the Sunday morning shows that he knew the president would be watching. The Russian ambassador was being interviewed; he was complaining that President Blake's actions were ill-conceived and very anti-Russian, and that the US President was making it so that Russian people feared him.

The phone rang again, and Brent picked it up. "The ushers office, Brent Williams."

Vice President Elizabeth Gentry came over the line. "Hi, Brent. It's Beth. Happy Sunday! What's on the president's schedule for today?"

"Howdy!" replied Brent. "Absolutely nothing. He even canceled church."

"Perfect. When does the first lady get back?"

"Not until tomorrow night."

"Okay, let me know if anything changes," Elizabeth requested. "Maybe I'll see you later. Thanks."

"You got it. Take care."

Brent received a text from the butlers confirming the president had his coffee in his bed at 7:04, and his breakfast was served in the family dining room at 7:35. Brent updated the ushers log with the information.

The doors to the president's elevator automatically opened as it stopped in the hallway outside of the ushers office, which meant it was being called to the second floor. Brent quickly jumped on, and as the elevator approached the second floor, he could see through the porthole window that the president was standing and waiting. The doors opened, and in walked the president, followed by the Secret Service agent. The president was wearing jeans and a nice sweater, his graying hair was at a stylish length, he looked good, but he always looked good.

"Good morning, Brent."

"Good morning, Mr. President."

"I'm going to go do my weekly radio address. Can you please tell Patrick it'll just be me for lunch, and I would like something light?" The president smiled and added, "But not too light."

As the doors to the elevator opened on the ground floor, Brent responded, "Absolutely." The president headed to the west wing, followed by the agent. Brent took the back stairs to get back to the ushers office.

Switching his mind away from his recent memories and back into cold, hard reality, Brent pulled his knees up to his chest as far as they would go, trying to convince himself that this maneuver was making him feel warmer. Being in total darkness and silence caused him to lose all concept of time. He wondered where he was, how long this would go on. Desperate to distract himself and pass the time, he reminisced about happier days. He focused on his job as an usher and on more normal times and then laughed to himself as he realized "normal" didn't describe the job of a White House usher.

Brent was convinced his job was one of the greatest in existence. He had been an usher for over eight years and had met five US presidents, dozens of world leaders, all varieties of celebrities, Nobel laureates, professional athletes, and even astronauts. At his most recent performance evaluation, Winston told Brent that he would be his choice to be the next chief usher, provided that Winston ever decided to retire. After which, he had joked that that would never happen.

He thought about Beth—VP Elizabeth Gentry. Only forty-two, and she could pass for someone five years younger. The woman reminded Brent of a cross between actresses Catherine Zeta-Jones and Demi Moore. Beth was a political rock star, Naval Academy grad, former Navy pilot, Harvard Law graduate. three-term congresswoman, the former vice president, and now, evidently, the president of the United States. She was a captivating and dynamic speaker, super-intelligent, and stunningly beautiful, a combination that made her wildly popular. The worst thing her few critics could say about her was that she was too ambitious. While President Blake's polling numbers were phenomenal, there had already been talk about Elizabeth Gentry being the presidential nominee in six years, after the current president completed his two terms. Brent felt fortunate to know her. He thought back to the first time they met.

It happened on a Friday night in late January, just over two years ago. President and First Lady Blake were hosting a private party, one of their first events in the White House.

At 7 p.m., twenty guests arrived in the diplomatic reception room for a cocktail party in the private residence. President and Mrs. Blake had just left the room with several guests to escort them to the second-floor. Brent stood by for any late arrivals; moments later, Vice President Elizabeth Gentry and her husband, retired Admiral James Curtis, arrived. Brent had met them very briefly the prior week when they attended the Inauguration Day customary coffee at the White House before heading to the Capitol for the official swearing-in. Brent didn't believe they would remember him and was pleasantly surprised when the VP and admiral walked right up and said it was nice to see him again.

Brent was caught off guard by Elizabeth Gentry's beautiful, intense gray eyes that seemed to pierce into him. He had forced himself to look away, then helped her with her long fur coat, revealing the attractive, dark red dress beneath it that showed off her amazing figure. The admiral looked most distinguished, and even though it was cold out, he refused to wear an overcoat. His perfectly tailored navy-blue suit fit him well. The man was in his late sixties but still looked very fit; his flattop was gray, but the shortness of his hair made him look younger than he was.

The admiral had stepped away to examine a painting, and the VP then asked Brent to share some of the history of the room.

"When the White House was built, this was the boiler room and actually the site of the first baby to be born in the White House," Brent had told her. "The mother was a slave, and the father was…" Brent paused for effect. "…Thomas Jefferson." The VP's jaw dropped, and the admiral, having heard this fascinating trivia, turned his head to look, then walked over to rejoin them after suddenly losing interest in the painting.

Both the VP and the admiral began asking all sorts of questions regarding White House history, lore, and trivia; they were legitimately fascinated. Brent escorted them from the diplomatic reception room and into the china room, where samples of china used by each president were on display. Brent pointed out the Lincoln china, which was still used but only on special occasions.

The VP had asked Brent about what his job as usher entailed. Brent had explained that the job title was a little confusing; it was a term used in England during the 1700s to describe the role of those who maintained the mansions and schedules of the great men who lived on the large estates. "The ushers office today is the managing office for the 132-room White House executive residence, the home of the first family, the eighteen acres of surrounding grounds, and management of the house's ninety-plus staff. It's the greatest job in the world!" Brent said.

The VP asked, "Are you a regular federal employee?"

"I am but serve at the pleasure of the president, however. The current executive residence staff has spanned several administrations, and one of the benefits is that we are the only group that offers continuity from administration to administration."

"How long have you been here?" inquired the admiral.

"President Blake is my third president. I have been here eight years. Chief Usher Bartholomew Winston has been here over fifty years and has served ten presidents."

They both reacted in amazement. Then Beth asked if the hours were long.

"Yes," said Brent, "but it's always invigorating so you never realize the long hours you put in. The schedule is unique. The chief usher works a regular Monday-through-Friday schedule unless there are large events on the weekend. Although, Chief Usher Winston seems to work just about every day—not sure how he keeps that up. The three assistant ushers work on a unique twenty-one-day rotation. Basically, we cover the awake hours of the president."

The admiral asked about the hours of the shifts.

"Day shift starts at 5:45 a.m. and goes until 2:30 p.m.," Brent explained. "The evening shift starts at 2 p.m. and goes until the president retires in the evening. The hardest part is being in charge of events, so anytime there's an afternoon or evening event, and say I'm on day shift, I end up working long hours. When there is a state dinner, I'll work from 5:45 a.m. until 2:00 a.m. the next day!"

Brent realized he was taking up a lot of their time, thanked them for their questions, and suggested he escort them to the private residence to join the other guests.

When they got to the top of the grand staircase and entered through the large, opened double doors, they were greeted by a butler holding a silver tray with champagne. The couple took a glass. Elizabeth handed one to Brent. The president stood in the center hall encouraging guests to tour the second floor and walk through all the rooms, mentioning to them that the ushers and curators were on hand to answer any of their questions.

Brent escorted the VP and admiral to the Lincoln bedroom, where he provided more history. By this point, other guests had gathered to listen. The admiral stopped to focus on the Gettysburg Address in the corner of the Lincoln bedroom. Brent could see that the VP was losing interest, so he invited her into the adjacent Lincoln sitting room, then they walked across the hall to the queen's room. They continued to talk as Brent showed her around, being interrupted often by other guests who wanted to meet the VP. As soon as the VP was free, she would seek Brent out to talk and learn more historical trivia. She asked how late Brent was working and whether it would be possible for them to get a tour of the public rooms downstairs. Brent told her he would be happy to show them everything.

The dinner party ended around 10:30 p.m. On her way out, the VP asked if they could have a raincheck for the remainder of the tour, and of course, Brent agreed.

Brent was amazed when the very next afternoon, the VP called him and asked if now would be a good time to get a tour of the public rooms. He responded, "Absolutely. The president and Mrs. Blake left for Camp David this morning. I have all the free time that would be needed."

"Great. The admiral is busy, so it'll just be me."

Brent thought back to that weekend and how fun it was showing VP Elizabeth Gentry all the rooms, including the bowling alley, main kitchen, family theater, even the carpenter and electric shops. She had seemed so interested and had wanted to see it all. They ordered pizza and ate in the ushers office. Brent brought up a six-pack of beer from the storeroom. The VP was so positive and fun. She had such great energy and even laughed at his jokes. She returned the next day to spend time in the White House library; by the end of the weekend, she began insisting that Brent call her Beth.

Brent was suddenly snapped back to reality when he heard a noise. He held his breath and listened. Nothing. He continued to sit in the pitch-black, cold darkness. He felt shaky and eventually passed out.

Chapter 7
2:30 p.m., Monday, March 2: The White House

Winston, Loretta, Jim, and members of the White House curators office reviewed the records of the Kennedy and Lincoln funeral arrangements. Winston then called the first lady's office in the east wing to begin the methodical planning for the funeral of President Blake.

The president's body would arrive from Walter Reed and lay in state in the east room of the White House all day Tuesday, then be transferred to the Capitol, where the casket would lay-in-state all day Wednesday. The funeral service would take place at the National Cathedral at 11 a.m. on Thursday, followed by the burial at Arlington National Cemetery at 1 p.m.

Meanwhile, the newly sworn-in president, Elizabeth Gentry, was eager to move into the White House. Winston, while busy making arrangements with his team regarding the former first lady's move out of the White House, was interrupted by a phone call from the new president. She told him to deal with her on all matters involving her husband and their move. Winston found President Gentry to be rather insistent on making the move happen as soon as possible. He then consulted with the White House curator regarding protocol and history.

It had been fifty-seven years since a president had died in office. Winston and the chief curator reviewed just how generous at the time the new president, Lyndon Johnson, had been with Jackie Kennedy. After her husband was assassinated, Johnson insisted on allowing Mrs. Kennedy to stay in the White House for as long as she needed.

Winston thanked everyone for coming, then asked Loretta to write up the plan, distribute it to the meeting attendees for review, and see if they could get it all finalized before 5 p.m. that day.

Winston was ready for a break, so he escaped to his private office on the mezzanine. He sat in his comfortable leather chair, leaned back, and closed his eyes. He thought about all the challenges he had faced over his years as an usher. What could possibly compare to what he was dealing with today? Perhaps the final days of the Nixon term in the White House— certainly one of the more tumultuous times he had faced during his time there.

***

Thinking back to people who had made a difference in his life, Winston remembered with fondness his mentor, Rex Scouten. Rex became an assistant usher in 1960 after serving thirteen years in the Secret Service. In 1969, he was promoted to chief usher, a year before Winston started as a military aide in the Nixon White House.

Rex was legendary. During his tenure in the ushers office, Scouten dealt with the Kennedy assassination, the Vietnam war protests, race riots, President Nixon's resignation, and the attempted assassination of President Reagan. But his most harrowing experience occurred before he even joined the ushers office. It happened while he was in the Secret Service as an agent, assigned to Truman's presidential protective detail.

The White House was built in eight years, with construction starting on October 13, 1792, and ending on November 1, 1800. In 1948, engineers determined that the building was so structurally weak that it was in danger of collapse. Therefore, from 1949 to 1952, a massive renovation and expansion took place, and the White House was completely gutted. It was determined that the exterior walls would remain from the original structure, but the inside was rebuilt with steel and concrete. The project necessitated then-President Truman's move across the street to Blair House, the president's guesthouse.

On Wednesday, November 1, 1950, the day was unusually warm, an Indian summer day in Washington. Rex, as part of the presidential protection detail, was at Blair House when two Puerto Rican nationalists brazenly attacked. President Harry Truman had been napping on the second floor and suddenly awoke to the sound of gunfire. He wanted to know what all the commotion was, so he barreled down the back stairs and attempted to open the door at the base of the steps. Rex was on the other side of the door using all of his weight to keep it closed, thus ensuring the curious president would remain out of harm's way. Several shots were exchanged, and a member of the Secret Service, Leslie Coffelt was killed. One of the nationalists was killed, shot by Coffelt, who miraculously got off an expert marksman shot as he lay dying from his own wound. The other nationalist was eventually subdued, and Rex succeeded in keeping the president out of the line of fire—although Truman initially was not too pleased with Rex when he realized he was the one to blame for keeping him from finding out what was going on!

Rex was the first modern-era usher, a consummate gentleman, and a well-respected man of principle. He did everything with class and developed close and long-lasting relationships with each of the presidents and first ladies he served.

In 1970, during Rex's second year as chief usher, President Nixon approached him and asked if he would consider hiring one of his military aides as an usher. Fortunately, for Winston, Rex agreed. And that was how Winston began his career in the ushers office. Winston and Rex had a mutual admiration for each other; the two spent endless hours working closely together.

By mid-1974, the Nixon White House was unraveling. Watergate dominated the news; the first family was suffering the effects of the ever-increasing revelations of Nixon's wrongdoings. Support for the president soon eroded on all fronts. Protestors could be heard from Lafayette Park chanting day and night: "Jail to the chief." The pressure was evident in the faces of the president, the first lady, and their daughters, Tricia and Julie. As hard as the president tried to put on a positive demeanor, behind the scenes, the executive residence staff witnessed a man in decline.

The president was often exhausted but too tired to sleep, and while early in his administration he would enjoy a late-night brandy, he now began to consume more alcohol. His drinking would start earlier as each day of that summer went by. The executive residence staff, as always, worked hard to maintain their professional dedication and focus on superbly serving the first family, but they were suffering as well. The tension was unbearable and taking its toll on the ushers, butlers, and housekeeping staff.

Winston recalled one hot July afternoon when President Nixon called the ushers office. Winston had great difficulty understanding the president because his words were slurred. The only thing he could make out was that the president needed help in the Lincoln sitting room. Winston quickly ran up the back stairs and entered the private quarters, where the only sound was the rush of air-conditioning through the vents. The temperature in the private quarters was abnormally cool, almost cold. Winston quickly strode toward the east sitting hall. As he passed the Lincoln bedroom, he could see the door to the Lincoln sitting room was open. He lightly knocked as he entered the room.

He smelled smoke and found a dozing president on the floor laying on his side close to the lit fireplace. The president's brandy glass must have slipped from his hand as it appeared to have rolled a couple of feet across the carpet. As Winston got closer, he saw there was a lit cigar on the floor, which was burning a hole in the rug. Winston picked up the cigar and quickly stomped out the sparks. This activity awoke the president, who slowly sat up and came to his senses. Before Winston could say anything, the president gave him a curious look while collecting his glass, and with his words still slurred, said, "Uh, Winston, is that my cigar?"

"Sorry, sir." Winston quickly handed the cigar to the president.

The president placed the cigar in his mouth, then adeptly emptied the remaining drops of Napoleon Brandy into his glass.

"Please bring me another bottle of brandy," Nixon asked with more clarity in his voice. "Oh, and bring one more glass. Henry [Secretary of State Henry Kissinger] will be joining me."

"Absolutely, Mr. President, and here you go." Winston had located an ashtray and handed it to Nixon.

"Oh, thanks. Ask the butlers to bring in more logs. This fire is dying. Also, tell the engineers to lower the AC to as low as it will go," Nixon directed.

"I'll take care of it, sir." As he stepped away, Winston glanced back at the president, who appeared comfortably seated on the floor and lost in thought, staring at the fire.

When Winston got back to the ushers office, he immediately informed Rex of what had happened. Rex's response was typical: He was always calm and composed. He thanked Winston and assured him he had handled everything properly.

The next few weeks were incredibly demanding as the ushers worked nonstop to help the Nixon's with their impending move. Even though the president had decided on July 23 that he would have to resign, it wasn't made official until the night of August 8, 1974, when the president made his resignation announcement in a nationwide address from the oval office. The president and his family would leave before noon the next day.

On the morning of the departure, Winston watched the display of graciousness and kindness exhibited by the president and Mrs. Nixon as they bid farewell to the executive residence staff. Mrs. Nixon was more emotional, but the president had become stoic; the lined wrinkles on his face had never been so apparent. Winston stood just feet away and could see the president attempting to muster his once confident campaign bravado, but it just wasn't happening. Mrs. Nixon hugged each of the ushers, followed by the president, who with no emotion gave each of the ushers a perfunctory semi-firm handshake. Rex was the last person inside the White House for Nixon and his wife to say goodbye to.

The Nixon's then exited the diplomatic reception room and headed to the Marine One helicopter that would take them to Andrews Airforce Base, where they would ride Air Force One for the last time. They walked across the south lawn on a hastily rolled-out red carpet. The ushers stood at the south portico and watched what would become an iconic scene: Richard M. Nixon, with a forced smile, waving vigorously from the top of the step of Marine One; then, with arms spread, he flashed a two-handed peace salute before disappearing in the chopper.

Rex Scouten would retire from the ushers office in 1986 as First Lady Nancy Reagan persuasively talked him into becoming the White House curator. Thus, Rex left the ushers office but worked another ten years as the White House curator. He and Winston remained close friends until Rex passed away in 2013.

Winston thought about all the years he had spent in the White House and wondered if it wasn't time for him to start planning retirement. He convinced himself he was still providing value, and as long as he was doing so, he should continue. But then he wondered if he was the best judge of his value. His thoughts were interrupted by a knock at his door. It was Mary the housekeeper.

"Winston, sorry to bother you," began Mary, "but can you please share with me the details and funeral plans for President Blake?"

"Of course, Mary. C'mon in and have a seat."

Mary Aaron, a confident and attractive woman in her mid-forties, came from a small town in North Carolina. She began working at the White House as a maid twenty-seven years ago. Ten years ago, she was promoted and became the first African American executive housekeeper, where she became responsible for managing a staff of ten maids and housemen in keeping the 132-room executive residence pristine. Never married, she'd tell anyone who asked that she was married to the White House—she didn't have time for anything else. Winston never confirmed nor denied the persistent rumors that Mary was his cousin. When asked, he'd only say that Mary's performance and work ethic were an example that everyone should strive for.

***

Winston answered the phone in the ushers office.

"Winston, it's Beth," the voice announced in his ear. "Uh, I mean, um, President Gentry. I need you, the curator, and your moving guys to meet me in the oval office." Before Winston could respond, she had hung up.

Winston and Assistant Usher Loretta, along with the operations team (AKA the "moving guys") and the entire curators office staff, stepped into the oval office, where the new president was with her chief of staff, Wendy Wolf. They were ordering west wing staffers to bring the chair from her former VP office to replace President Blake's chair. The Blake west wing staff were moving in slow motion; many of them were emotional.

President Gentry looked up, acknowledged Winston, and then said to the group, "Good, I need your help." She stepped over to the chief curator, slipped her arm through his, and announced, "I want this awful rug replaced, and do I have to use the Resolute desk? It's so big and way too old."

"We have a warehouse in Springfield, Virginia that has in storage most of the White House collection," the curator mentioned. "I also brought my laptop to show you items, including desks, rugs, chairs, settees, and paintings."

"Excellent. Let's sit over here." She motioned toward the two sofas fifteen feet away and added, "I need this all done immediately."

Winston turned to face the ops team and several of the curators and quietly told them to go back to the executive residence. Then he and Loretta joined the president and the curator to help with the selections.

Gentry continued. "Before we get started, I just want you to know that I have asked all of President Blake's staff to tender their resignations. This is completely routine. I will have my folks in place by the end of the day. Of course, Wendy will remain as my chief of staff, and Jill Turner who was my press secretary while I was VP will remain as my press secretary. I will hold a press conference later today. Winston, what's the status of the east room?"

"Well, Madam President," Winston began, "President Blake's body will be lying in state in the east room all day tomorrow. We need to construct the elaborate catafalque, the structure that will support the coffin—"

President Gentry interrupted, "I know what that is! How much time do you need?"

"Several hours. At least six."

"Good," approved Gentry. "My east room press conference will start at five. Your guys will have plenty of time to get the 'elaborate catafalque' set up afterward."

Winston worried about the strain on his staff members who would be needed for many extra hours in the days to come. He kept his concerns to himself and responded simply with, "Of course."

Loretta busily took notes.

President Gentry was approached by an aide who whispered in her ear. Gentry could be heard responding, "Tell Wendy we're good for the five o'clock press conference." The aide nodded and quickly left the room. "Okay, let's pick out some furniture," President Gentry said with a smile.

After thirty minutes of reviewing and confirming the president's selections, the curator finalized everything. Wendy Wolf walked in and handed President Gentry a note. A stern look came over the president's face as she read aloud, "The FBI is charging Brenton A. Williams with killing the president." She stood and said to Winston and the chief curator, "That will be all for now."

Chapter 8
3 p.m., Monday, March 2: Interrogation Facility, Undisclosed Location

There was a sudden flash as the lights came back on. Brent squinted, trying to adjust his eyes. A door swung open, and several individuals entered the room. A bright orange jumpsuit was thrown toward Brent, and he was ordered to get dressed. Brent stood and immediately wobbled from dizziness. He was so unstable that he needed to sit back down to dress himself. After getting dressed, he watched as a man crouched next to him.

"Brent," began the man who was too drenched in shadow from the overhead light to make out in any detail, "I'm Dr. Andrews. You went into insulin shock, and we administered a glucagon rescue kit. How are you feeling?"

Brent was surprised by the warmth and concern of this individual, quite a contrast to his previous experiences in this place. "I'm feeling better," he managed. "Just a bit lightheaded."

"They'll be providing you with some food very shortly." The doctor stood and left before Brent had a chance to thank him.

Three uniformed DC police officers circled around Brent, helped him stand, and then placed him in handcuffs and shackled chains around his ankles. Brent feared he was about to be led to the gallows.

A man in a dark suit wearing a fedora stepped forward and began to speak. "Brenton Augustus Williams, you are hereby being charged with the assassination of the president of the United States. There are three separate charges: Number one, you are charged with first-degree murder; number two, you are charged with concealing an illegal and deadly substance; and number three, you are charged with violating the Secret Service Directive 501 lockdown order. You have the right to remain silent. Anything you say can and will be used against you in a court of law. You have the right to an attorney. If you cannot afford an attorney, one will be appointed for you. Do you understand your rights?"

Brent stared blankly at the man; he did not hear anything after "Assassination."

The man in the dark suit impatiently repeated, "Brenton A. Williams, do you understand your rights?!"

Brent hesitated, stammered, and then uttered a weak "Yes."

The man in the dark suit looked toward the DC police officers and said, "Okay, he's all yours. Get him out of here."

Chapter 9
5 p.m., Monday, March 2: The White House

The press were packed and waiting in the east room as Winston and Loretta slowly slid open the large, mahogany pocket doors, revealing for the TV audience the brightly lit and expansive view of the state floor main hallway with its long red carpet.

At 5:01 p.m., one of her aides gestured to her, and the new president exited the red room. TV viewers watched as she walked the long red carpet toward the lectern in the east room. She wore a designer, charcoal-gray skirt suit, white blouse, and Christian Louboutin patent leather pumps. Her dark hair was pulled back tightly into a bun. Her makeup was perfect; she looked determined and confident. The endless lightning-like flashes and nearly deafening sound of the electronic camera clicks suddenly silenced as President Elizabeth Gentry took her position at the podium. She nodded to the several dozen members of the press, then began:

"Thank you for gathering under such short notice. I have a brief statement to make, then will take a few questions." She gripped each side of the podium and looked straight into the camera. "My fellow Americans, we meet today with heavy hearts. Our tremendous loss has saddened not only our country but the entire world. President Blake was a man who guided us flawlessly for the past two years. He was not only my role model, but he was also my friend."

Gentry took a deep breath, appearing to fight back her emotions. "I have spent time grieving with the first lady and have assured her that she can take as long as she needs for her moving arrangements. In regards to the investigation, an individual has been charged. The FBI will be making a statement later today.

"I have a lot of work to do and hope to have the support and prayers of the nation as I move forward. God bless the United States of America."

Members of the press immediately began yelling questions. President Gentry pointed to a reporter in the front row.

Reporter 1: "Mrs. President, can you please comment on the fact that a White House usher has been charged in the murder of the former president?"

"We're all shocked by this, and rather than comment any further, we should wait until after the FBI briefing." She then pointed to another reporter.

Reporter 2: "President Gentry, how well did you know Brenton Augustus Williams?"

"He worked here in the White House, in the ushers officer. That's all I'll say for now."

Several reporters yelled questions, and Gentry looked to the far back of the room and pointed to a reporter.

Reporter 3: "Mrs. President, the AP is reporting that Usher Brenton Williams was found with a deadly toxin, the very same toxin that killed the president. Can you offer any thoughts or an opinion on this?"

Gentry looked sullen and paused for effect. "That's a very disturbing report, and I look forward to the FBI briefing." She then pointed to a reporter in the third row.

Reporter 4: "Thank you, Mrs. President. Bridgette Chasemore, Agence France-Presse. Can you tell us how long you knew Brenton Augustus Williams and how you would rate his performance?"

"I believe I met him over two years ago when we came into office. As for his performance, and any other details, I'm not going to discuss specifics or answer any more questions on this until the investigation is completed." Gentry then pointed to a reporter directly in front of her in the first row.

Reporter 5: "Mrs. President, can you share with us your highest priorities?"

"Right now, my job is to assure all citizens of the United States and our allies that everything is under control. We have had a very smooth transition in a remarkably short period of time. My plans include following President Blake's agenda. I will have much more on this in the week ahead."

President Gentry pointed to a reporter to the right of the one she just answered.

Reporter 6: "Madam President, Rob Forrester, CNN. Can you comment on the reports that are emerging that Brenton Williams was radicalized in Pakistan and is an Islamist jihadist?"

Gentry took a deep breath and with a grim look, said, "I have not been made aware of this reporting. If true, it would be most disturbing." She pointed to a reporter in the second to last row.

Reporter 7: "Madam President, can you please provide any updates on the amassing of Russian troops along the Polish border of Ukraine?"

"We were aware that Russia has had military exercises scheduled for some time now. The US was not aware they involved crossing Ukraine to the Polish border. We will have more to report on this later." President Gentry gestured to a reporter in the middle row.

Reporter 8: "Jerome Barton, BBC. Mrs. President, the BBC has learned that President Blake was working on a top-secret allied coalition plan, primarily with Great Britain and France, to end the Russian occupation of Crimea and eliminate the Russian troop presence in Syria. Can you comment on this, please, and more importantly, do you plan to follow through on the Blake plan?"

Gentry looked visibly annoyed. "There is no truth to this, and even if there were, I, as president, would never comment on such hypotheticals." With that, President Gentry swiftly nodded, said thank you, and then immediately left the east room as reporters continued to shout questions after her.

Chapter 10
6 p.m., Monday, March 2: DC Jail

Brent surveyed his new surroundings. He was in a roughly six-by-eight foot cell. In the corner was a stainless-steel sink, and next to it, a toilet attached to the wall. As he looked around, he took note of concrete block walls on three sides and open bars spanning across the remaining side. He was surprised at how clean the bars appeared; they were painted the same pale-yellow color that matched his walls. It was quiet; while he could see other cells across from him, they were all dark. He had a small bed frame with a mattress, over which a new-looking navy blue blanket had been folded. No pillow. The lighting was not particularly good, but the temperature was much more comfortable than it had been in the dark, cavernous dungeon he had been held in for what may have been a day or more—he wasn't sure. His biggest luxury was his new orange, cotton overalls. He was barefoot but comfortable.

A guard appeared with a tray of food. He placed it on the floor, then unlocked the door to the cell. Two other officers appeared, along with a nurse. They brought Brent's meal in, and the nurse reported that she was there to administer his insulin, which she did. Then they all left. Brent said thank you, and the last guard to leave looked back; he appeared annoyed by the delay of his exit. "We're not supposed to talk to you," the guard said. "We're only here to make sure you don't kill yourself."

Brent slowly shook his head, then the aroma of the food reminded him of just how hungry he was. He devoured some sort of chicken and potato stew, surprised by how good it tasted. He drank the entire bottle of Dasani that had come with his tray of food but decided to hang on to the small package of peanut butter crackers for later.

As Brent sat on his bed in silence, no longer hungry, his mind again wandered back to happier times. He smiled as he recalled his first day in the White House. He had just turned twenty-eight the day before and felt very anxious as he walked down Pennsylvania Avenue and up to the White House northwest gate, Post A4. The Secret Service uniformed officer spoke through a microphone from behind thick glass and asked how he could be of help. Brent showed his ID while explaining he was reporting for duty as the new assistant usher. A Secret Service sergeant came out through the door and greeted Brent.

"Hey there," the sergeant greeted with a broad smile. "I'm Sergeant Jack Woodard. You're the new usher?"

"Yes, sir."

The sergeant held out his hand. "Well, welcome to the White House! We're going to be working a lot together. Hand me your pass. I'll show you how to scan in." Brent handed over his pass and watched the sergeant tap it to the reader. He then asked Brent to enter his pin on the keypad. Brent entered the six-digit code and heard a buzz as the lock was released, and the sergeant pulled open the door for Brent to walk through.

Once inside the Post A4 guard house, the sergeant announced, "Guys, this is Brent Williams, the new usher."

The three officers all offered warm hellos and welcomed Brent. Brent was then invited to walk through the magnetometer, which emitted a beep.

Sergeant Woodard motioned for Brent to back up. Then pointing, the Sergeant continued. "Empty your pockets into this bin, and throw your backpack up on this conveyor belt, then walk back through." Brent obliged. No beep this time.

"Congrats!" bellowed out the overly friendly sergeant. "You'll be doing this for the next forty years!"

Brent thanked the officers and grabbed his backpack. As he walked out the door, he heard one of the officers radio ahead to the officer standing at the north portico: "New usher headed your way."

The view of the White House mansion as he walked up the sidewalk adjacent to the north drive was spectacular. With each step, the beautiful and famous façade became larger and larger. To his right, Brent could see reporters doing their live standups. He thought about how he would be one of those blurry images walking in the background of their shot. Rather than stare at the camera, he looked straight ahead, convincing himself he belonged.

Brent briskly walked up the steps at the north portico, and the uniformed officer smiled and welcomed him. Brent walked in through the front door and paused to take in the pristine view of the grand foyer. To his immediate right, the double doors to the ushers office were propped open, so he walked in. Inside, Winston was seated, reading *The Washington Post*, and Jim, the assistant usher, was at his desk on the phone. Jim saw Brent and offered a thumbs-up. Brent smiled and returned the gesture.

Winston looked over the top of his newspaper, saw Brent, and in one swift motion folded and then flipped the newspaper paper onto a nearby table. He stood and held out his hand. "Welcome, Mr. Williams. We've been waiting for you."

"I'm glad to be here, sir," said Brent.

"Leave your bag," Winston instructed. "I've got just ninety minutes to give you a quick tour. Follow me."

Brent followed Winston out the rear door of the ushers office and down the back stairs.

"We'll start with the shops and non-public rooms. I want the staff to meet you. Tomorrow, I'll have one of the curators give you an in-depth guided tour of the public rooms, and later this week, I will get you familiar with the private quarters. Hopefully, we'll have an opportunity to meet President and First Lady Blake."

Winston showed Brent the main kitchen, storekeepers office, grounds office, carpenter shop, electric shop, engineer shop, flower shop, housekeepers office, butlers room, curators office, and accounting office. They had traveled through so many basement sub-levels, Brent had no idea how to get back to any of them.

At almost ninety minutes into their tour, Winston looked at his phone and said, "Great, my meeting with the first lady has been delayed by five minutes. Let me show you one more room. Winston took Brent to a room that was under the north portico. Brent couldn't believe it when the lights came on; there it was, a beautiful modern bowling alley.

"You can thank President Truman for this. Although when he had it installed it was only one lane. We modernized it a few years ago and added the second lane." Winston reached down near the ball return and flipped a switch; a humming could then be heard as the lane lights illuminated. It looked to Brent like any other professional bowling alley he'd visited. Winston kicked off his shoes and picked up one of the bowling balls. Carefully, the older man lined up his shot and then delivered a perfect roll down the middle of the lane. *Strike!* The pins reset, and Winston motioned for Brent to take his turn.

Brent kicked off his shoes, grabbed a ball, lined up his shot, and took a three-step approach. Just as he was releasing the ball, his feet slipped out from under him, and he hit the floor, landing hard flat on his back. Brent raised his head just in time to watch his ball roll into the gutter. Winston had to lean against the wall, he was laughing so hard.

Winston, Jim (the evening usher), and several of the executive residence staff were in the ushers office watching Wolf Blitzer on CNN.

"Brenton Williams had spent time in Pakistan, and CNN has learned that the Office of Director of National Intelligence is now looking into the probability that Williams had been radicalized," Blitzer informed the public in his reliably matter-of-fact tone.

"We're now going live to the Department of Justice for a briefing being held by the FBI, and we understand that the attorney general may make comments as well, and yes, we can see the attorney general is at the podium. Let's go live."

Blitzer stared straight ahead, then his image was suddenly replaced by the chaos of the briefing room. On screen at the front of the room the middle-aged, stern-jawed attorney general could be seen, and behind him stood several others.

"Good evening," said the attorney general. His dark eyes scanned the room with severity, which immediately silenced the room's other occupants. "Brenton Augustus Williams at this time has been charged with three counts: murder one, concealing an illegal and deadly substance, and violating the Secret

Service lockdown order. Mr. Williams is presently being held in DC jail and is scheduled for arraignment tomorrow morning. I will now hand it over to FBI Special Agent Vance Clayton, who is the FBI lead for the investigation. Agent Clayton?"

Winston recognized Clayton and several others from the meeting in the map room early that morning.

"Brenton Augustus Williams has been charged with Section 22-2101," announced Clayton as the agent took the attorney general's place at the podium. "Murder in the first degree, premeditated killing of the president. Anyone found guilty of assassinating the president faces either the death penalty or life imprisonment. Williams is also being charged with concealing a deadly substance, and he has been charged with violating an order of the United States Secret Service. My involvement is primarily with the murder charge. We have other agents and US attorneys working through the other charges." The hundreds of clicks from the still photographers' cameras were almost deafening.

"And for everyone's edification, allow me to review the basics and the process we will be following. Assassination cases are investigated by the Federal Bureau of Investigation, which can and will seek assistance from any other federal, state, or local agencies, to include the branches of the US Armed Forces. Brenton Augustus Williams will be taken to

DC Superior Court tomorrow morning for arraignment, and if the judge so decides, a bond setting. The United States attorney for the District of Columbia, with the assistance of the FBI, will be working to prosecute all of Mr. Williams' criminal violations that occurred here, within Washington, DC.

"Mr. Williams has the right to a defense attorney; if he does not have one already, one will be appointed for him. Williams' defense attorney will represent Williams during the various hearings that will take place. If and when the case ends up going to trial, the defense attorney will work to put forth the most appropriate defense possible. That concludes our statement. We will provide additional briefings as warranted." Reporters began yelling questions as Agent Clayton, the attorney general, and others walked away.

The once-again chaotic scene of the briefing room was replaced by Wolf Blitzer's head just above the CNN banner on the ushers office television. "You have been watching a live briefing by the Department of Justice and the FBI. Let's go to White House Correspondent—"

Winston muted the TV. "I hate the way they always go and tell us what we just heard," he muttered. Facing the gathered staff, he said, "I need all of you to go back to work. I'll keep you posted on developments." The assembled staff sauntered out.

Winston had been up for over thirty-six hours; he was beyond exhausted. He said good night to Jim and then walked into the first-floor pantry, poured a large glass of Bordeaux, and headed down the service elevator to the ushers suite in the sub-basement to spend the night.

***

8 p.m., Hay Adams Hotel

Loretta walked through the lobby; she was very familiar with the route. She pulled the keycard from her purse, entered the elevator, swiped her card through the reader, and pressed number seven. As the elevator rose, she looked in the mirror and touched up her lipstick. The elevator doors opened, and she walked toward the door to room 706, swiped her card again, and entered the room. She heard the shower running, popped her head in the bathroom, and announced her arrival with, "Hello, love."

A voice from the shower responded, "Hiya, babe. Pour us a drink. I'll be right out." Loretta smiled and went back to the bedroom to admire the spectacular view from the double-balcony door windows that looked out upon the north side of the White House. Night had fallen, so the entire front facade was all lit up. She poured two Blanton's, took a sip, looked in the mirror, removed her chignon, and shook out her hair, which fell to beyond her shoulders. She then undressed, took another sip of her drink, placed the two glasses on the bedside table, and then climbed into bed to await her amour.

***

9:50 p.m., the Ellipse, south of the White House

The dark figure on a rental scooter was only a blur as they sped down 17th Street in DC. Just past E Street, they pulled off to the sidewalk and parked. The light traffic allowed the dark figure to jaywalk across the street and follow the walking path toward the Ellipse.

***

As President Gentry and the admiral admired the dessert the butler had just laid before them, Chef Patrick Sullivan knew he was done for the evening. He left the second-floor kitchen and headed to his locker in the White House basement, where he slipped off his chef's frock, threw it in a laundry bag, pulled a sweatshirt on over his head and grabbed his coat. He then exited the White House via the east appointments gate, A1. He joked with the officers on post, said his good nights, and headed south on East Exec to get to his car parked on the Ellipse.

The dark figure wore a hoody, resembling any other jogger in the park. No one seemed to notice the figure crouch down next to the Subaru Forrester. The beep to unlock the door signaled Patrick's approach.

Patrick placed his remote back into his pocket and proofread the text he was about to send out: *I feel badly how we left things this afternoon. Can we please meet, take our time, and talk?* Before he hit send, he got into his car. As he reached over to close his door behind him, a dark blur appeared from his back left. He felt the high-voltage surge go through his body and blacked out.

***

At 11 p.m., Secret Service Uniform Division Officer Jeff Hill had finished his shift. He was exhausted and just wanted to get home, so he decided not to bother stopping at the uniform division's locker room in the basement of the executive office building, where most of the guys at the end of their shifts changed out of their uniforms and into civilian clothes. As he approached his car on the Ellipse, he noticed Patrick Sullivan's vehicle still sitting next to his. Over the years, the Secret Service and executive residence staffers had grown familiar with one another's vehicles. Jeff thought it strange that tonight, with no special event going on in the White House, Patrick hadn't left yet. As he got closer, it appeared that Patrick was in his car.

Officer Hill walked up to the driver's side. *Is he sleeping?* Jeff wondered. He pulled the flashlight from his gun belt, turned it on, and looked in the car. Patrick was slumped to the left, leaning against the window. Jeff saw blood on the front of his shirt. Hill took a few steps backward and called the Secret Service joint operations center (JOC).

Hill then went to the other side of the vehicle and used his nightstick to shatter the glass, careful not to destroy the scene. He reached in, opened the door from the inside, and then moved farther in to check for a pulse. None. He radioed back to the JOC to report that the individual did not have a pulse and that the victim was Patrick Sullivan from the executive residence staff.

Within minutes, several Secret Service officers arrived on foot. More came in their vehicles, red and blue lights flashing. A Secret Service sergeant approached, then looked in the Subaru. He radioed JOC to report what he had seen, then instructed them to notify US Park Police and the DC Metropolitan Police Department (MPD). Within minutes, dozens of Secret Service agents, along with MPD, Park Police, and DC Fire & Rescue personnel, were on the scene. DC Fire paramedics ultimately declared the victim was deceased, at which point DC Fire called the DC medical examiner's office, requesting that they respond and officially record the incident.

The Ellipse is under the law enforcement jurisdiction of the Secret Service and the US Park Police. Since the Secret Service was the originating agency on the scene, the Secret Service crime scene unit was dispatched. That unit made it clear that the

Secret Service, along with the US Park Police, would manage the scene with MPD to assist only if needed.

A Secret Service lieutenant walked several steps away from the activity to find a quiet spot, then phoned Captain Scott Saras, the overnight watch commander.

"Captain, I'm on the scene and wanted to provide you with the latest. We've confirmed the identity from his White House pass around his neck. It's Patrick Sullivan, the sous chef. It appears he was killed by a self-inflicted single shot. Entry point was under his chin. He was still holding the gun, a Baretta 21A, .22-caliber, equipped with a silencer. MPD ran a check. The only firearm registered to Patrick Sullivan was a Ruger Wrangler .22-caliber. And Scott, we found what appears to be a suicide note. It says he was upset about the president's death, and the note infers Brent Williams killed the president."

"Oh, Christ. Okay. Maintain the scene," the captain instructed. "I'm on my way."

Chapter 12
3:50 a.m., Tuesday, March 3: The White House

Winston thought for sure he was dreaming. The knocking got louder and louder. Abruptly, he realized he was not asleep. Someone was banging on the door to the basement ushers suite. He jumped out of bed and fumbled for the light, then rushed over to the door to find one of the White House night engineers with a uniformed Secret Service duty captain.

"Winston, I've got some horrible news."

Winston stared blankly at his friend Captain Scott Saras; a handsome, athletic man whose big, broad shoulders took up almost the entire doorway. A seasoned member of the Secret Service Uniformed Division, he and Winston had worked together for years. Winston thanked the engineer for escorting the captain and invited Saras into the suite, where they each took a seat.

"What now?" asked Winston.

"Winston, Patrick Sullivan was found shot to death on the Ellipse. It appears to have been a suicide."

The Ellipse was situated between the White House and Washington Monument. While Winston parked on West Executive Avenue between the west wing and the executive office building, the assistant ushers parked adjacent to the White House on East Executive Avenue. The rest of the executive residence staff parked farther away on the Ellipse.

Winston took a deep breath. Feeling stunned, slowly shaking his head, he asked, "What happened?"

"He was found in his car with a gunshot wound to his head. It may have happened last night around 10 p.m., just after he left the White House."

Winston leaned forward and began massaging his temples. After a moment he looked up at Captain Saras. "Oh, my God. What led you to believe it was suicide?"

"He was in his car. It was locked. No sign of a struggle, and we found a note," reported the captain.

"What did it say?"

"It was short, said something to the effect that the death of President Blake was just too much to handle and how he had suspected Brent and that he could not forgive himself for not doing enough to prevent it."

Winston stood and began to pace a few steps back and forth as he thought. "My God. I remember how upset he looked while the medics were trying to revive the president, but I had no idea he was that bad off. I should have been more aware."

"Winston, don't beat yourself up. You can never stop someone who is emotionally unstable and intent on killing themselves."

Winston stopped pacing, pinched his lower lip as he thought. "I would like to inform the First Lady and the new president. Do you know if the press has gotten this yet?"

"Not unless they listen to the DC police scanner."

"Well, actually, some of them do. I better get dressed. Thanks, Scott."

"Of course, Winston. I'm just sorry I had to bring you such bad news."

***

5 a.m., Tuesday, March 3: The White House

Winston poured his second cup of coffee. Soon, the majority of the staff would be arriving. He needed to alert them fast and then take care of his top priority: the first lady. He would inform President Elizabeth Gentry later. He looked up; as usual, CNN was on the ushers office TV. Thankfully, nothing about Chef Sullivan yet. They were still busy dissecting the president's press conference and the FBI statement from last night.

Secret Service Special Agent in Charge Greg Leidner walked into the office carrying a travel coffee mug and sat in a vacant chair near Winston.

There was concern all over his face as he took his seat. "Winston, I'm so sorry about Patrick. It was a shock to all the guys on the detail. How are you holding up?" he asked.

"Greg, I'm doing my best. Neither the staff nor the first lady knows yet, so I've got to deal with that. Then, we have to be ready for President Blake's casket, which arrives at 8 a.m."

"Right. The military just coordinated with us to make sure they're no delays getting the caisson through security." Greg then lowered his voice to prevent anyone else from hearing. "So, how's Brent doing?"

"No clue. I've been so busy with everything here, I have not had a minute to think, let alone try and visit him."

"Winston, I know Brent better than anyone, and absolutely none of this makes any sense. There's a lot more to this than we know."

"No doubt. Right now, I can't figure out any of it. I know Brent didn't do anything wrong." After a pause, Winston changed the subject. "So, how are you all adjusting to the new president thus far?'

Greg rolled his eyes. "Let's just say she's demanding. I started to say high-maintenance, but that's not fair. Let's give her a few months."

"Good idea. I'll do the same," Winston declared. "Now I've got to set up the meeting with the staff. Thanks for coming by Greg. I've always appreciated your trust, help, and insight. Thanks."

"Winston, you can always count on me for anything. Good luck today!"

Both men stood and shook hands.

Winston composed an email to all the residence staff announcing that there would be a mandatory meeting in the basement staff lunchroom at 6:30 a.m., making sure to put "do not be late" in bold font.

He glanced at his watch. It was after 6:15. Winston wondered why his assistant had not arrived yet. The day shift started at 6, but typically, whoever was on duty would arrive by 5:45 at the latest. Maybe when he redid the schedule, he had accidentally left the shift unassigned. He pulled up the schedule and was relieved to see he had not made a mistake; Loretta was scheduled for this morning. He thought, *Loretta was never late for anything.* Winston grabbed the desk phone and keyed in her number.

She answered on the first ring and in a rushed voice said, "Hi, Winston. Sorry. I got a late start. I'm almost there."

"That's fine. I just wanted to make sure everything was all right. I scheduled an all-hands meeting at 6:30 in the lunchroom. You need to be there."

Loretta responded, "Okay. See you there."

***

Winston walked into the basement lunchroom; it was filled with the majority of the staff. The curators and budget staff typically arrived after 7 a.m. Winston would brief them later.

He stood in front of the room. "Team, thank you for gathering on such short notice. I have some very distressing news to share." Winston paused as Loretta arrived. Since there were no seats available, she stood just inside the doorway, leaning against the wall. Winston was annoyed that she was late and did not appreciate being interrupted. He tried his best not to show his displeasure but knew it must have been obvious. He continued, "I have some very grim news to share. Patrick Sullivan died last night." There was an audible gasp in the room.

Loretta sensed her legs going weak. She leaned back against the wall for support. Her stomach turned, and she instinctively placed her hands over her abdomen. Winston watched with concern as Loretta bolted from the room. He heard others in the room crying but went on, "I don't have all of the details at this point, and any speculation would be unfair to Patrick's family. I will share more once I know more. In the meantime, President Blake's casket is arriving at 8 a.m. and will lay in state in the east room for twelve hours. Mrs. Blake has been phenomenal. Even in her grief, she has asked me many times how the residence staff are doing. So, please, let's show the world what high-caliber professionals we are. Thank you, and if anyone needs to talk to me, I will make time available for you."

Winston made a quick exit. He found Loretta still in the hallway, walking away very slowly. He approached, noticing how pale she was. Tears streamed down her face. He guided her into a nearby utility room where they would have privacy.

"Loretta, are you okay?" he asked.

Loretta looked at Winston. Her mouth opened, but no words came out. She looked down and slowly shook her head. Finally, after a long pause, she said, "I'm sorry. This is such a shock…. I'm having difficulty understanding. Winston…" She hesitated, seeming to struggle to find the right words. "We had kept it a secret, but Patrick and I had been in a relationship."

Winston was totally caught off guard. In the twenty-four years he had known her, he had never seen any evidence of Loretta having any type of relationship. "I'm so sorry—I had no idea."

"Please. Please, tell me what happened," Loretta begged.

Winston decided to share what he knew, ending with the discovery of Patrick's suicide note.

Loretta closed her eyes and began to sob. "No. Oh, my God! Oh, my God!"

Winston held her and softly offered, "I want you to take some time. For now, let's go to the basement usher suite, where you can get yourself together. Then go home. I've got everything covered here."

Chapter 13
7 a.m., Tuesday, March 3: DC Jail

A different nurse injected Brent's morning insulin. After she left, Brent finished the last of his oatmeal. There were two guards seated and facing him from outside his cell; they were maybe ten feet away. Yesterday, he had been aware that guards had been stationed somewhere in the vicinity of his cell, but they had not been visible.

Two additional guards appeared, and the four of them approached in unison and unlocked the cell door. They told Brent to stand in the middle of his cell. He was surprised to hear that he had a visitor and they needed to cuff his hands and shackle his feet in order to take him to the visitor room.

With a guard on either side of him, one in front and one behind, Brent was escorted through several corridors and then led into the kind of room that he had only seen before in movies. It had seats for the prisoners facing their guests on the other side of a partition made of heavy, bulletproof plexiglass. A phone was present. Brent was thrilled to see his best friend, Secret Service agent Greg Leidner. Brent sat opposite him, staring into his friend's eyes through the plexiglass barrier. Brent's chains rustled as he picked up the phone to talk.

"Man, am I happy to see you!" Brent gushed.

"Me too," Greg agreed. "Hey, remember: Everything we say, they're listening to it."

"I don't have anything to hide.... Dude, what the hell is going on? I have no idea why or how I ended up here."

"It's not looking too good for ya, man. Why did you have that toxin? And what's this shit about you being in Pakistan? They're saying you were radicalized."

"That's total bullshit!" Brent yelled incredulously into the phone. "I have no clue about any toxin or how anything may have ended up in my suit! Pakistan? Are you kidding me?! That was years ago, when I was in my early twenties, and I declared that trip on my security papers! I only went there to accompany my aging stepfather, who was old and frail at the time. I just wanted to make sure he got to see his family. It was an amazing trip. The Pakistani people were friendly, warm, and most respectful. No one talked to me about Islam, ever!"

Greg was concerned for his friend, trying his best to be positive. "Hopefully, they'll be able to figure out that you were never radicalized."

Brent did a quick glance around the room to see if anyone could hear. "So, what are you hearing? How did all this happen? And Beth is now president of the United States? Unbelievable!"

Greg lowered his voice. "I talked to Wendy Wolf last night. She and some of the ladies in the VP's—uh, excuse me, the president's office—mentioned something about you and the vice president. Dammit! I need to refer to her as President Gentry. Anyway, there is talk that you had a thing for her, and they're wondering if you had an infatuation and that was why you did what you did—so she could become president."

Brent leaned so far forward he was practically standing, his phone cord stretched to the max. "Jesus Christ, Greg! Listen to yourself! You believe that shit?"

"Of course not! I'm just letting you know what you're up against."

Brent sat back in his chair. "Crap. That's probably why Beth is keeping her distance from me," Brent realized.

"Could be."

"They let me make two phone calls late yesterday afternoon. One was to you. Did you get my voice mail?" asked Brent.

"Yes, of course—about Frank Osborne."

"Yes, I want him to be my attorney," Brent asserted.

"Good idea. I always liked Frank. He's one of the guys. He was just leaving the Secret Service when I was coming on board. And now he's, like, number ninety-seven on the *Forbes* top billionaires list."

"Actually, he's number ninety-one." Brent smiled. "See, Greg, you've still got a chance! Frank went from Secret Service to the US attorney's office and finally to K Street, where he's now making billions!" Brent switched to a more serious tone. "Anyway, my second call was to Frank. I left a voice mail telling him my arraignment was at 8:15." Brent glanced at the wall clock. "In just about an hour from now."

"When I got your message, I decided to do a quick check. Here's my file on him." Greg held the bio page printout up to the glass for Brent to read:

> **Frank Osborne**, forty-eight, twice married, twice divorced. Undergrad and law degree from UVA. Career started as uniformed officer in the Secret Service. Was promoted to a lead agent position as a presidential protection detail agent. Went to the Department of Justice, served as a US attorney. Spent time on Wall Street, and today, he's a very successful investor and K-Street lawyer, well known for representing corporate and political leaders in a variety of noteworthy cases. He has been

instrumental in providing behind-the-scenes political strategy to numerous high office holders from both sides of the aisle. Frank's net worth is among the highest in Washington.

"Yep, that's all correct," Brent approved. "Greg, Frank's a good man. I'll never be able to afford him, but if he can at the least attend my arraignment tomorrow, that would be really good."

Two guards approached and announced that their time was up.

"I'll let you go, man. I'll be back." Greg paused. "Oh, shit, I forgot—they found Patrick Sullivan dead in his car last night. Looks like he shot himself."

Chapter 14
8 a.m., Tuesday, March 3: The White House

The caisson pulled by six horses and escorted by a military honor guard, representing all the branches of the Armed Forces, majestically rolled through the northwest gate from Pennsylvania Avenue and approached the north portico.

The former first lady, Winston, and President Elizabeth Gentry stood in the grand foyer and watched as the soldiers lifted and brought President Blake's casket up the steps and in through the north portico door, then headed to the main cross-hall and into the east room. Mrs. Blake, guided by Winston, followed the procession while President Gentry stood back. The soldiers methodically lifted the casket and placed it on the catafalque, which was positioned directly beneath the large center chandelier. There was no press other than one pooled TV camera that captured the events for live broadcast.

Winston escorted the former first lady to the edge of the casket, then he stood back to allow her time to herself. Mrs. Blake gently touched the draped American flag that ornamentally covered the casket. She then kneeled on the small ledge of the catafalque and prayed. After several minutes, she stood and looked to Winston for guidance. Winston stepped forward and offered the first lady his arm, which she took. Together, they slowly walked out of the east room, passing President Gentry in the grand foyer without so much as a glance. Winston then took the first lady upstairs via the president's elevator and returned to the state floor. As soon as he stepped off the elevator, President Gentry was there to meet him.

She stepped right up to Winston and pressed her face within inches of his so that no one else could hear. "I want that woman out of my house so my husband and I can move in. No delays. Make it happen!" Before Winston could respond, Gentry turned on her heel and rushed down the back stairs, heading toward the oval office.

Back in the ushers office, CNN was again the television station of choice. They had just aired the event in the east room. Now, a news anchor announced, "We have breaking news and are now going live to CNN's Kasha Garrett reporting from DC Superior Court."

Winston's weary eyes settled on the uber-serious, middle-aged face of Garrett on the wall-mounted TV as she began. "Yes, DC Superior Court Judge Rufus Queen, in a surprise move, has just set accused presential assassin Brenton Augustus Williams bond at a record $275 million. Judge Queen stated that in determining Williams' bond amount, he took into consideration that Williams would not be a flight risk, and if Williams were to somehow post bond, he would be under house arrest, and the court would implement sophisticated electronic measures to ensure compliance with the bond measures. Brenton Williams' attorney, the well-known litigator Frank Osborne, argued that the bail was excessive for an individual who had no record. Judge Queen ignored Osborne and announced the trial would take place in forty-five days. This drew an immediate protest from Osborne, who said the defense needed at minimum 120 days to prepare. Again, Judge Queen ignored the attorney."

"Thank you, Kasha," said the CNN anchor. "We now have more breaking news. CNN has just learned that White House sous chef Patrick Sullivan was found dead last night in his car parked on the Ellipse near the White House. There are unconfirmed reports that Sullivan was despondent over the death of President Blake and that he took his own life. Sullivan, as we previously reported, had prepared the president's final meal on Sunday night and was the one who alerted staff that the president had collapsed. CNN is working to get additional details and will be reporting on this and other developing stories."

The phone rang. Jim, who had come in to relieve Loretta, answered. He held the phone out for Winston, telling him it was Chief of Staff Wendy Wolf.

Winston pressed the receiver to his ear. "Yes, Wendy."

"Oh, Winston, we feel so horrible over here in the west wing with everything you're having to deal with. I'm so sad. I didn't know Chef Patrick very well, but during the few encounters I had with him he was always nice."

"Yes, Patrick will be missed. Wendy, thank you. You're always so considerate and supportive of the ushers office. We're getting by."

"Well, please let us know if there is anything we can do," Wendy offered. "Oh, and the president wanted me to tell you that she is perfectly fine with the current executive residence staffing, especially the executive chef, and she would like to offer some suggestions for both Assistant Usher Brent and Sous Chef Patrick's replacements."

Winston was caught a bit off guard, thinking President Gentry's reaction to be highly inappropriate, but he kept his demeanor positive. "Of course. I'm ready to meet with her any time to discuss it."

"Perfect. Thank you, Winston. Call me personally for anything if needed."

"Absolutely," replied Winston. "Will do."

Chapter 15
11 a.m., Tuesday, March 3: DC Jail

Attorney Frank Osborne glanced down at his Baume & Mercier watch as he sat at the small table in the DC jail attorney/prisoner conference room. Older in appearance than his forty-eight years, Frank had dark hair and with its professional dye job, it looked completely natural. His full beard was nicely trimmed, and his slightly overweight physique was greatly improved by his tailored suits and designer shoes. Frank, known for his wit and sense of humor, was an exceptional orator and champion debater, often quoting Lincoln, Churchill, or Shakespeare to make his point.

Frank took a moment to visually survey the room and believed it would be sufficient for his purposes: no windows, just one table and two chairs. The door opened, and three DC police officers escorted Brent Williams into the room. Brent shuffled along slowly so as to not trip over the shackled chains around his ankles. Frank was concerned by what he saw. Brent was pale, looked like he hadn't slept for days. His usually well-coiffed brown hair was totally unkempt, he needed a shave, and he walked as if he were in pain. When he looked up to see Frank, he smiled, Frank could see Brent's pale blue eyes were totally bloodshot.

Frank asked the guards to remove the shackles and handcuffs, but the guards responded that it was against policy—presidential assassins were to remain in chains whenever not in their cells. Osborne questioned if there was such a policy, but the police officers ignored him as they left the room and shut the door. The sliding of the deadbolt could be heard, locking the two in the room.

"Brent, we should be okay to discuss anything in here. The room is not wired. How are you doing?"

"Frank, first of all, thank you for showing up," said Brent with emotion. "I wasn't sure if I would end up this morning with a court-appointed lawyer, or what would happen exactly."

Frank motioned for Brent to take a seat and then took the other seat, which was across the table from him. "I got your voice mail, and Greg Leidner stopped by my house early this morning. I asked him why he didn't just simply call. He said this was too important and that he wanted to meet with me face to face. We had a good talk. He did share with me what Wendy Wolf told him. You should know you have a really good friend in Greg," Frank said.

Brent grimaced. "Oh my God! Wendy's story is total bullshit! I like Beth, but it's nothing close to an infatuation, dammit!" He took a breath, then continued. "And yes, I agree, Greg's like the brother I never had."

"Cool. Okay, I need to know more about Wendy Wolf." Frank pulled out a notebook from his briefcase, which he placed on the table and opened. He flipped to the first page and tapped his finger against a line of neatly written cursive. "Here's what I have: Wendy is a forty-four-year-old former attorney, was a close friend and top advisor to Vice President Elizabeth Gentry, and now is chief of staff to President Gentry. They both went to Harvard Law at the same time. Wolf spent time as an intelligence analyst with the CIA. She also worked at the Securities and Exchange Commission. Anything I'm missing?"

"I didn't really know her, but I knew who she was when I worked for the ODNI." Brent explained. "She had a good reputation. I never met her until President Blake and VP Gentry came to the White House. I do think she's really cute."

"Well, thank you for your in-depth analysis. I do have eyes!"

"Look, Frank, in regard to your fees, I've got some savings that—"

Frank interrupted with, "Brent, let's figure out fees later. Right now, our focus needs to be on getting you out of here and resolving all this, and/or worse case, preparing for your trial. So, let me start with some questions. And before I begin, I need your commitment to total honesty, full disclosure, and complete detail on every aspect of this case. Let me make this perfectly clear: I am the one person you need to be open and honest with. Do you understand and agree?"

"Of course, but ya know, I've been completely honest with everyone!" Brent tried to use his hands to emphasize his point, but the chains restricted his movement.

"Hold on a sec." Frank stood, went to the door, and then knocked. The officer opened the door, and Frank told him to get his sergeant. .

Moments later, the sergeant arrived, and Frank greeted him with a smile. "Darius, how ya doing? More importantly, how's your son?"

The thin brown sergeant with closely cropped white hair grinned and responded, "Hey, Frank. Great to see you, and my boy's great, in his second year at Maryland. He may start at safety next season."

"I'm impressed! And fear the turtle!" said Frank. They both laughed. "Hey, do me a favor…. The officers mentioned something about a policy preventing my client from being shackle and handcuff-free. Can you help us with that?"

"No problem, Frank. They're just being overly cautious." The sergeant called in the officers and told them to remove the chains.

"Darius, thanks," said Frank as the guards left with the chains and cuffs in tow. "You're the best. Can I please ask you one more favor?"

"Of course. What do you need?"

Frank handed him a $100 bill. "Can you get us some subs and beer and use the change to treat yourself and your guys?"

Darius took the bill. "I'm on it. See you in a few."

The door closed. Brent massaged his wrists, then looked up at Frank. "Thanks. Is there anyone in this town that you don't know?"

Frank smiled. "Don't forget, I spent a lot of time in law enforcement before landing my current job. But the most important thing is to just be nice to people. Okay, let's get back to it. I've read the police, medical, and court reports and will be asking some follow-up questions pertaining to them, but I wanted to start with some general background so that I have a complete picture of the entire context. Tell me about your relationship with then-Vice President, now President Elizabeth Gentry."

"Beth and I have always worked well together," recalled Brent. He slid his chair back and crossed his legs. "We're friends."

"Brent, in order for me to help you, you're going to have to share much more. Tell me about your so-called 'friendship' and everything else."

"Well, starting two years ago, as soon as President Blake came into the White House, I met Beth," Brent began. "She was really cool, fun, and fascinated with White House history. I gave her many long tours. We got along great. She asked me to help her on various projects. Eventually, we started working together on White House events. As each event ended with great success, she would insist that I help her on additional projects, some of which were even outside of the White House. Everything was above board, and Beth kept Winston informed and she often lauded my efforts directly to President Blake."

"Were you attracted to her?" asked Frank.

"Attracted?" Brent repeated. "Well, she's absolutely gorgeous, and I'm a man, but I know my place. She's the vice president and married!"

"So, I'll put that down as a yes. Were there ever times you felt things were getting too close?"

Brent considered the question. "I'm not sure it's fair for me to suggest things were getting too close, but I admit, I did wonder six months ago during the state dinner for the president of Brazil when she dared me to accept a challenge."

"Interesting. Do tell."

"As you know, during events, the White House ushers mix and mingle with guests. We essentially blend in, which makes our job of supervising the event that much more effective, and I have to admit, fun! Typically, we're always in business attire—a suit and tie—but state dinners are formal, so we're in black-tie. This particular evening, Beth was in an amazing, blue sequined formal dress that looked as if it had been painted on her. She was receiving quite a bit of attention. Dinner had just finished, and the guests were moving from the state dining room to the east room for the after-dinner entertainment, a tribute to Rodgers and Hart. The band was basically covering the duo's greatest hits from 1918 to 1933—not really my cup of tea!

"Well, evidently Beth wasn't too thrilled about it either. She motioned me to follow her to a dark corner of the green room. She had this devilish grin and said, 'Let's get out of here!' I laughed and asked if she was nuts or drunk. She laughed and said both, but then said she had only two glasses of champagne. She told me she wanted to see how good I was, and I could prove it by sneaking her out of the White House undetected. Well, I'm not one to pass up such a challenge. So, I told her to meet me on the ground floor near the back stairs and that we could not take the elevator because the Secret Service had a camera watching it.

"Minutes later, the two of us met and went down three levels to the sub-basement. From there, it was a bit tricky. We traversed the passage between the White House and the east wing, but the Secret Service had a camera on the barred gate. So, we walked through the basement storage rooms and avoided the cross-hall, which was also monitored by a camera. At the far end and near the barred gate, I stepped in front of the gate while Beth hid out of sight. I waved to the camera, which was normal routine. The Secret Service guys in the JOC saw me, pressed a button, and unlocked the gate. As I walked through, I quickly flipped up a yellow legal pad in front of the camera while holding the door for Beth to dash through undetected, then I swiftly pulled the pad away. This would have appeared as a brief split-second blackout on the camera, which I knew the guys at the JOC would simply attribute to their old camera equipment flickering.

"Beth and I then navigated the remainder of the east wing basement corridor until we got to the iron ladder stairs, which led to the rear of the family movie theater. We climbed up, and I told Beth to pull her shawl up over her head. Then I escorted her out of the east wing and through A1. At the appointments gate, I explained to the officers that I was helping one of the dinner guests who had become ill. Once we got out and onto East Exec Avenue, success! We were laughing like kids as we walked to Pennsylvania Avenue, then to 15th Street, where Beth hailed a cab.

"At that point, I was thinking, *What on earth?* We get into the cab, and she says 'Watergate!' I asked her what was at the Watergate. She told me she had a condo there that she used as a hideaway now and then. It was off the grid, so to speak. The Secret Service didn't know about it. I reminded Beth that we only had fifty-five minutes before she needed to be back on the state floor."

"So where did she leave the admiral?" Frank asked.

"When we left the state floor, he was walking into the east room to see the Rodgers and Hart tribute, which was more fitting to his era than most!"

"Okay," said Frank. "Go on."

"The taxi drove us up to the front of the Watergate complex. Beth looked at me waiting for me to pay, so I threw the guy a ten for an eight-dollar fare and jumped out, following Beth as she quickly walked to a side entrance of one of the buildings in the complex. She pulls a plastic card out of her tiny purse and swipes it through a reader to gain access, and in we go. We get on an elevator and go up several floors to her penthouse. We walk into her place, which is really nice. She goes to a shelf, where she had several decanters of liquor, and pours two glasses, hands me one. She then toasts me for getting her out of the White House without being detected. We clink glasses and drink. I remark at how good it is, and she says, 'It should be.

It's a special Macallan twenty-five-year single malt.' I looked it up later. It's considered to be the Rolls-Royce of single malts at $2,300 per bottle!"

"Please tell me you walked out of there with a bottle!" exclaimed Frank.

"No. I could never do that! Anyway, we drink our scotch, and after a few minutes of small talk, she gives me a tour of the place. it's incredible—two bedrooms, a large living room, and a study. The place is amazing, but the one thing I noticed was that the ceilings seemed low. I had heard that complaint about the Watergate. Having been built in the 1960s, it didn't have the advanced architectural features of more modern condos in DC. Anyway, she invites me to the balcony, which has a magnificent view of the Potomac. Man, it was like a dream.

"As we're leaning against the railing enjoying the view, she leans against me and whispers in my ear, 'We can do this often.' I looked into her eyes. I couldn't resist. We were about to embrace, and I swear to you, both of our cell phones went off within a split second of one another. My call was from a high school friend, so I ignored it, but she answered her call, and I could actually hear a man's voice ask, 'Where are you?' She whispered a response: 'I'll call you later.' I then looked at my watch. It was 10:30, so I told her we only had ten minutes to get back to the White House. She sighed and said, 'Got it. Let's go.' So, now you know the whole story."

"How'd you get her back in the White House?"

Frank and Brent were both a little startled by the sudden knock at the door. It opened, and two officers brought in a bag of food and an ice-cold six-pack of Dog Fish 60 Minute IPA. Frank thanked the officers, took out two beers, and then reached into the bag and pulled out two wrapped twelve-inch subs.

Frank handed a sub to Brent. "By the way, that is a great story!"

Brent opened the beers. He stared at the food in front of him, mesmerized. The smell of the fresh deli meat and onions awoke his senses and made him realize he was absolutely famished. He slowly unwrapped his sub and savored the first bite. He then took a sip of his beer, closed his eyes, and smiled. For a brief instant, everything seemed normal again.

"These are great subs," Brent commented after he swallowed his first delicious bite. "And how did you remember my favorite beer?"

"Dude! The last time you spent the night at my place, it was after we drank, I don't remember how many of these!"

"Yeah, that was when my life was normal."

"Well, I'm gonna do everything I can to help you, but friend, your life will never be normal. Okay... finish the story, please!"

"Okay. Where'd I leave off? Oh, getting her back to the White House... So, we took a cab. She sits really close to me, like, practically on my lap! It's a short cab ride to 17th and Penn. She got out as I paid. I let her get about fifteen feet ahead of me. As she approached the northwest gate, I kept going past, but I was close enough to hear her explain to the surprised Secret Service officers that she had gone out because she needed some fresh air. They of course immediately let her in. As I continued my walk down Pennsylvania Avenue, I looked to my right and watched as she walked up the north drive to the north portico and in through the front door. As it turned out, she walked in just as the east room entertainment had ended and the guests had started to exit."

"What did you do?"

"I continued walking all the way around to Post A1 on East Exec and entered the entrance as I would normally do. A shift change for the Secret Service had just occurred, so there were all new officers on post, a few said hello but none of the guys asked me anything about seeing me exit with a sick guest sixty minutes earlier. I got back to the ushers office. Everyone hanging out in the office thought I had been in the east room watching the show."

"So, what do you think coulda-woulda happened?" asked Frank.

"I've thought about it a lot, my being single, Beth growing bored with her aging Navy admiral husband… I dunno. If there had been more time, who knows? I was certainly intrigued. Yes, okay, I'll admit it. I'm attracted to her. There was definitely chemistry between us. But that was it. Nothing more, and believe me, it was never as Wendy Wolf described—as me having some sort of John Hinkley Jr./Travis Bickle from *Taxi Driver* infatuation!"

Frank chewed a bite of his sub. "So, how have things with you and Beth been ever since?"

"Cordial. I mean, we still joke around a little, but it's different. Nothing romantic. Nothing close to that night on the balcony."

"Is this how it happened with you and the social secretary from the last administration?"

Brent, about to take a bite, stopped and lowered his sub. "No. That was totally different. Well, I guess it was different. I mean, it was nothing like it was with Beth, and of course, the social secretary and I had a true relationship. It lasted two years. It was not hidden."

"That led to your divorce, right?" Frank reminded him.

"No, my marriage was pretty much over when I came to the White House eight years ago. It took two years for my divorce to be finalized. During that time, I was legally separated and free to date. So, I did. The woman I dated just so happened to be the social secretary."

Frank put his beer down: "Glad to see you're moving up!" They both laughed.

"This has been really helpful. Good info. I've got to leave soon but know this: I'm gonna get you out of here!" Frank assured. "Don't lose faith. Give me time."

"C'mon. Stay for one more beer."

"What the hell." Frank opened another beer. "I've got nothing better to do than hang out in a DC jail."

Chapter 16
8 p.m., Tuesday, March 3: The White House

The horse-drawn caisson carrying President Blake's casket departed the White House via the NE gate en route to the Capitol rotunda. Winston stood in silence with the former first lady at the north portico. Once the caisson was no longer visible, she turned toward Winston, and he escorted her back to the second-floor private quarters. He was about to leave when Mrs. Blake asked him to sit with her in the west sitting hall. They sat on the sofa in silence for several minutes before she spoke.

"Winston, I know it's been a little over two years, but in a good way, it feels more like twenty. You've always made us feel truly comfortable here and made it a real home for us. My husband thought the world of you, and oftentimes at dinner, he would relay to me historical tidbits you had shared with him. I would love to know, who was your favorite president?"

Winston smiled. "Why, Mrs. Blake, President Blake was my favorite." They shared a hearty laugh.

"Winston, you're the consummate diplomat!" she exclaimed. "So, let me ask it this way, who was your second favorite president?"

"I sincerely liked all the presidents I have served. I owe a great deal of gratitude to President Nixon, who made it possible for me to serve in this job. I have worked for ten presidents and have been honored to have met three others: presidents Johnson, Eisenhower, and Truman. I count my blessings and cherish each and every moment that I have had in this job."

The first lady peered at him. "Winston, has anyone ever mentioned to you that you resemble the actor Morgan Freeman?"

Winston smiled. "Yes, I get that a lot. In fact, one time, back in the Reagan White House, the social office staff talked me into pretending I was Morgan Freeman for a party the Reagans were having with close personal friends. Mrs. Reagan was even in on it! My job was simply to walk around with a cocktail in my hand. Well, turned out the joke was on me, because in the middle of my 'performance,' the real Morgan Freeman walked up to me. Everyone was laughing at my expense. I had been set up!"

"Oh, Winston, that's absolutely hilarious! Tell me more about where you're from and about your family."

"Well, I was born in Salisbury, North Carolina. I never knew my dad. He was killed in World War II during the Battle of the Bulge, and I was born eight months later. My mom never remarried. She raised my three older brothers and two older sisters and me. My brothers are all gone. Two were killed in Vietnam, and the oldest one died a few years ago. My sisters are still around. They are in North Carolina."

"Winston, oh, my God. I had no idea you lost two brothers in Vietnam. That's so tragic, so unfair."

"Yes, that's why, after I graduated from college, I joined the Marines and served two tours in Vietnam. Like a fool, I thought I could make a difference. It was really hard on my mother."

"Tell me about your parents," requested the first lady.

"My dad was a carpenter," Winston began, "who got drafted. His first action was during D-Day, the Normandy Invasion, June 1944. He served over six months in France and then came home at the end of 1944 for his mother's funeral, but they only allowed him to stay for a week and then sent him back, and he was killed shortly thereafter. My mom worked with her parents who were sharecroppers on a cotton and tobacco farm. She eventually attended nursing school at night and became a nurse."

"Amazing," commented the first lady. "What a story, and your mother was an incredible woman to have raised six kids. Wow."

Winston: "Yes, my mom was amazing. We were also lucky that both she and my dad came from big families, so I had grandparents and lots of aunts and uncles helping out."

"So, I know you went to college," she recalled. "Did any of your siblings go?"

"My oldest brother got his degree. He ended up as a teacher and then became a high school principal. None of the others went to college except for me. I went to the same college my oldest brother did, but instead of doing something with my degree, the day I graduated, I enlisted in the Marines and ended up in Vietnam."

"Your mother must have been so proud of you! Is she still alive?"

"No, she died eight years ago, at age 101. She was in great shape, worked until she was in her nineties!"

"That's incredible! Did she ever come to the White House?"

"Many times. The last was when she turned one hundred. President and Mrs. Obama had her for dinner, along with my brother, two sisters, my son, and me. It was the highlight of my mom's life! My mom passed just over a year later, and Mrs. Obama came to the funeral."

"Wow. I wish I could have met her," offered the first lady. "So, tell me about your son. He's Winston Jr., right?"

"Yes! We call him Win and he's quite a man. He's a doctor in San Diego, where he's married to a wonderful woman, Gwen, who's a hospital administrator. He's forty. She's thirty-five, and to anticipate your next question—yes, they're trying to start a family." Winston beamed.

"That's fabulous. I can tell just how proud you are by hearing you talk about him. Tell me about your wife, Connie. I recall you introducing the president and me to her. It was our first weekend in the White House."

"Mrs. Blake, you have an excellent memory. So, way back when, Connie was a part-time professor at Howard University. We met while I was taking her class on forensics. It was love at first sight. It wasn't long before we were married, and we must have done something right because we were married for forty-six years. As you know, she died in an auto accident a year and a half ago."

Mrs. Blake looked down and slowly shook her head. "Yes, it was so tragic. She had retired from the government, right?"

"Yes, she retired a few years ago after a forty-year career with the NSA [National Security Agency]."

"That's quite an accomplishment. So, Winston, how much longer do you believe you'll work here?"

"That's a very good question. In six months, I'll be seventy-six, with fifty-one years of federal service under my belt. That could make for a logical time for me to go. But since when have I ever been logical?"

They both laughed.

"You'll know when it's time," she assured. "Just don't let anyone push you out! I worry that the new president may be a little too ambitious, meaning micro-managing. Do you have thoughts on who would be the best person to take over as chief usher once you retire?"

Winston felt himself smiling again. "Yes, our new president is indeed ambitious." He shifted his weight. "My choice to take over for me was Brent, but obviously, now everything has changed."

"I know right now it looks very bad for Brent, but I feel in my heart he did not do the things they are suggesting," the first lady said with certainty.

Winston: "I hope you're right, Mrs. Blake. I hope you're right."

Chapter 17
5:45 a.m., Wednesday, March 4: The White House

Winston took the elevator from the ushers basement suite, stopped in the pantry to pour himself a cup of coffee, and then walked into the ushers office. He said good morning to Jim, who was at his desk. The office TV was on. A CNN anchor was reporting on the long lines of people waiting to see the president lying in state in the Capitol.

The anchor on the TV screen continued, "The line has grown throughout the night with no end in sight. The president will lay in state in the rotunda until tomorrow morning when a hearse will take President Blake's casket to the National Cathedral for an 11 a.m. service. After the service, at approximately 12:30 p.m., the funeral procession, led by a horse-drawn caisson, will take President Blake's casket to Arlington National Cemetery."

Winston turned down the volume so he could attend to the normal morning routine. The housekeeper, chief florist, electric shop foreman, and engineers' foreman all stood in and around the ushers office doorway, waiting to receive their directions for the day.

"Good morning, all. Please come in," requested Winston. The department heads did so and all exchanged good mornings.

Winston began. "Mrs. Blake, God bless her, has agreed to move out of the White House tomorrow morning. I am finalizing the schedule of the moving trucks. All of your staff will need to put in a full day tomorrow. Mrs. Blake will dine alone this evening, and there will be no overnight guests. And, as always, I will keep you up to date throughout the day via email. Thank you and have a good day."

The staff left the room.

***

At two o'clock, with everything relatively quiet, Winston decided to get in a workout. While most of the executive residence staff enjoyed golf, Winston preferred cycling. Throughout his entire adult life, he had been an avid cyclist. Nowadays, he enjoyed cycling around the DC area. He had a few bikes, nothing extravagant, just basic models. His oldest, a twenty-year-old Schwinn SuperSport, had been relegated to the shed in his backyard in Bethesda. His primary long-distance bike was a Giant 27-speed, which he often rode back and forth to the White House. His favorite bike was the hybrid Novara Big Buzz he had bought from REI in 2016. This particular model he kept at the White House, and whenever time permitted and the temperature was above forty, he would get out for a ride.

Winston told Jim, still seated at the ushers desk, "I'll be back in just over an hour. Call me if needed."

He nodded, and Winston headed down to the basement usher suite. There he changed into his biking gear, put his helmet on, and retrieved his bike from the far wall of the bedroom. He checked the tire pressure. Perfect. He left the suite, and rather than use the president's elevator, he walked around to the service elevator and took it up to the ground floor, thus avoiding the formal areas of the White House by exiting through the back of the main kitchen. He traversed the tradesman's hallway and exited out the east side of the mansion, then walked his bike to the east appointments gate. He scanned his ID, and the uniformed Secret Service personnel on duty waved to him and opened the vehicular gate for Winston to ride through.

He rode south on East Exec, then at moderate speed, rode four times around the Ellipse before heading the 3.3 miles to the southern tip of Haines Point. The weather was crisp, to say the least—fifty-one degrees and breezy with borderline gale-force winds—but it felt good to get out and keep his speed up for maximum cardio. Winston cherished the opportunity for the break to clear his head and feel the freedom of being on his bike. During his fifth loop around Haines Point, his phone rang. Winston pulled over and retrieved his phone. He recognized the phone number as belonging to the ushers office.

"Hello. This is Winston."

"Hi, Winston, the first lady just called for you," reported Jim.

Winston thanked him, then rang the main White House admin operator and informed her that he was returning Mrs. Blake's call. "Stand by while we ring her." A few seconds later, the operator said, "On the line."

"Hi, Mrs. Blake," Winston said immediately. "Sorry I missed your call."

"Hi, Winston. I wanted to invite you to join me for dinner tonight."

"That is so nice of you. I would be honored to attend. Thank you."

"Oh, wonderful. See you at 6:30."

"Perfect. See you then." They both said goodbye, and Winston put his phone away, then checked his watch: 3:45 p.m. *Wow*, he thought. He had no idea he had been riding for ninety minutes. He headed back to the White House, took a long, hot shower, and then put on a fresh shirt and a new suit.

***

At 6:30 p.m., Winston took the elevator to the second floor and walked into the west sitting hall. He found Mrs. Blake on the sofa, legs, crossed, facing him.

Mrs. Blake was wearing a knee-length pink knit dress. She leaned forward and held up her glass of red wine. "Winston, would you like something to drink?"

"Thank you," said Winston as he took a seat next to her. "I'll have what you're having."

Mrs. Blake pressed the buzzer on the coffee table in front of them, to call for the butler, who arrived a split second later. She smiled at him and asked that he bring Winston a glass of wine. Winston also smiled and nodded to Nathan, the butler, and off he went.

Winston turned to his right so he could better face the first lady. "Mrs. Blake—"

"Call me Beverly."

"Of course. Beverly, I wanted to let you know that all of your items, except what you will need for tonight and tomorrow morning, have been loaded into the truck at the south portico. The truck will depart tomorrow morning and should arrive at your home in Philadelphia early afternoon."

"That's perfect, Winston," Beverly responded. "Thank you for everything. That'll work well. I'll be visiting my daughter in West Chester for lunch and should make it to our…" She paused to correct herself. "…to *my* home by mid-afternoon. And if I'm not there when they arrive, my housekeeper will let them in."

Nathan walked in with a single glass of red wine on a silver tray and leaned toward Winston, who took the glass and thanked him.

Beverly smiled. "I would like to take the butlers and chefs with me to Philadelphia. I'm sure President Gentry will get on just fine without them." They laughed. "Seriously, it's going to be quite an adjustment. I have a wonderful housekeeper who takes care of everything, but she's hardly at the level of your staff."

"I remember when President and Mrs. Carter left," Winston reminisced. "They, too, wanted to take the staff. In fact, they offered one of the butlers a job. Fortunately for us, he stayed at the White House."

"I actually am looking forward to being home," she revealed. "John and I have a wonderful home with a beautiful courtyard. I've missed it, but I'm a little nervous, wondering what it will be like without him."

Winston asked, "Will your daughter be able to spend some time with you?"

"Yes! As I mentioned, we're having lunch tomorrow, and she's planning to stay with me for a couple of weeks, starting this weekend. I'm so happy for that."

Nathan came into the room to announce dinner was ready.

As they stood Beverly said, "Winston, I hope you can understand, but we're having our dinner in the yellow oval room. I have not been able to enter the family dining room since John's passing."

"Of course," replied Winston.

Winston and Beverly walked together to the yellow oval room, located at the midway point of the second-floor private residence.

A fire was burning in the fireplace, and there was a four-foot round table toward the south end of the room set up for them. The sun had just set, and they stood admiring the magnificent view starting over the south lawn and stretching back to the Washington Monument. Everything was artistically distorted due to the historic, 200-year-old blown-glass windowpanes.

After a moment, they turned to admire the dinner table. "The table is beautiful," commented Beverly. Her eyes widened. "Wait, could it be…? Are we using the Lincoln china?"

Winston smiled as they both took their seat at the table. "Yes, I thought it most appropriate for your final dinner in the White House."

"I've only ever seen this in the china room downstairs. I had no idea we had enough for place settings."

"Actually, we have just enough for twelve settings," explained Winston. "We last used it in the 1990s when the Bushes hosted Queen Elizabeth for a private dinner—in this very room, as a matter of fact."

Beverly reached across the table and affectionately touched Winston's hand. "Winston, this is so thoughtful of you. Thank you."

They both read the identical calligraphed menu cards above their plates.

Medallions of Main Lobster and Cucumber Mousse
Aurora Sauce
Galettes Fines Herbs

Roasted Pheasant
Dauphine Potatoes
Bouquets of Vegetables

Watercress and Belgian Endive Salad
St. Andre and Chevre Cheese

Pistachio Marquise with
Fresh Raspberries

"Of course, and I have to admit, I had inside information on what the menu was for tonight, and with the pheasant, I selected a wonderful pinot noir: a bottle of the 2014 Chateau Rayas La Pialade Cotes du Rhone," Winston mentioned.

"Oh, my. I so wish John was here to enjoy this."

"Well, Mrs. Blake—excuse me, Beverly—I have a feeling he's watching."

"I know you're right," agreed Beverly.

Soft piano music could be heard from the baby grand piano in the main cross-hall.

Winston, seeing Beverly's content reaction to first hearing and then recognizing the music, added, "I thought it would be nice to have Michael from the Marine Chamber Orchestra play for you this evening."

"He's the best," she said. "John and I loved to listen to him. Thank you for thinking of that."

Two butlers walked in carrying trays and served the first course, which was complemented by a 2018 Jordan Chardonnay.

As they worked on their meal, Beverly commented, "This is so wonderful. I love lobster, and this wine is perfect."

"Jordan Chardonnay was President Reagan's favorite," Winston recalled. "We had it often. Of course, back then, the bottles were from the 1980 vintages."

They sat in silence, enjoying the music as they ate.

The butlers gracefully appeared from nowhere and cleared the first course dishes, then were back in an instant with the main course: the pheasant. After the plates were in place, they replaced the white wine glasses with red ones and poured the Cotes du Rhone.

"Winston, this pheasant is outstanding," Beverly commented. "Where is it from?"

"We have a purveyor in the Shenandoah Valley near Strasburg, Virginia. We've used them for years and have never been disappointed."

After the meal, the butlers brought in a bottle of 1984 Dom Perignon.

"I'm not sure if you were aware, but we have a temperature-controlled room on the mezzanine level of the basement that we call the Nixon wine cellar because President Nixon accumulated an incredible collection of fine wines and donated them to the White House when he left office in 1974. Only the ushers have the key to this room. Over the years, we've occasionally added select wines, so the inventory remains at around three hundred bottles. These included extra special wines. Hence, I selected the '84 Perignon tonight for I believed it would be most appropriate for this your final dinner in the White House."

"I had no idea there was a private wine store hidden in the basement. How fascinating—and by the way, this is my favorite champagne."

"For the Reagans' final dinner in the White House, I found a 1964 Dom Perignon that we served to them," Winston recalled.

They touched their glasses and wished each other luck.

"Winston, thank you for such a special evening. I will remember this fondly as one of the more special moments of my time here. Everything was beyond wonderful."

They both stood, and Beverly gave Winston a hug. Winston felt her arms wrap around him, delicate yet with a strength that belied her age. In that moment, he admired her more than ever. Winston allowed himself one indulgent second and closed his eyes. Her beautifully styled graying hair was spun up in a stylish bun, and a loose strand tickled his nose. He smiled just a little. Beverly was an amazing lady...and had been amazing *first* lady. And her husband, a great man. Wistfulness tugged at him.

He knew the White House would never be quite the same.

Brent had just finished the last of his dry oatmeal when four guards appeared. One of them greeted Brent with: "Rise and shine, bright eyes. Someone out there must love you very much. Your bail has been posted."

Brent was shocked into momentary silence, then finally managed to ask, "Are you serious?"

"As serious as a DC jail cell," answered that same guard. Apparently, the guy thought he was a comedian. "Let's go!"

One of the officers handed Brent a large, clear plastic bag that contained his hastily folded clothes.

Brent quickly jettisoned the orange jumpsuit and got dressed. He was then led through a maze of corridors, and after several checkpoints, ended up at a counter. The officer behind it slid a paper bag toward him. It contained his personal items: shoes, belt, iPhone, wallet, keys, and watch.

The officer spoke. "Here is your release order form that you must read and sign. It states that your release conditions, which include checking in weekly to DC Pretrial Services in person or by phone and weekly drug testing. You are being released under the high-intensity supervision classification, which requires you to wear a GPS monitor on your ankle at all times, and you shall abide by a curfew. You must be inside your residence between the hours of 11 p.m. and 6 a.m., and you are not allowed to leave Washington, DC. Any violations of the release order will result in your immediate incarceration. Your trial date has been set for forty-five days from today. If you do not appear for trial, the $275 mill that was put forward for your bail will become the property of the Superior Court of Washington, DC. Do you have any questions?"

Brent signed the form and then asked, "Where do I get my ankle bracelet?"

The officer nodded to the escorting officers, who then took Brent into the next room, where a very large lady in uniform instructed Brent to roll up his right pant leg. He obliged, and she motioned for him to place his foot on a stool. She then attached the GPS monitor around his ankle, took a photo of it with her cell phone, then pointed to the officers and ordered, "Go with them." Brent thanked her, but she never looked up from her paperwork. The officers then escorted Brent to the main entrance to the DC Jail building, where his attorney, Frank Osborne, stood waiting.

Frank smiled. "I told you I was going to get you out of here!"

"Frank! Thanks so much! You have no idea how glad I am to be getting out of this place!"

"Hold on one minute," Frank instructed. "You can't walk outside without a disguise. Everyone knows you, and everyone wants you dead!" Frank reached into a plastic bag. "Here's a hat and sunglasses. When we walk out, keep your head down. We're lucky the press hasn't found out yet that you posted bail."

Brent and Frank exited the DC jail building and briskly walked to Frank's black BMW X7, which was illegally parked right in front of the building.

After Brent buckled in on the passenger side next to Frank, he took a deep breath and looked over to Frank. "Thank you. Thank you. Thank you." Then looking around the dashboard and center console. "Mind if I plug my phone in?"

Frank, pulling out of the lot, gave him a wave. "Go right ahead." He frowned. "Oh, there's no plug." Frank pointed. "You just lay it right here, and it automatically charges."

Brent laid his phone on the center console as instructed.

"So, we're going to my place in Georgetown. I don't want you seen in or around my K Street office."

They arrived at Frank's historic, three-story brick home near N and 33rd in Georgetown. Frank pulled around to the rear entrance to the garage to avoid being seen.

The two men entered the main level of the home. Brent was wide-eyed as they walked down a hallway passing several rooms. The impressive dark, wide-plank wooden floors were partially covered with beautiful Persian rugs. Various original works of art tastefully decorated the walls. There was a noticeable aroma of vanilla throughout, almost like a fine pipe tobacco. Frank led Brent into a modern kitchen and motioned for him to have a seat on one of the comfortable-looking stools at the bar. Frank then pressed a button on the Jura coffee machine and within seconds coffee was filling a mug.

"We've got forty-five days," Frank told him, as he loosened his tie, removed his suit jacket, and draped it over one of the vacant bar stools. "And that's if your case goes to trial."

"I like the sound of 'if,'" replied Brent. "So, how can that be possible?"

"This should never go to trial. I'll explain more later. For now, let's get you ready for what your new life is going to be like. President Blake's funeral is in a few hours. Crowds started pouring into town yesterday and Brent, look at me. President Blake had a seventy percent approval rating. As far as everyone is concerned, you ended his life. There are ten thousand Jack Rubys waiting for you."

Frank's cell phone buzzed. He glanced at a text message. "Shit! The word is out." He then reached for the remote and turned on the TV.

Wolf Blitzer's familiar face appeared, offering the public the latest hot news. "…bail amount was $275 million, a historically high figure. Brenton Williams certainly did not have the means to pay that."

A CNN legal expert now monopolized the TV screen. "Frank Osborne has been known to pay high bail amounts for his clients in the past, but we don't believe he ever paid over a million dollars."

"That's because I never had to," Frank mumbled, eyes on the screen.

"We have also learned that the conditions of Brent Williams' bail require that he wear an ankle monitor and he is not allowed to leave the district. We understand that he lives in the Dupont Circle area and that reporters have already started gathering near his home."

Frank turned to Brent. "Is there a back entrance to your condo?"

"No, it's an old, two-story building. Just one entrance."

"Then it's settled. You'll stay here at my place," Frank announced. "I'll have Melinda, my assistant, go by your condo and get whatever you need."

"But the release order stated I must stay at my residence," Brent pointed out.

"Correct. I'm taking care of that," Frank assured. "For the foreseeable future, you'll be my tenant."

"What's this going to cost me?"

Frank answered, "275 million!"

Chapter 19
10 a.m., Thursday, March 5: The White House

Loretta walked into the ushers office after having been off since early Tuesday morning. Winston thought she looked rested and greeted her warmly. "How are you doing?"

"I'm still numb, but I think I need to be here," she said. "Focusing on work will help."

"Please know, what you shared with me the other day will remain in complete confidence," Winston assured.

"Thank you, Winston. I value your trust more than you know."

"Good. Let's go join Jim. He's in the state dining room awaiting the first lady."

Beverly Blake stood in the state dining room, dressed in black. She thanked the entire executive residence staff, who had gathered to bid her farewell. Emotions were running high and could be felt throughout the room. Winston handed his handkerchief to the first lady, who gracefully accepted it, wiping away tears. She bid goodbye to each individual staff member, then allowed Winston to escort her to the south portico. They walked past the moving van to the limo that would take her and President Gentry to the

National Cathedral for the funeral service and then to Arlington National Cemetery. From there, she would leave Washington.

President Gentry appeared after walking over from the oval office, and in an exaggerated and inappropriate tone as if heading to a pep rally, encouraged everyone to get in the limo.

The first lady had invited Winston to accompany her to the funeral, but this was overruled by the new president, who insisted Winston's priorities were to ensure a smooth household transition.

Mrs. Blake hugged Winston and thanked him for everything, then got into the limo with President Gentry.

At the south portico, staff members were loading the van with the last of the former first lady's belongings.

Winston gave a polite nod as President Gentry and former First Lady Blake's limousine left the south grounds. As soon as the motorcade was out of the southwest gate, Winston signaled to the Secret Service to allow the two moving vans that were waiting at the northwest gate to enter the north grounds. These vans contained the belongings of President Gentry and her husband, Admiral Curtis.

The activities now taking place in the White House were very much as they would be on the inauguration day of a new president, only rather bizarre in that it was all happening on the same day as the former president's funeral.

Washington, DC was packed with people; all the streets had been blocked between the Capitol and Arlington National Cemetery. The funeral procession slowed, giving Winston and his staff the extra time they would need to complete the move before President Gentry got back to the White House.

Confounding the process were the two dozen young staffers that President Gentry had obligated to "help" the executive residence staff with the move. The residence staff had been handling presidential family moves for over two hundred years. Now they not only had the pressure of a time-constrained move, but they also had to essentially babysit two dozen painfully inexperienced west wing staffers!

Chapter 20
8 p.m., Thursday, March 5: The Swann House,
Northwest DC

The Swann House, located in upper-northwest DC, is an 1880s Victorian mansion that now serves as a high-end bed and breakfast.

Frank and Brent were the first to arrive. They sat in the living room surrounded by period pieces from the late 1800s. Swann was very relaxing, and most importantly, it was quiet and private.

Secret Service Agent Greg Leidner, accompanied by Chief Usher Bartholomew Winston, walked into the Swann House. As soon as Winston saw Brent, he immediately walked over, and the two hugged.

"Brent, I'm so sorry I never made it to visit you in jail," apologized Winston.

"Winston, don't be ridiculous. I knew you had a few million things keeping you busy. How did everything go today?" Brent asked.

Winston sighed. "Miraculously, we got Mrs. Blake moved out and the Gentry's moved in, in spite of two dozen well-meaning and painfully young west wing staffers helping us! Only a few things were misplaced, and just two things were broken that we're aware of at this point!"

The four men sat down and opened the cooler that Brent had brought. They passed around Yuengling beers. Greg opened his laptop.

"Gentleman, I hope you found this place without any problem," Frank began. "I love the Swann House and have used it in the past during times when I needed a semi-secluded location that doesn't get a lot of attention. As you all can see the house exudes character. The furnishings are all tasteful period pieces. I find it one of the more beautiful bed and breakfasts in Washington. It has even been visited by presidents. President William Howard Taft attended a wedding here in 1912."

Brent quipped, "Taft was the heaviest president by a long shot. I wonder how he made it up all those steps to the entrance!" The men chuckled.

Frank continued. "There is an impressive list of past owners, notable guests, and famous visitors from the140-year history of this place. I have made arrangements with the general manager to book the Swann for the entire month. We'll use this as our primary meeting and planning location. We will be the only ones here. The Swann House staff will come in early mornings when we're not here. I may have some of my legal team join us if and when necessary.

"Oh! And before I forget, I have new cell phones for each of you. These are basically burner phones, meaning once we're done with them, they will be destroyed. Use these phones for all calls and texts between the four of us. Now listen closely, we will only use the Signal app for our communications. Signal is an encrypted messaging service. It's used by *The Washington Post* for their informants—not that I would know anything about that. But bottom line, it's the most secure way to send and receive texts and make phone calls. The app is already installed on each of your phones as is each of our contact data. Any questions?" The room was silent. "Good. We will meet here at 8 p.m. most nights of the week. If we need additional meetings, they will be scheduled. Greg is on vacation leave for the next few weeks so he will be dedicated to our efforts. And by the way, Greg, just how much leave do you have?"

"I've got a lot saved," Greg informed them. "Plus, since I am law enforcement, they allow me to carry over an additional 360 hours. So, in other words, I can take up to fifteen weeks of leave if needed."

"Jesus, man!" exclaimed Frank. "I run my own law firm, and I don't take that much!"

"Uh, Frank, we all felt really sorry for you last year when you and your friends took eight weeks to sail across the Atlantic, and then you stayed in France for…what? Another eight weeks?" Winston gave him a look.

"Oh, yeah. There was that!" Frank recalled. "Okay, let's get focused." Frank looked directly at Brent. "All of us here agree that we will help you beat this. No one can stand the injustice of an innocent man being framed and imprisoned." Frank then stood as if he were in a courtroom and walked back and forth. "So, the White House has not yet released the autopsy report and as such, the press does not know the official cause of death. But we do know from Monday's press conference that the Associated Press, in their question to the president, mentioned that Brent 'was found with a deadly toxin,' which they followed up with, 'the very same toxin that killed the president.' How did they know this? I mean, we know it, but nothing has been officially released to the press."

Greg spoke up. "My sources in the White House press office tell me a draft of the autopsy was personally leaked by the new press secretary. She only provided it to the Associated Press because she was trying to send a message to CNN that the White House now controls information, not them."

"Great," sighed Frank as he retook his seat. "They're having a pissing contest. But the bottom line is, there has been no official release of the cause of death. We need to be prepared for when they do release it because that will put more heat on Brent—and Brent, just so you know, based on information you shared with me from our Tuesday morning conversation and other information that we have since been able to obtain, I think you'll be impressed at how much we've been able to accomplish thus far. But before we get to that, I've drafted a guide for my opposition research team that I want us to briefly review."

"Opposition research?" questioned Brent.

"Yeah, I use 'em for all my cases and for helping some of my friends who are running for office. So, in your case, they're gonna do opposite-of-opposition research. In other words, these are the guys who will work the positive spin about you into the media, 'cuz right now, friend, the picture ain't too good for ya!"

"Cool, let's get started," said Brent.

Frank's eyes moved to everyone in the room, then he adjusted his view down to the screen on his Mac. "Team, this is Brent's basic bio. It's good and needs to be out there ASAP. Okay, you grew up in Howard County, Maryland, went to public schools, you were a C-plus student..."

"Really?" muttered Brent. "We gotta mention the C-plus part?

"Yep, but don't worry. It gets better: You graduated from the University of Maryland summa cum laude with a bachelor's in science degree in information systems. You attended Johns Hopkins and earned an MA in government with a certificate in intelligence.

You married at age twenty-four. No children, divorced at age thirty. You spent four-plus years working in the intelligence community, received an award for excellence in leadership, joined the White House at age twenty-eight, and have been there eight years. All of your performance evaluations have been exemplary. Former presidents, first families, and senior staff have nothing but great things to say about you. Is there anything else that we should highlight?"

"Yeah," said Brent. "I once hit a half court three-pointer at the buzzer, but we still lost."

"Very funny. Is there anything else that would help your image? Are you dating anyone? So, you had told me you dated the former social secretary and that ended, right?" inquired Frank.

"Yeah, it ended. We're still friends, and no, I'm not dating anyone now."

"Okay, then this draft is good to go," Frank decided before turning to Greg. "Greg, please report on your progress."

Greg placed his bottle of beer on the table and then sat forward a little. "A couple of significant items. One: My friends at the NSA were able to confirm that the phone call that then VP Gentry received on her penthouse balcony that night when you, Brent, were with her was from Patrick Sullivan."

"Patrick? Wha…huh? What the hell are you saying?!" demanded Brent.

"We're saying things are not as they seem, or rather, not as someone wants everyone to believe," Greg informed him. "I checked with my NSA contact who sent me the phone logs. Elizabeth Gentry and Chef Patrick shared over one hundred calls and five hundred texts over the past six months, including five calls the day the president died!"

"How could she be so stupid to use her cell phone?" Brent asked incredulously. "She must have known how easy it would be to track."

"True," Greg agreed. "Except she never used her phone. Gentry used a series of burner phones purchased by Wendy Wolf. Like Frank said, we've been busy the past few days!"

"I have what I affectionately call 'observers' all over DC," Frank explained. "One of them is the midnight watchman at the Watergate—who has photos of Chef Patrick and then-Vice President Gentry together on the balcony of her penthouse. Brent, I know you had a special relationship with Beth Gentry, but she was playing you, man. She made you feel like you had this 'thing' and that maybe it would evolve into something. Well, guess what? She was having a 'thing' with Patrick too. Patrick had been on the very same balcony that you were on—only he went a lot further!"

"Yeah, let's just say he went all the way," Greg interjected. Brent shook his head. "Holy shit!"

"And ever since you rebuffed her, she's worked very hard to fabricate evidence against you," Greg continued.

"All of our evidence thus far points to Elizabeth Gentry having orchestrated the assassination of President Blake," concluded Frank. "And Brent, you were to be her facilitator. Meaning she believed she could manipulate you into poisoning the president. But she had a backup plan in case you failed her, which you did. Hence, her affair with and manipulation of Patrick."

"There's more," Winston finally chimed in. "Remember Greg mentioned there were two significant things we uncovered? My buddy that works forensics for the DC police tells me, they're starting to look closely at Patrick's suicide note and have a lot of questions."

Brent's eyes widened. "Oh, my God! Wow! This is great! Let's go to the FBI!"

"Hold on! The more we uncover, the more we realize how well Gentry planned this," Winston said.

"Exactly," Frank agreed. "We need more evidence and to figure out just how far this reaches."

"We're a long way from going to the FBI with anything," Greg seconded.

"Shit, so I can still end up in prison, or worse, the electric chair?" Brent asked, looking from one man's face to the other in the group.

Frank smiled. "Probably would only be life in prison."

"Wonderful, thanks. I feel much better."

Frank handed out more beers.

Brent took a gulp of his beer. "So, all this is encouraging, but what about my interrogators, whoever those guys were? They kept asking me about my trip to Pakistan and whether I had been radicalized."

Frank responded. "Yeah, those guys were a specialized team made up intelligence community interviewers, they were from the military, and the NSA. They knew you hadn't been 'converted.' They also were very familiar with your security clearance filings, which you submitted when you joined the White House. They were told to ask you those questions from someone high up in the administration—and we believe Elizabeth Gentry pushed for that line of questioning."

"Jesus!" Brent's mind was reeling as he struggled to take all this in. "So, what about the toxin?"

"Brent, how many times have I warned you about leaving your personal Mac open and unlocked while you were in the ushers office?" Greg asked, giving Brent a withering look.

Brent grimaced. "Uh, once? Well, maybe twice?"

Greg glared. "More like a half-dozen times! So, we believe you made it a bit too easy for a 'bad actor' to use your laptop to access the dark web and create all sorts of nasty evidence showing that you bought the botulinum toxins."

"Maybe so, but I had those vials in my possession!" Brent reminded him.

"You're always leaving your suit coat on the back of your chair," Winston added. "Think of all the times you walked back to the pantry to get breakfast, lunch, dinner, or to go to the bathroom, thus leaving ample opportunities for someone to have easily slipped something in your pocket."

"Wow, this is so disturbing," whispered Brent. "Winston, do you have thoughts on any other executive residence staff that could possibly be involved with this?"

Winston made an unpleasant face. "God, I hope not. I have shared this with Frank and Greg only. I was aware that Elizabeth Gentry and Patrick were having an affair—I knew from the start. I also heard the talk coming out of the VP's office that you and Elizabeth were getting too close. But I knew the truth. I knew Elizabeth Gentry was using you. I just never fathomed the extent or purpose. I never believed I needed to say anything because I had complete confidence in you. She's the one I never trusted."

"Wow," said Brent for perhaps the tenth time during that conversation.

"We have a lot of ground to cover," Frank pressed. "Our primary objective is to get you, Brent, off. Hopefully, we can get the charges dismissed, or worst-case scenario, we go to trial and win. But that's absolute worst-case. A trial can go on for months!"

"Brent," Winston began, "it would be best if you gave me the key to your closet in the basement usher's suite. So far, no one has thought to ask about that yet, and I just want to check to make sure there's nothing out of the ordinary in there that could incriminate you."

"Sure," Brent said. He reached into his pocket, pulled out a very familiar keychain, and removed a single key, which he handed to Winston. "Thanks for thinking of that, although the only things in my closet are my tux, shoes, an extra business suit, books...oh, and two bottles of Basil Hayden's that the social office gave me for Christmas a few years ago."

"A few years?" Greg repeated. "What have you been waiting for?"

"The right time," answered Brent.

"So, a few years of occasions with your friends, you never had the right time?"

"Okay, guys, stay focused," Frank butted in. "I'm looking into a story from years ago. Rumor has it that during Elizabeth Gentry's campaign for Congress, a story came up that she received special favors, which gained her admittance to the Naval Academy, but those stories were quickly squelched and never became an issue. So, it may very well be that it happened. We have uncovered evidence that she had an affair with the naval officer that was the chair of the admissions who, less than eighteen months later, mysteriously drowned in a boating accident. Think about it…a Navy man drowning? None of this passes the smell test.

So much involving her seems to have been part of a greater plan, everything orchestrated or even choreographed somehow. Two years before her election as VP, she marries sixty-eight-year-old Admiral James Curtis, Naval Academy grad who saw action in Vietnam, Lebanon, Panama, and Iraq. He retired with the rank of admiral four years ago, then immediately married then Congresswoman Elizabeth Gentry, a woman twenty-six years his junior. This was surely a calculated marriage of convenience to enhance Gentry's stature in her quest to be a candidate for higher office and ultimately her role as vice president.

Shortly after her election as VP, when the transition team was underway, the admiral was often rumored to be a candidate for various administration posts; i.e., joint chief, secretary of defense, secretary of state, etc. However, he never advanced beyond media speculation and was never given serious consideration due to persistent questions regarding his health as he has a bad heart, and more importantly, to concerns about his overall temperament. I feel sorry for the guy.

So, the question becomes, does Elizabeth Gentry have a dark side? I think this group knows the answer to that, but the public sees her as brilliant and beautiful, with great energy and presence. And the best that her few critics can come up with is that she's maybe a bit of a micromanager."

"So, we have our work cut out for us," Greg concluded.

Frank added, "These eight o'clock meetings will be where we verify our findings and document our proof. I think we've covered enough for our first meeting. Let's meet tomorrow at the same time. Meanwhile, I'll work to get more definitive information pertaining to the suicide note. Winston and Greg, I need you to continue to observe and note anything and everything, but I need you to be exceptionally careful. You guys are in the line of fire, so to speak. I don't want Elizabeth Gentry or anyone else having the slightest suspicion about what we're doing."

The men stood.

"Thank you, gentlemen," said Frank before his eyes settled on Brent's. "C'mon, Brent, you're in my custody. And lucky for you, I have some Macallan at my place. No, not the gazillion-dollar kind, but a decent twelve-year."

Chapter 21
7 a.m., Friday, March 6: The White House

Winston answered the ushers office phone: "Good morning, ushers office. Winston speaking."

President Gentry spoke. "Winston, my husband will be moving into the solarium. I will need you to convert it into a bedroom. He will need a full bath up there. How long will that take?"

"I will have the plumbers and carpenters draw up the design," promised Winston. "I would think, if we rush it, it will take us six, maybe eight weeks."

"You have one week. Make it happen," she demanded. "In the meantime, let's move him into the Lincoln bedroom." The line went dead.

Winston called housekeeping to let them know that the admiral would be using the Lincoln bedroom until further notice. He then called the White House plumber and told him to meet him in the carpenter shop.

Before Winston could head toward the shop, the phone rang. It was the direct line of their new chief of staff, Wendy Wolf.

"Good morning, Wendy," Winston answered. "How are you this morning?"

"Great," replied Wendy. "Just trying to stay ahead of the 'lady hurricane' that's living above your office." She let out a short laugh.

"Aren't we all?" agreed Winston.

"So, the president and admiral have invited seventeen of their friends for dinner tonight. They want dinner at seven and a top-rated movie shown in the east wing family theater at eight, followed by a bowling tournament."

"Perfect, I'll get a list of the best movies available," Winston assured. "Shall I share that with you, the admiral, or the president?"

"Oh, God," groaned Wendy. "I don't have time for this. Um, get a list, email it to me, and I'll see what I can do. What suggested menu do you have?"

"We can get top-rated beef from Chapel Hill farm in Virginia. I would suggest the chef's knife boneless New York striploin, and we'll prepare it with potatoes and a medley of vegetables, Served with a 2017 Amici Cabernet Sauvignon from Napa. And the pastry chef will come up with something fabulous for dessert."

"That sounds perfect," Wendy decided. "Include all that in your email. Thanks, hon!"

Winston hung up the phone and looked up to see both the plumber and carpenter foreman standing in the doorway of the office. "We thought it would be easier if we came up to you," they said. Winston smiled, thanked them, and suggested they go up to his private office.

Before Winston could make it to the steps, the president's elevator, with its automatic security stop, opened in the hallway near the ushers office. Winston told the guys he would be with them in a minute as he jumped onto the elevator. The doors closed, and he stood there, running mentally over his schedule as the elevator rose gently.

The doors opened on the second floor; President Gentry walked onto the elevator, followed by an agent. The president wore a dark gray pantsuit with a white turtleneck underneath. Her hair was tied back. Winston thought she looked very nice. She had a strong aura of class and confidence.

"Good morning, President Gentry," greeted Winston.

"Hi, Winston. There will be twenty-five for dinner tonight. I'd also like a movie and bowling to be included. Get the menu to Wendy."

"Will do."

The elevator doors opened on the ground floor. Before the president got off, she turned to Winston and added, "I've also invited Roman and Claire Mirov to overnight tonight." She lowered her voice so only Winston could hear. "They're big-time donors." No longer in a low voice, she went on, "I want them in the queen's bedroom. I'll have Wendy handle the clearances with the Secret Service, but I need you to arrange for a car to pick them up from Reagan National. They have their own plane. I believe they should be arriving at eleven. Confirm with Wendy. Make sure we prepare a very nice lunch for them. Serve it in the family dining room. I'll try to attend."

"All sounds great," said Winston.

The president dashed off toward the oval office, and as she looked back over her right shoulder, she waved and called out, "Thanks, Winston!"

Since he was already on the ground floor, Winston decided to go directly to the main kitchen to inform the chef of the lunch plans and the updated dinner guest total.

Once back in the ushers office, after conferring with Wendy, Winston called the White House garage, officially known as the White House Transportation Agency, which provided a fleet of vehicles with military drivers for transportation services to the first family, White House senior staff, and official visitors of the first family. "Hello, Sergeant. This is Winston. Could we please have a car pick up two guests of the president?"

"Of course, Winston," said the sergeant over the phone. "Just tell me who, when, and where."

"Mr. and Mrs. Roman Mirov, arriving at Reagan National General Aviation, private aircraft operations terminal at 11 a.m.," Winston relayed. "Please bring them to the south portico."

***

Winston's cell phone rang. He looked at the number and answered, "Hi, Wendy."

"Winston, just wanted to make sure you're all set for the Mirovs. These are very important guests who provided large contributions to Beth during her time in Congress and again when she ran as vice president. We want to make sure everything is perfect for them."

"We shall handle them as if they were royalty," promised Winston. "I will personally greet them when they arrive. I've ordered their car. They should be here by 11:15."

"Good. Please let me know once they arrive—the president wants to stay informed on the matter. Thanks, Winston." The phone went dead. Winston checked his watch: 11 a.m.

Winston had gotten into the habit of learning as much as he could about houseguests in advance of their arrival. So, from his private office, he did a quick internet search on Roman Mirov. Apparently, the man was a Russian oligarch who had made his fortune as a commodities and shipping magnate. He also found that Mirov had contributed $250,000 to a PAC for each of Elizabeth Gentry's three congressional campaigns and another $500,000 to the Blake-Gentry PAC for president. *One point two mil in just over six years*, Winston mused. *No wonder Wendy said they were important*!

A navy-blue Chevrolet Impala Premier pulled up to the south portico. Winston opened the rear door for Mrs. Mirov while the military driver opened the door for her husband.

Winston shook each of their hands, introducing himself and welcoming them to the White House.

The three of them stood admiring the view of the south grounds as the military driver departed.

Mr. Mirov, a jovial, rotund man probably in his mid-fifties, adjusted the dark raincoat over his dark suit as he straightened. "Hi, Winston, I'm Roman, and this is my wife, Claire." Clair smiled and said hello. He had a Russian accent; hers was deep-south. With a big smile, he added, "And if you can't tell from our accents, we're from Atlanta, Georgia."

Claire could have passed for a southern belle, her forty-ish age lines barely visible under layers of makeup. She was tall and blonde and spoke with a very thick southern accent. "We're so happy to be here. Do you know if Beth will be joining us for lunch?"

"I know she's going to try her hardest to be there," Winston replied.

"It would be nice if she could." Claire leaned in, smiling in a mock-conspiratorial fashion. "I'll tell you a little secret, Winston. President Blake was a nice man, but we only supported him because of Beth. We've known her from the time—since she was in the Navy—and we were her biggest donors when she ran for Congress. We could not be happier that she is now president."

Winston nodded. "Well, it sure is nice that she has longtime friends like you. I know she's thrilled that you took the time to visit. How about we go inside, and I can take you to your room, then maybe show you around a bit before lunch?"

"Winston, I can tell from your accent that you're also from the South!" noted Roman.

"Yes, sir. I'm from North Carolina." Winston reached for their suitcases and was quickly brushed aside by Roman.

"Well, from one southern gentleman to another, I'll carry my own bag," he asserted boisterously.

Winston smiled, picked up Claire's bag only, and led them into the White House.

As they boarded the president's elevator, Winston asked, "Have either of you ever been to the White House?"

"I was here for a Clinton state dinner, but this is Claire's first visit," replied Roman.

As they got off the elevator to enter the private residence, they were all surprised to see President Gentry standing there. She hugged Roman, then Claire.

"I have cleared my afternoon schedule so I can spend time with my dearest friends," announced Gentry.

Claire squealed with delight, and Winston backed away unnoticed.

Chapter 22
1 p.m., Friday: March 6, Frank's House,
Georgetown

Frank sliced the cold cut sandwich diagonally and placed in on the plate in front of Brent. "So, Melinda from my staff is on her way with the stuff she picked up from your place. She said there were fourteen reporters camped out on the sidewalk directly in front of the door to your building!"

"Oh, man. My neighbors must hate me."

Frank placed his sandwich on a plate and sat on the kitchen stool adjacent to Brent. "Let me again be perfectly clear about this, Brent. Right now, everyone hates you!"

"Crazy. So glad I don't have to deal with being in the public right now. Thanks again, man. I really appreciate everything you're doing for me."

"I've got your back," Frank reminded him. "But we need to figure out exactly how everything happened. At this point, what we believe is that Sullivan poisoned the president, then Gentry had him killed. We need much more detail, and we need proof—empirical evidence beyond any reasonable doubt. Greg will report on his progress tonight."

Frank's cell phone rang. He put his sandwich down, whipped his hands on a napkin, and stopped chewing while he answered the phone. "Slow down, slow down!" he said into the phone. "Start from the beginning. She said what exactly?" After a long pause, he added, "She told the press this?! Okay, get on it. I'll talk to Brent."

Frank shook his head and hung up the phone. For a moment he just looked up at the ceiling with his eyes shut. Then he took a deep breath and reopened them, swinging his disbelieving stare toward Brent. "Priests, jumping the White House fence to infiltrate the White House? What the fuck? You actually said that?"

Brent blinked. "Wait. *What*?"

"Your ex-wife just told the press and a bunch of TV media that you told her one of the best ways to attack the White House would be for twenty-four men dressed as priests to jump the fence all at once…that the Secret Service would hesitate to shoot the priests long enough to give them a big head start on entering the White House?"

Brent rolled his eyes. "Oh, Jesus. Uh, yeah, I told her something sorta like that *ten* years ago! It was before I was even at the White House!"

"Well, she's now telling the world that you had premeditated thoughts on how to kill the president!

Jesus Christ, Brent, you're killing me! What other shit is out there that's gonna bite us in the ass?"

"Calm down. It was a total fantasy. Fiction. Stupidity. Nothing real!"

Frank took a breath and spoke very slowly. "Okay, start from the beginning. Tell me everything you told her. Everything!"

"It was totally my imagination…," Brent recalled. "I told her I thought the best scenario for a gate jumper to make it inside the White House would involve two dozen men dressed as priests, all in black robes to conceal their weapons but with their priest collars visible. Twelve would approach from the north side of the White House, the other twelve from the south side. The men would wait until a peaceful Sunday morning, then, at exactly the same time, they would all jump the fence, spread out, and rapidly walk toward the mansion.

"The Secret Service counterassault team would respond with total confusion, due in part to the physical geography. Several jumpers all at once, now advancing from both the north and south grounds, this would cause all sorts of resource constraints. The Secret Service would not know where to start, and then, once they got their response organized, which one of them would be willing to shoot a priest? Based on this scenario, out of the twenty-four jumpers, I figured that surely a handful would make it all the way inside."

"You're an idiot!" Frank snapped. "Though, actually, I can see some merit to your idea. But damn, all the stories about you being radicalized are now going to be front and center. Everyone will believe you had been plotting with Jihadist extremists to kill the president for years!"

Brent rubbed his chin thoughtfully. "You wanna hear my idea for a White House hang-glider attack?"

"Shut up!"

Chapter 23
2:30 p.m., Friday, March 6: The White House

Assistant Usher Jim Allen walked into the ushers office to relieve Loretta, but she was not at the desk. So, he took a seat and read the ushers log to get caught up.

Loretta walked in. "Hey there. I was just upstairs with the houseguest."

"Howdy," said Jim. "How are things?"

"Another crazy day in paradise."

Jim nodded. "Yeah, I'm trying to get used to Winston's new schedule. I was really enjoying my day until after lunch when my wife asked me why I wasn't getting ready for work. I told her I was off, to which she replied, 'That's not what the schedule taped to the fridge says!' I looked at the schedule and said, 'Dammit!'"

Loretta smiled in commiseration. "Yeah, well, this was supposed to be my weekend off."

Jim's brow creased. "Where's Winston?"

"I think he's down in the carpenter shop. President Gentry has ordered us to convert the solarium into a bedroom and move the admiral into it."

"Solarium?" Jim repeated, frowning. "What the heck?"

"*And* she expects a full bath to be installed up there as well. She told Winston to get it done in one week." They both laughed.

"What's next? She gonna ask us to install an indoor pool in the yellow oval room?"

"Hey, nothing would surprise me at this point," Loretta commented.

"We haven't had any opportunities to talk." Jim leaned back in his chair, all his attention on her. "So, what's your take on everything? You don't really think Brent did what they're saying, do you?"

Loretta sighed, looking thoughtful. "At first, I thought, *No way, not possible*. But I gotta tell ya, with all this stuff coming out, I'm starting to wonder. I mean, the whole jihadist thing... And today, they said he had a plan for priests to jump the fence. So, you have to wonder, who thinks like that?"

"Oh, heck, Loretta, I've sat here late at night talking to the Secret Service about ways someone could attack the White House." He paused and offered her a lopsided smile. "And please don't ever tell anyone I said that!"

"Well, I'm tellin' ya, with each passing day, it's looking worse for Brent."

Jim, not aware that Loretta and Patrick had been in a relationship, continued. "So, get this: Last night, the guys in the kitchen were telling me there's no way Patrick would commit suicide. They told me he was about to accept a very lucrative job offer at the Four Seasons. And listen to this! He was about to propose to his girlfriend that no one knew about. On top of that, they said the reason he was leaving the White House was because he was bored and didn't really like the Blakes. That sure doesn't sound like someone considering suicide."

Loretta sharply inhaled, fighting to not display any reaction. "Uh, c'mon, I don't believe those guys. I haven't heard anything like that. In fact, I've heard just the opposite. Patrick was very happy working for the Blakes, and—"

The phone rang. She dutifully answered, "Ushers office, Loretta Fitzgerald." Loretta listened for a few seconds. "Yeah, he just got here, and I'm on my way out." She wrote something down on a sheet of paper on the desk. "Okay, I'll let him know. Okay…bye." She stood to leave and handed the piece of paper to Jim. "Winston wants you to contact this upholsterer and see if they have the blue room chair material. President Gentry wants to make a sofa with it."

"Oh, great," muttered Jim. "I wonder if this'll be for the new solarium suite?"

Loretta, upset over what Jim had revealed about Patrick, was anxious to leave as fast as possible. "See you tomorrow."

"Alrighty," said Jim agreeably. "Oh, wait. Quick question: Next week is my anniversary, and last year, you suggested I take my wife to that Middle Eastern restaurant on Florida Avenue…"

Loretta stood at the top of the back staircase, holding a little too tightly to the railing. She felt her hand grow damp and shake a little as she paused after her first step down. Loretta quickly turned to look back at Jim. "Maydan."

"Yes! It was fabulous. So, do you have any thoughts on something a little different?"

Loretta smiled wanly. "Have you been to Russia House on Connecticut? I've been several times. It's different. Very authentic. I like it a lot."

Jim grinned. "Perfect! I'll make a reservation. Thanks!" Before he could ask her how she knew of Russia House, Loretta was rushing down the steps. "Gotta run. See ya."

***

Winston waited until the last of the thirty-five guests were seated at the four round tables set up in the private residence within the yellow oval room. He then headed down to the ushers office, where Jim was busy on the computer updating the usher log.

The electrician—and the designated projectionist for the movie to be shown later that night for Gentry and her guests—walked into the office. "We still good for an 8 p.m. showtime?" he asked.

Winston gave a quick nod. "Yes, you should be ready to go at eight, although it might be a little after that." The electrician left, nearly bumping into Mary the housekeeper on his way out.

Mary stepped into the office. "How's it going?"

"Well," Winston began, "when you figure that the guestlist I was given this morning went from seventeen to twenty-five, and then from eleven to twenty-seven, and we just seated thirty-five, I would say it's all going terrific! The executive chef is ready to punch someone or something, and the butlers have earned sainthoods, the way they so graciously adapted to all of President Gentry's spur-of-the-moment demands. And to top it all off, I had a minor confrontation with the admiral when I suggested he limit his cigars to the Truman balcony, at which point the man deftly reminded me of who owns the house for the next eight years. I couldn't bring myself to correct him by suggesting it is the 'people's house!' So, all in all, a fine first event for the new family!"

Mary shook her head. "Oh, my God, Winston, I think you're the one deserving sainthood!"

"Hardly, but thanks. So, I'm going to leave it to you, my trusted assistant Jim, and the butlers on the front line upstairs. I'll be back later." Winston stood, offered Mary an abbreviated bow, and then exited the office, descended the back stairs, and headed to his car on West Exec Avenue.

***

The sun had just set, but it was still light out. Loretta sat in bed in her quaint one-bedroom, fourth-floor condo at 1725 New Hampshire Avenue in northwest DC. She wore her most comfortable flannel pajamas, her down comforter pulled up to her shoulders. She was on her third glass of wine and already knew the wine would never dull her aching heart. She kept hearing Jim say over and over again: *He was about to propose to his girlfriend.* While she and Patrick had a torrid affair, she never had any idea that he considered her anything more than a sex object. She had always suppressed her feelings for him because she didn't want to end up hurt.

"Patrick was the first guy she had dated since college, which was such a long time ago. He had been fun, handsome, cultured, and a great lover. She often fantasized about a life together but always fought to not

182

allow herself to think that would ever be a possibility. So, she had kept her dreams in check. She was crushed with guilt that she had broken up with him the very day he died, and now she would never be able to tell him her true feelings. She did feel a connection to her current love interest, but that had only been going on for a short while, and she really only started it because she believed Patrick was fooling around. She now wondered if anyone could ever take Patrick's place.

Loretta and Patrick's secret relationship had lasted over two years. There were gaps in their time together, during which Loretta had remained faithful, though she wasn't so sure about Patrick. She fondly reminisced on how they got their start.

It began the night of a rehearsal dinner two years ago. These dinners provided an opportunity for the chefs to prepare and receive feedback on the meal that was scheduled to be served for the upcoming state dinner.

With Winston gone for the evening, Loretta had stood by in the private kitchen located on the second floor of the executive residence and observed as the executive chef, Patrick the sous chef, and the pastry chef used the lack of food on the plates being brought back in by the butlers as a barometer of how the meal was going.

They all shared the extra bottle of wine, and after a couple of glasses, Loretta caught Patrick looking at her. She was not used to having a man's attention on her and had soon felt her pulse quicken.

At the end of dinner, the first lady, Mrs. Blake, came into the kitchen, gave a warm smile to Loretta, and then began talking directly to the chefs.

"Hi, team! We loved the dinner, starting with the Alaskan salmon in the champagne jelly. That was incredible, and the veal for the main course was amazing. Everything was perfect. And that dessert? Wow. Those cherries... I left my menu card on the table. What did we call that?"

The pastry chef, in his heavy French accent, said, "Mrs. Blake, that is the bombe with fresh cherries. Please tell me, that wasn't too heavy on the chocolate, was it?"

"Oh, my. Heavens, no." She faced the butlers. "In fact, if there is any left, my husband would like more."

One of the butlers was already preparing the plate. "Of course, Mrs. Blake. And shall I prepare a little plate for you as well?"

Mrs. Blake laughed. "Yes, but who said anything about little?"

Everyone laughed along with the first lady.

Loretta enjoyed watching the exchange, then blushed when her eyes met Patrick's, and he winked at her. Her eyes quickly darted around the room to see if anyone had noticed, then she bit her bottom lip and bashfully looked down. She had been sensing these vibes from Patrick the past month or so and had kept trying to ignore the attention, but she was enamored with him. Plus, she was lonely and longed for some physical intimacy.

She and Patrick found themselves alone in the service elevator later that evening, and the next thing Loretta knew, they were kissing. Loretta pressed the button for the basement level, and then they resumed their embrace.

They awoke in bed early the next morning in the ushers basement suite.

***

Loretta's personal cell phone buzzed. She looked down to see a message left by her current love interest. Deciding to ignore it, she poured another glass of wine and continued crying.

Chapter 24
8 p.m., Friday, March 6: The Swann House, NW DC

Frank, Brent, Greg, and Winston sat in front of the TV with their beers.

CNN's Anderson Cooper was on. The dapper reporter continued with the news of the day.

"We've learned additional details on what may have been a prior plot that Brenton Augustus Williams came up with to kill the president. Earlier today, CNN was present when Sara Lexington, Brent Williams' ex-wife, held a press conference during which she shared what her ex-husband had told her a few years ago. A plan he had to attack the White House with priests. Here's the interview."

CNN cut to a setting outside of a suburban house in Maryland, where Brent's ex stood at a small podium with a half dozen mics attached to it. In front of her, a dozen or so reporters jockeyed for the best position, with major network TV cameras set up behind them. Sara read from a prepared text:

"I am not going to answer questions. I am just going to share with you something that has disturbed me ever since the president was assassinated and my ex-husband was arrested and charged with the murder. A few years ago, Brent told me about his idea on how to successfully attack the White House." Sara detailed Brent's plan on how priests could be used to infiltrate the White House, then added, "I have never told anyone this story, but I feel it's my duty as an American to let people know what my ex-husband was thinking. Thank you."

Cooper's face reappeared on the TV screen. "This perhaps is very revealing and does help us understand more. Brenton Williams may have been planning for some time now to kill a president. We're joined by Dr. Stanislaus Friedman of the Berkeley School of Psychology and the author of *Criminally Insane Minds of the Modern Era*. Dr. Friedman, what do you make of this?"

"Well, Anderson," began Friedman, "I believe this gives us a clearer view of what was in Brenton Augustus Williams' mind. He is exhibiting behavior similar to someone who has become radicalized, and he very well may have been working with Islamist jihadists to plan a sensational terrorist act for some time. I find other relevant indicators in his background, Brenton Williams had an advanced degree in intelligence from Johns Hopkins. My thought is, he had premeditated his actions starting as far back as his college years. Additionally, his work in the US Intelligence Community may have been all part of his plan to gain knowledge on the highest levels of security involving the White House. This case is most disturbing. Scholars will be writing about this for years to come."

"Thank you, Dr. Freidman. Let's go to our panel of experts, starting with CNN Legal Advisor and former White House Counsel Gerard Lang. Gerard, good evening. How would you set up the defense for Brenton Williams?"

"Good evening, Anderson," said Lang. "That will be a very difficult job for anyone. Fortunately for Brent Williams, he has Frank Osborne, but I don't see Frank having much hope of building a successful strategy in this case. We are still awaiting the official release of the autopsy, but if as rumored the president was poisoned, and also as rumored Brenton Williams was found with traces of whatever substance was used to kill the president, then I believe we're looking at a trial that could very well set speed records in obtaining a conviction of Williams."

"Very interesting, Gerard," Anderson said. "The White House said it will not release the autopsy results until after the funeral. We expect it to be released early next week. When we come back from break, we will hear from the rest of the panel."

Frank turned off the TV, then invited the team to help themselves to more beer.

"We're losing the spin," lamented Frank. "Brent, your ex's press conference came out of left field. We should have covered this in our first meeting last night, but let me ask, is there *anything* else we need to know about you? Any other plots, plans, murders, girlfriends, nude photos, movies, etc.?"

"No," Brent replied adamantly. "I sure can't think of anything, but if I do, you all will be the first to know—well, hopefully before the media reports it!"

"Good." Frank nodded his approval. "Greg, do you have any updates to share?"

"I'm making some progress on the question of Elizabeth Gentry's acceptance to the Naval Academy," reported Greg. "I have a witness affidavit that Gentry and the chancellor of admissions had an affair. I also have the autopsy results from the chancellor's death. He did drown. However, he had a reasonably high amount of barbiturates in his blood. This was never investigated, which is strange. I'm working on that aspect."

"Good. Anything else?" asked Frank.

"Yeah. I'm not sure that this is relevant, but it is interesting: Wendy Wolf spent a lot of time in Annapolis while Elizabeth Gentry was at the Naval Academy," added Greg.

"We find this interesting because then-Vice President Gentry told me that she and Wendy didn't meet until Harvard Law, which was after the Naval Academy and after her four years in the Navy," Winston pointed out.

"Hmm. That is weird," Frank agreed.

"I've got something else," Winston said.

Frank gestured to him. "Please."

"The housekeeper told me there were two prescription bottles for cariprazine in President Gentry's bathroom vanity cabinet. I looked it up—it is used in the treatment of schizophrenia, bipolar mania, and bipolar depression."

Frank's eyebrows shot up. "Oh, wow! Are we sure they're for her and not the admiral?"

Winston frowned. "No, I can't be sure. I did go up and look at the two prescription bottles. One was nearly empty. The other was full. Get this: The patient name on the label was Gwendolyn A. Wolf, Wendy's full name."

"And do we know who the doctor is?" inquired Frank, before addressing Greg. "Greg, I need you to check this out."

Greg nodded. "Already on it."

"Thank you. Anything else, guys? No? Okay, I've got something, and I'm already handling it, but I wanted you to be aware. My friends at the SEC tell me that they were contacted by their partners in the US Attorney's Office, and as you may know, the SEC and the US attorneys are a very close group. They share everything. My SEC contacts said the US attorneys were told this afternoon by someone in the west wing to investigate my holdings in Apple. The west wing seems to be suggesting that I benefited from insider trading because I profited $700 mil. Their records aren't even current—my profit to date is $930 mil. Anyway, this is just another prong in the effort by the White House to discredit and destroy Brent and anyone on his defense team.

"Just so you all know, there is absolutely zero justification for any investigation into my investments, and this will fizzle out in a week or so. My job is to figure out where the next attack may come from, and I wouldn't put it past Elizabeth Gentry to go physical once all else fails. Because of this, early this morning, I assigned extra security for us. The folks I've assigned to this won't be in the White House but will be everywhere else. You all won't even notice them unless, of course, they are needed."

Frank's eyes moved across the room. "So, is there anything else we need to address tonight? No? Okay, then. Thank, you gentlemen. Have a pleasant remainder of your evening."

Chapter 25
6 a.m., Saturday, March 7: The White House

Winston carried his breakfast tray into the ushers office; he was lost in the aroma of the bacon and eggs when the phone rang.

He put his tray on his desk and lifted the phone. "Good morning. Ushers office, Winston speaking."

"Oh, good. You're in," said Gentry. "How soon before the admiral can move from the Lincoln bedroom to the solarium?"

"The plumbers tell me they'll have the plumbing completed by Wednesday, and the carpenters should have their work done by next Saturday."

"I was hoping for sooner, but I guess that'll have to do. Hey, dinner last night went very well. Pass my regards to the chef."

"Excellent and will do," replied Winston.

"One of the butlers… Uh, I forgot his name…. Oh, yeah. Harley, that's it. He's a bit too slow for my liking. Please let him go. Make it happen."

The phone went dead.

Winston thought about Harley; he had been a dedicated butler since the Ford White House. Winston hoped that President Gentry would allow him to convert Harley from a butler to a doorman, a position in which Harley would run the elevator. Something of a slower-paced position. Anything rather than fire him. Winston decided that due to her coolness on the phone, he would not call her back but wait until he had the chance to see her in person.

Winston went back to his breakfast.

Mary the housekeeper came in and took a seat. "Good morning, Winston."

"Good morning. How'd it go last night?" asked Winston.

Mary scoffed. "You mean this morning? The final guests didn't leave until 3 a.m."

"Oh, my! And the president was up early," Winston told her. "She just called me!"

"Well, the overnight houseguests, the Mirovs, left a few minutes after 6 a.m. The butlers carried their bags."

Winston nodded. "Right. I ordered their car to pick them up at six. So, tell me about the party."

"After the movie, the bowling was short-lived," Mary recalled. "The president gave a tour, took everyone to the oval office, and they all ended up in the pool without bathing suits! We made sure there were plenty of towels, and the butlers served hot chocolate."

"Sounds like quite the party," mused Winston.

"The president turned in at 1 a.m., but the party raged on."

"What about the admiral?"

"He was the life of the party!" Mary exclaimed. "He led everyone in a cigar-tasting contest, followed by a scotch blind taste test! He escorted the final guests to the gate at 3 a.m.!"

"That's pretty amazing for an old guy."

"I bet you could keep up with him!"

Before Winston could respond, a Secret Service agent stuck his head in the office and said, "Looks like the president and admiral will be heading out for golf. The president called the staircase directly a few minutes ago." The "staircase" was the presidential protective detail (PPD) control room on the ground floor of the White House.

My God, Winston thought. They were going out to play golf just six days after President Blake's assassination? It seemed as if the official period of mourning was over. *These people only care about themselves!* he thought in disgust. "Where are they playing?"

"Holly Hills Country Club, near Frederick, and we're taking Marine One," replied the agent.

Winston said under his breath, "That's certainly ostentatious."

"I'm sorry, what was that?" asked the agent.

Winston said more loudly, "That's a very nice course."

Not long afterward, the roar of the Sikorsky SH-3 Sea King—more commonly known as Marine One—could be heard as it landed on the south grounds, blades whipping the air.

Winston rode the elevator up to the second floor. Minutes later, the president, followed by the admiral, walked from the cross-hall and toward the elevator.

Winston wished both of them a good morning.

Gentry glanced up at him. "Oh, good morning. Where are our clubs?"

"The valets just carried them out to the chopper," replied Winston. He entered the elevator with the admiral and president, closed the doors, pressed the ground floor button, and then pressed the buzzer to signal the president was moving.

The admiral said with a big, warm smile, "Hey, Winston! What a great party you threw for us last night. We had a blast. Your team was great. They had everything ready even before I thought to ask! Please thank them for us."

"Thank you, sir. I will be sure to let the staff know."

The doors to the elevator opened on the ground floor. As the president stepped off, she asked, "Did you take care of the staff adjustment we talked about?"

Winston, now walking with the president toward the diplomatic reception room, answered, "Will handle that now, ma'am. Would you consider allowing Harley the job of running the elevator? That way, we don't have to terminate him."

"Uh, yeah, sure. That should be okay. Oh, I'm having a working lunch in the west sitting hall at one. There will be ten of us, including the admiral. Let's have sandwiches."

"We'll have everything ready," promised Winston. "Enjoy your round."

"Winston, I need for you to attend the lunch as well."

Winston glanced at Gentry, hiding his surprise. "Certainly. Is there anything I should prepare for?"

"Nope, just be there."

"Yes, ma'am. Enjoy your game."

The president and her husband walked out through the south portico doors and onto the south lawn toward Marine One.

Winston stood beneath the south portico canopy. He laughed as the admiral, just prior to entering the chopper, turned back to look at him and gave the famous President Nixon peace-sign salute.

Thirty minutes later, Harley was officially a doorman, and the executive chef was preparing lunch for twelve. He was a good chef with a great attitude, especially considering he was working ninety hours a week now since, in addition to his regular duties, he was also handling the family meals until a replacement for Patrick could be hired.

While the president and admiral were playing golf, Winston decided to survey the private quarters. He exited the elevator on the second floor and walked through the double mahogany doors and into the private quarter's main cross-hall. Straight ahead, he could see through the open door and into the TV room. To his right was the west sitting hall, and to his left was the wide corridor hallway leading all the way to the very far-away end: the east sitting hall. He went right and entered the west sitting hall, then looked in through the door to his right to see the family dining room, where just six days prior, President Blake lay dying.

He could not believe it hadn't even been a week since it happened. Directly across the doorway to the dining room was the entrance to the master bedroom, where he could see the maids putting clean sheets on the bed. He walked in and said hello. One of the florists was in the corner putting the final touches on a fresh flower arrangement. Winston walked through the doorway that led to what had traditionally been the First Lady's bathroom, now being used by President Gentry as her bathroom. Winston leaned into the bathroom and noticed the medicine cabinet was open; the two medicine bottles he had inspected the day before were still there.

Winston then went to the opposite end of the second floor toward the east sitting hall; he passed the yellow oval room on his right. Next was the president's office. Then he walked up the slight incline to the Lincoln bedroom on the right, where the admiral was temporarily being housed. The Lincoln bedroom had actually been Lincoln's office when he was president. During the Lincoln White House, the famous bed had been used in another guest room. Eleven-year-old Willie Lincoln died in that bed, then was embalmed in the green room. For her remaining time in the White House, Mrs. Lincoln refused to enter either the guest room or the green room. The bed was not moved to its present location until 1902, after all the offices of the president were relocated to the newly constructed west wing.

Winston stood in the doorway of the Lincoln bedroom and turned to see Mary approaching.

"The room is perfect. We didn't have to do a thing," she remarked.

"Yes, it certainly is one of my favorites, with its history, and especially after the most recent restoration. That really makes it perfect," Winston said.

"Oh, no, I don't mean that!" protested Mary. "I mean, it's perfect because each morning the admiral makes his own bed, and he cleans the bathroom! This morning, when I asked if we could change his sheets, he laughed and told me not to worry about anything with him and for me to just leave fresh sheets once a week and he'd take care of it! I thanked him and told him he would be the first ever to do this. He had just smiled and headed to breakfast."

"I may have misjudged him," Winston realized. "He seemed rather aloof and not too pleased when I suggested he smoke his cigars on the Truman balcony instead of inside the White House. But this morning he was very warm, very appreciative of the staff's efforts last evening."

"Well as far as smoking cigars, he listened!" said Mary. "Last night, he seemed to take pride in telling all the guests there would be no smoking inside the White House. Cigars were limited to the Truman balcony or the south grounds."

Winston left the Lincoln bedroom, gave a quick glance at the queens room across the hall, then took the hidden back staircase from the second floor to the third floor and checked the seven bedrooms and billiards room. Satisfied all was in order, he headed back to the ushers office.

Chapter 26
1 p.m., Saturday, March 7: The White House

Winston stood outside the south portico and witnessed another majestic landing of Marine One. He never tired of the 60 mph winds blasting all around him. Once securely on the ground, the rotors stopped turning, and the front side door of Marine One was lowered open from the inside. A marine in full dress uniform stepped out and made a sharp left toward the rear of the chopper, where he opened the rear door, then returned and stood at attention at the first door. An agent opened the inside door separating the cabin from the exterior door area, then stepped off the chopper and headed across the lawn to his right. Moments later, the president walked out, followed by the admiral, and walked across the south lawn. A few staffers exited the rear door of the helicopter, followed by the valets who carried the golf bags.

The president and admiral walked toward the south portico, and once they were under the canopy, Winston asked, "How'd you hit 'em?"

The president smiled. Winston thought, *Wow, a smile. That's a first.* She said, "Better than usual."

The admiral, walking closely behind her, winked at Winston. "I hit an eighty-nine! First time I've broken ninety in, well, let's just say a long, long time."

Winston nodded. "Excellent!"

Once inside, as they boarded the elevator, Winston told the president that the luncheon guests were ready to come up whenever she was. She requested that they be brought up in exactly five minutes. Winston was trying not to be concerned over the fact that she had mysteriously invited him to the luncheon as well.

At 1:06 p.m., Winston went to the state floor to gather the staff who had assembled for the working luncheon.

The max the president's elevator can hold is eight, but all nine luncheon guests were able to squeeze in. Winston pressed the second-floor button. As they arrived on the second floor, the president and admiral, looking stylishly casual in their golf garb, greeted the staff as they got off the elevator.

"Thank you all for coming," said Gentry. "Grab any seat in the west sitting hall. We'll be eating on trays."

After everyone had been seated, the president spoke. "I've asked the butlers to hold off on bringing in the lunch until after we start the meeting. Since we've only been in office less than a week, let's quickly go around the room and do introductions. Just say your name and position."

"Wendy Wolf, chief of staff."

"Jill Turner, press secretary."

"Donna Carpenter, White House chief counsel."

"Scott Giambattista, political affairs."

"Ellie Wigglesworth, cabinet affairs."

"Dean DePriest, office of communications."

"Trevor Antolik, constitutional expert."

"Joseph Toreski, ethics advisor."

"Steven Albano, national security advisor."

"Admiral Curtis." He then stood up at attention. "I am proud to be the first husband!"

Everyone laughed.

The president then nodded toward Winston.

"Bartholomew Winston, chief usher."

"Okay, tomorrow marks one week since I have been president," announced Gentry. "I need to select a vice president. We'll start with our expert in constitutional law, Trevor."

"Thank you, President Gentry," Trevor said. "It's rather straightforward. Under Section 2 of the 25th Amendment, if there is a vacancy in the office of vice president, the president then nominates someone to fill the vacancy. If a majority of both Houses of Congress agree, that person becomes the vice president."

"Thanks, Trevor." Gentry then raised her voice and looked toward the kitchen. "Guys, you can bring lunch in." She then faced her staff. "Some of you may be wondering why I've invited Winston to be at this meeting. Well, for the two years and two months that I have known him, and especially the past six days as I've gotten to know him a lot better, Winston has proven to me beyond any reasonable doubt that he is solid and dependable, and I now realize he is the underpinning for the success of any administration. Jackie Kennedy once said, 'The chief usher is the most powerful man in Washington next to the president.' I believe her! Winston, thank you for all you've done to help the admiral and me settle in. I know I have been demanding, maybe, just a little bit at times." This got a big laugh from the staff, after which the president continued, "But you, with your herculean efforts, have handled everything with the grace and dignity that define you. Thank you, Winston!"

Winston was moved and said, "Thank you, President Gentry. Your words mean more to me than you know."

The butlers whisked in, carrying two silver trays of sandwiches, followed by a tray of chips and another tray covered with pitchers of lemonade and iced tea. The food was placed on a side table, and while everyone was getting their meal, the butlers placed TV trays at each person's seat.

Once everyone was seated, the president announced, "I will need a list of names to be considered for vice president."

The admiral said, "I vote for Winston!" Everyone laughed.

"The VP needs to be eminently qualified," said Gentry. "And, of course, someone that will help get us votes in two years! I would like to see the first draft of the list by this time next week. Wendy, what else do we need to address?"

"Madam President, as you heard in your 4 a.m. briefing, the Russian military exercise is no longer a crisis," began Wendy. "National Security Advisor Albano will be providing you with another briefing, which is scheduled for…" As Wendy was bringing up the calendar on her laptop, Steve Albano said, "Eight a.m. Monday, ma'am, if that works for your schedule." Wendy quickly added, "Yes, that's correct. Monday, 8 a.m."

"Perfect," said the president. "Anything else, Wendy?"

"Yes. The speaker called to remind you the fiscal year budget submission is due on Wednesday. Next Tuesday, you are hosting the state arrival and dinner for Jean-Claude Marchal, president of France. As of today, you have twelve more senior White House staff vacancies to fill, and this morning, the secretary of commerce announced his retirement, so you will need to nominate a candidate. And finally, the queen has invited you to the palace. We need to discuss possible dates. And that's basically it."

The president shifted her gaze to the usher. "Winston, you need to provide Wendy and me with a crash course on how these state arrivals work, what our menu options are, entertainment, everything, the works."

"Of course, Mrs. President. Have you had time to select a social secretary?" Winston inquired.

"Oh, hell, no," groaned Gentry. "I need one of those?" Everyone laughed. "Can't you be it for this event?"

Winston frowned. "Ma'am, we should talk."

This got everyone laughing again, including the president.

"Winston, Wendy will make time on my calendar for us, ASAP. And Wendy, you said there are twelve more vacancies?"

"Yes, twelve."

"Okay, please stay after this meeting so we can address that. Everything else can wait. No more work talk! Please eat up, everyone. We don't need the leftovers!"

***

Mid-afternoon, the phone rang in the ushers office. Winston answered. It was the president. "Winston, let's meet regarding the state dinner. Can you come up now?"

"On my way." Winston grabbed the state dining room seating chart, the list of guests, and a printout of the menu and took the elevator to the second floor.

Winston walked into the second-floor cross-hall and looked toward the west sitting hall but did not see the president. He figured the next most logical place would be her private office, which had previously been known as the treaty room. This was where President William McKinley performed the signing of the peace treaty with Spain that ended the Spanish-American War. The room had also been used as a meeting room for presidential cabinets and private offices for more recent presidents.

Winston walked into the room. It was empty. He stepped back in the hallway and headed back toward the west sitting hall, where he heard the president yell, "We're in here!" Winston followed the voice to the family kitchen, where he found the president with Wendy. Both ladies were drinking chocolate milkshakes. The president handed one to Winston and said, "Oh, my God. These are so great. Adam, the guy that works in the main kitchen, made them for us."

Winston was a bit surprised but smiled and took a sip. "Mmm," he said as his lips left the straw. "Very good."

"Okay, tell me everything I need to know about state dinners," instructed Gentry.

"Well, luckily, we had been planning for this dinner for several months. A lot of the prep work has already been done. The guests have been invited and have RSVP'd. I brought the list in case you wish to make any changes, and if so, we should do that today." Winston handed the list to the president, who then handed it off to Wendy. Winston continued, "Here's the menu. Mrs. Blake had approved it, and everything has been ordered. The wines came in yesterday." Winston handed over the menu to Gentry, who briefly looked it over before passing it off to Wendy.

"Winston, I'm not going to change any of this," Gentry decided. "I will have a lot of input on the next one, but let's go with what's been planned."

"Thank you, Mrs. President. That makes the job much easier."

"I've attended six of these so far, but I would like to hear from you about the whole process, the timing involved, etc. Oh, and are there any fun people on the guest list? Who's the entertainment? Hopefully not a Hodges and Heart tribute this time around?" The president wrinkled her nose and made a face.

"The entertainer is American cellist Yo-Yo Ma."

Gentry nodded. "Oh, excellent. I love him!"

"Yes, he has performed here before. He was invited to perform at this event because he was born in Paris, and obviously, with this being the French state dinner, it made perfect sense."

Wendy studied the guest list. "Oh, cool. I see Julia Roberts is coming."

"Is she still married to Lyle Lovett?" asked Gentry.

Wendy glanced at her. "That ended, like, twenty-five years ago!"

"Oh."

Wendy's eyes widened with mounting excitement as they lowered down the list. "George Clooney! Daniel Craig! Denzel Washington! Wowsers! This is going to be great!"

The president's hand shot out. "Give me that list!"

Trying to redirect the focus, Winston continued, "State dinners typically have 126 guests seated at thirteen round tables in the state dining room. A host is assigned to each table, and each host has a direct line of sight to the president."

Gentry semi-listened to Winston, eyes still glued to the guest list. "The Senate minority leader… Hmm, does he have to be there?"

Winston nodded. "Yes, I'm afraid so. It's protocol."

Gentry frowned. "Well, then, can we give him, like, the worst seat?"

"There really isn't a bad seat, but you certainly can make changes as you choose. I brought a seating chart with all the tables. We can arrange it as you see fit."

Wendy pointed to the list. "Oh, wow. Did you see this?!"

"Okay, I'm putting this guest list down so that you'll have my undivided attention," announced Gentry. "That means you too, Miss Wendy!" They laughed.

"We do a slightly modified French service," Winston continued. "Basically, we serve four courses. For Tuesday night, it will be: first course: supreme of smoked trout, mouse of celeriac sauce verte, and Fleuron's; second course: roasted filet of beef bearnaise sauce, mushroom in potato bordure, and asparagus polonaise and buttered carrots; third course: endive radicchio and bibb salad, herbed capri cheese, and French bread; dessert: dried pear souffle and caramel sauce; and wines: Stag's Leap Wine Cellars White Riesling 2016, Clos Pegase Cabernet Sauvignon 2010, and Scharffenberger Crémant.

"What's potato bordure?" asked Gentry.

"It's smoked trout and mushrooms served with potato. It's outstanding," said Winston.

"So, is the Scharffenberger Crémant a champagne?" inquired Wendy.

"Basically, yes, but technically, Crémant is a group of sparkling wines made with the same technique as is used in champagne but from outside the Champagne region, so it cannot be called champagne."

"So, that will be used for the opening toast?" asked Gentry.

"No, the champagne is served after dessert. The toasting wine will be the Stag's Leap white Riesling."

Gentry frowned. "I sure hope I don't look like an idiot."

"You won't," assured Winston. "The maître d' will be just behind your seat. Count on him to guide you, and he will ensure you have what you need. Plus, I will be observing from the cross-hall and am only steps away if needed."

Gentry nodded. "Good to know. Okay, give me a quick overview of the entire event, starting with the state arrival."

"Fortunately, you have a chief of protocol, Ambassador Clark. She will be briefing you next week on all the aspects and specifics, but I can share the basic steps—"

Winston was interrupted by Wendy, who was just getting off her phone. "Mrs. President, we have something we need to address immediately."

Gentry faced Winston. "Winston, my apologies. We'll pick this up at a later time."

Winston stood. "Of course, Madam President."

Chapter 27
4 p.m., Saturday, March 7: The White House

Winston picked up the direct line from Post A4, the northwest gate.

"Winston here."

The Secret Service sergeant said from the other end of the line, "Hey, Winston, we have an envelope for you that was just dropped off."

"On my way." Winston hung up, then looked out the window. A sunny day. He left his coat behind but grabbed his hat—he never missed the opportunity to wear his fedora when going outside. He held the hat and walked out of the ushers office and through the door that led to the grand foyer. He nodded to the Secret Service officer who was stationed near the front window, then put his hat on while walking through the north portico doors. He nodded to the officer on post just outside of the doors, descended the steps, and then followed the north drive the 140 yards to the northwest gate.

Winston entered the rear of the small building designated as Post A4. He greeted the four officers and was met by Sergeant Bamberger, who was at the x-ray machine as the envelope addressed to "Chief Usher: White House" came out after its scan. The sergeant handed Winston the envelope, which had no return address.

Winston examined it. "Who dropped this off?"

The officer at the window facing Pennsylvania Avenue turned and responded, "It was an old woman. We all thought she was homeless."

Winston shook his head and thanked the officers. As he headed back up the north drive to the White House, he looked at the envelope curiously, then opened it. Inside was a plain piece of paper with a typed message:

This is about your case. Midnight tonight. Meet at the WMAL Tower site. Green Tree & Barnett Road. Chad

Winston got back to the ushers office. Loretta was not there, so he sat at the desk. He kept thinking, *Chad? Who the heck is Chad?* Winston suddenly broke out in a cold sweat. He was well familiar with the WMAL tower site, a wide-open, eighty-acre field with four majestic, three hundred-foot broadcast towers. WMAL bought the property during the 1920s and used it as their center for broadcast operations. Due to advancements in technology and diminishing popularity in AM radio, WMAL recently sold the acreage to a developer, and plans were underway for a massive residential development. The site was just a few minutes' drive from Winston's house. WMAL kept the fields mowed and allowed the locals to walk their dogs on the property. He and his late wife, Connie, had frequented the site, where they would walk Baron, their German shepherd.

Winston's heart ached as he thought back to that horrible night eighteen months ago. It was just after sunset. Winston was at the White House working a state dinner, and Connie had just left the WMAL fields after walking the dog. The man in the Chevy Suburban was focused on texting and did not look up in time to see the woman and dog walking to their car. Connie and the dog did not survive the 45-mph impact. Winston arrived on the chaotic scene as emergency crews were working to free his wife's body from beneath the vehicle. They told Winston that she had died on impact. Their dog had survived, but his injuries were so severe he had to be put down on the spot. Winston had never gone back to the site. He wondered why someone would suggest meeting there now.

After several minutes, he put the mysterious note in his vest pocket. Needing a distraction, Winston reviewed the ushers log already up on his computer screen. He scrolled back and read the entries for the past week, focusing on the days before the death of President Blake. He scrolled back and forth several times, looking over all the entries. He paused, marked a section of the text, and printed it out. He slid open the mahogany cabinet drawer near his knees to reveal the printer and grabbed the sheet that had just been spit out of it. Winston looked it over, then used his burner phone to take a picture of it. He then printed three more copies.

Winston texted the team: *Guys, I'm working on something that I think may be significant to the case, but I need more time to put it all together. How about we cancel our 8 p.m. meeting and meet tomorrow instead? Sunday at 8 p.m.?*

Frank was the first to text him back with: *Works for me. I'm in Annapolis following a lead, and I would have a hard time making it back tonight. So, let's go with tomorrow night. Thanks.*

Greg then responded with: *Got it.*

Brent was the last to text with: *Roger that, see all y'alls tomorrow.*

Winston then texted Greg: *You available to meet in an hour or so? I've got something I want to run by you.*

Greg's text lit up his screen within seconds: *Sure, meet me in the Willard's Round Robin Bar at six.*

Winston replied: *See you then.*

Chapter 28
6 p.m., Saturday, March 7: Willard Hotel, Round Robin Bar, Northwest DC

Winston exited the White House through Post A1 and walked onto East Exec Avenue. The weather was overcast and breezy. Temperatures were in the low fifties. It felt cold. Winston was glad to have his hat but wished he had grabbed his overcoat as well, though it was only a one-block walk to the Willard.

The Willard is one of the grander hotels of Washington and had been in operation since the early 1800s. It is said that when Abraham Lincoln arrived days before his first inauguration, the front desk failed to recognize him, and for a brief flurry of moments, things got a bit awkward for the president-elect.

Winston walked through the large revolving door and entered the hotel. He was immediately noticed by a few of the staff who perhaps thought he was Morgan Freeman. Winston smiled, quickly strode through the lobby, and then entered the hallway on his right, which led to the Round Robin Bar. He acknowledged the bartender with a nod but avoided any of the available seats at the round, marble bar. He didn't see Greg, so he backtracked until, at the end of the entrance hallway, he found a table for two that would be more private than the main area of the bar. He took a seat, careful to position himself so that he would see Greg when he arrived, and checked his personal and then his White

House phone—no messages on either. He looked up just in time to see Greg walk in.

"Hey, man," greeted Winston. "Thanks for coming."

Greg removed his overcoat, draping it on the back of his chair as he nodded to the bartender to indicate they would be ordering drinks.

Greg sat down and smiled at Winston. "I need a drink."

The bartender came over to their table. "What can I get you, gentlemen?"

Winston replied, "Kettle One martini, straight up, dirty, with lots of olives. It's how I get my green vegetables." The bartender responded with a half-smile, then looked at Greg.

"I'll have a double Basil Hayden's, one large ice cube. Thanks."

The bartender nodded and walked back to the bar.

"So, during this, your vacation, have you had time to do anything fun, or has Frank kept you busy on this stuff?" Winston asked.

"He's kept me busy," Greg assured him. "The one good thing is that I am able to sleep a little longer in the mornings. Normally, I'm up at five just so I can get in here before all the traffic, but for the past week, I've been getting up about 6:30, which is a luxury. I guess for you, nothing's changed. Do you ever go home?"

"Not really. Ever since Connie died, I don't have anything to go home to. So, I'm perfectly fine staying in the basement usher suite four to five nights a week." Winston laughed a little. "It makes my commute pretty nice."

The bartender placed their drinks on the table. The men thanked him. "I'll be back to check on you," said the bartender, then he stepped away.

Winston raised his glass to Greg, and the men toasted to a solid case.

"Okay," Winston said after taking a big breath. "I've discovered something that needs more investigation."

Greg nodded in approval. "Great!"

Winston pulled out a printed copy of the ushers log and gave it to Greg. "This is the ushers log starting the Friday prior to the president dying. Look at all the visits from Dr. Jenkins. Four of them. Plus, the president stopped by the doctor's office on the ground floor. This is highly irregular. President Blake, other than being a diabetic, was in good physical condition. I think his former doctor may have gone upstairs to the private quarters a total of three times in the two years he was the president's physician, and two of those times were for Mrs. Blake because she was having indigestion."

Greg looked up from the sheet. "Did you see President Blake on that Friday?"

"Yes, I saw him when he came over to the executive residence at 1:30, and when he went back at two o'clock. He was perfectly fine at that point. He was looking forward to a quiet weekend. Brent saw him on Saturday and Sunday. We need to check with him, but Brent didn't report anything out of the ordinary."

Greg's mouth pressed into a thin line. "This is all very strange. You know, I looked into all the prescriptions that Dr. Jenkins had written. I'm not quite done with my report. I'll present everything at the Swann House tomorrow night, but he did write a bunch for Wendy, and other than the prescriptions for insulin for the former president, I did find one that was different. It was for cobalamin—that's vitamin B12. It helps with all sorts of things, including energy. Nothing that would raise any red flags."

Winston gave a half-shrug. "Yeah, his former physician prescribed that for him too. I remember seeing it in his bathroom a year ago. But why did

President Blake and Dr. Jenkins meet five times? I wonder if there is a way for us to get the records from the doctor's office on the ground floor of the White House."

"Well, that's totally in your purview," Greg pointed out.

"Exactly. I'll take care of it."

"I'm sure all of those records are automated," Greg mentioned.

"No doubt. Damn, I need Brent. He'd be able to get into the system."

Greg frowned. "Yeah, well, he's not gonna be getting into the White House any time soon."

The bartender appeared and asked if they would like another drink. Greg was about to order another, but Winston said, "I'd like a glass of sparkling water." Greg quickly added, "Make that two."

The two men sat in silence for a couple of minutes.

"I'll check with our friends at NSA. I'm sure they can gain access to the system containing the medical records."

"Good. Do it!"

The bartender brought their waters, and Winston handed him a fifty before Greg could get to his wallet. The bartender said he'd be right back with the change.

Greg: "Damn, you beat me to it. I'll get you next time."

The bartender came back with $14 in change. Winston handed him a $10 and thanked him.

Winston and Greg walked out of the Willard together. As they got to East Executive Avenue next to the White House, Greg asked, "You going home tonight?" Winston responded with a wink and said he already was home and wished Greg a good night.

***

When Winston got back to the ushers office, Loretta was seated at the desk and reported that the president and admiral had just come back from using the sauna in the cabana next to the pool and were in for the evening. Winston thought, *Great, a quiet Saturday evening*. Winston went up to his private office and leaned back in his comfortable high-back leather desk chair. He gazed at the family photos on his desk. The 8 x 10 wedding photo of his son and daughter-in-law were the most prominent. He couldn't believe it had been five years since that beautiful fall day in San Diego. Win looked so handsome, standing next to Gail in his tux—tall, thin, short hair, and closely trimmed beard. He could be a model. And Gwen, so cute and absolutely adorable. The two of them had become so successful, and Winston was proud and impressed how they never forgot their African American heritage and had created a charitable foundation to help disadvantaged minority youths. What a couple! Winston grabbed his phone.

"Hi, Dad!" Win said immediately. "How are you? I was just about to call you."

"Great. What's up?"

"We're pregnant!"

Winston gasped. "What?!"

"Yep, it's official."

"Oh, my God! This is the best news I've had in a long time. Congratulations. I'm so happy for you two. How's Gwen?"

"She's fine. It's early. We're not telling people yet. We want to get through the first trimester."

"Of course. I'm so happy, I have tears in my eyes. Do you have a due date yet?"

"Well, it's only been six weeks. The doctor estimates November 11th."

"That's perfect. She taking vitamins? Getting plenty of rest? Not drinking alcohol? Only moderately exercising? Um, is she—"

Win interrupted with "Dad, remember, I'm a doctor! We're following all precautions, and our obstetrician is world-class."

"Yes, good. Great. Sorry, I'm just so excited for you guys!"

"Her next appointment is in two weeks, and they'll do an ultrasound, so I'll send you the images."

"Yes, please! I can't wait."

"Dad, we'd love to have you visit when you can, and especially at Christmas. This year will be very special, and we want you here with us."

"Absolutely! I am there when you need me. You can count on it. God, how I wish your mother was here to experience this."

"I have thought about her a lot. I'm sure she's smiling."

"Yes, I'm sure too."

After they hung up, Winston leaned back in his chair. He felt so wonderful, he couldn't get the smile off his face. After twenty minutes of reflecting on the great news, Winston had one more call to make and then would investigate what the chef was making for dinner.

Chapter 29
11:55 p.m., Saturday, March 7: WMAL Tower
site, Bethesda, MD

Winston pulled over to the side of the road at the prescribed location and turned off the engine. It was very dark; the only visible light was from the blinking red lights atop the four mammoth radio towers in the open field to his right. Winston checked both his White House cell and the burner phone. No messages.

The longer Winston sat in his car, the more he felt uneasy. He couldn't stop thinking about how he was sitting there parked at the place of Connie's death. His emotions began to get the better of him. Suddenly, he felt closed in. He gulped for air, finally cracking a window. The sudden rush of cold air and the familiar hum of traffic from the nearby DC beltway helped calm him down and bring him back to present day, though memories from the worst day of his life, just eighteen months ago, still clung to him.

Lost in thought and staring straight ahead, Winston saw the flashing of headlights from a car in the distance. He continued to stare in its direction. Less than a minute later, the lights flashed again. Winston reached over, lifting his fedora off the passenger-side seat. He took his time getting out of the car and slowly closed the door. Outside felt even colder because of the bitter wind. Winston adjusted his scarf and made sure his hat was securely on. As he looked up, he caught sight of the stars scattered across the sky, but with no moon out to brighten things, it was impossible to make out where the car was that had flashed its lights. A lull in the beltway traffic made it possible for him to hear the thump of two cars' doors closing. Winston now watched two individuals approach with flashlights pointed straight down. Once they were within twenty feet, they shined their flashlights directly at Winston, who instinctively shielded his eyes.

A man's voice called out, "Winston?"

Winston lowered his hand and nodded. The two lowered their flashlights. As his eyes adjusted, Winston could see two men who now stood about ten feet away. One appeared tall and thin, while the other was just the opposite: short and stout. They both wore dark trench coats, gloves, and no scarves. The fat man wore a black cowboy hat and a white, button-down shirt, he had a gray beard. The skinny guy had a pockmarked face, he wore large earmuffs, his coat was closed, the top of his dark-hooded sweatshirt was visible, and he was wearing a Baltimore Ravens cap beneath his hood.

The short, fat man spoke first. "We're Chad."

The man had what Winston thought could be a Russian accent. The two men took another step closer.

The tall, skinny man offered, "Yah, we like the name Chad cuz we thought it made us sound young."

Winston found the man to be irritating; something about him grated his nerves. And it was obvious that these two men were anything but young. The annoying skinny guy's English was not good; he, too, had an eastern European accent, possibly Russian. The fat man pointed to the field and said, "I'm told there will soon be 190 houses built here." When the fat man raised his arm, his coat shifted, revealing what Winston could plainly see was an automatic pistol, similar to the government-issue 9mm Sig Sauer. Winston was very familiar with the Sig, having used one during his numerous invites by his Secret Service friends to the firing ranges in the basement of the old post office building in DC and at the Beltsville training center. The skinny guy kept his hands out of his pockets, likely due to the oversized and clumsy-looking gloves he was wearing. He seemed more concerned about trying to keep warm than anything else.

"Is that what this is about?" Winston asked. "You want to talk about real estate?"

"No, Mr. Winston," assured the fat man. "But before we start, I hope you don't mind, but we need to check you for weapons or a wire." He motioned to the skinny guy, who stepped over to Winston and asked him to spread his arms. Winston complied and was patted down.

The skinny guy reported in poor English, "He good."

Winston addressed the fat man. "What is your name, and why are you armed?"

The fat man responded, "Don't you worry, Mr. Winston. My name is not important, but my message is. And in my line of work, my superiors require me to be armed. But, Mr. Winston, rest assured we are not here to harm you. We simply want to spend a few minutes talking."

Winston rolled his eyes. "So talk."

The fat man responded, "Let's walk."

The two men extinguished their flashlights and guided Winston toward the towers. The three of them slowly trekked along the path, which was well worn by the dog walkers. Winston could tell the men were familiar with the layout of the field as they had no difficulty following the path without light. The wind increased as they reached the open field. The path was bordered by patches of two-foot-high dead ragweed. Soon, there was barely enough space for the fat man and Winston to walk together. They were nearly shoulder to shoulder as the skinny man followed three paces behind.

Winston broke the silence. "What do you two want? What's this all about?"

"Mr. Winston," began the fat man, "we're here to share with you a concern from close friends of ours and thought this location would convey the seriousness of the matter."

Winston becoming agitated. "Get to your point now!"

"Certainly. We need for you and your little club to cease and desist your charade of an investigation."

Winston frowned. "I don't know what you're talking about. Who sent you here?"

The skinny man from three steps behind them chimed in with, "Shut the fuck up and listen."

"Let me make this clear for you," continued the fat man. "We have concerns about your so-called defense team, and lucky for you, we're here to help. In a matter of days, you will be receiving detailed information that will prove beyond any reasonable doubt who killed President Blake, so we need you to stop your activities now. That's all we're asking. Stop wasting everyone's time. Do not continue any further investigation. Understand, we're all concerned for you. What I mean, Mr. Winston, is gosh, it would be just so sad if by some chance you were to experience any other type of tragedy. Wasn't it bad enough what occurred here eighteen months ago?"

Winston's blood ran cold as the fat man continued with "We think it would be so unfair for you and/or those you love to again experience something unfortunate and tragic."

Winston stopped walking. He turned and faced the fat man, leaning forward so as to be eye level with the small, rotund man, and said in a steely voice, "Stop threatening me, or I'll demonstrate to you up close and personal what damage that Sig Sauer you're carrying can do to a man. Do I make myself clear?"

The fat man nervously smiled and took an uneasy step backward, trying not to trip on the high weeds. "Mr. Winston, we're just having a nice conversation here. All we're doing is trying to help you out by providing some friendly advice."

Winston gritted his teeth. "We're done here." He turned and nearly walked into the skinny man, brushing past him. "Get outta my way, dog breath." Winston walked away, leaving the two men behind in the field.

When he got to his car, he leaned against it and felt his heart pounding not from fear but from anger. His thoughts again raced back to his last time there, his anger soon fading into sadness. He took a deep breath and looked around, then hurriedly got into his car, started the engine, hit the gas, and pulled the wheel hard to the left. His tires squealed, and then he immediately had to hit the brake to avoid an oncoming car. The car swerved to miss him and flew by. It was a Mercedes-Benz GLS-Class SUV, very similar to the one he and Connie were planning to buy. *What kind of idiot speeds on this road?* he thought. His mind flashed with images of the speeding Chevy Suburban that had killed his wife.

Winston composed himself and slowly drove away. He looked in his rearview mirror to see headlights from where the two men that had met him had parked. Winston turned at the next street, turned off his lights, and waited as they drove by. Winston then continued driving; less than a mile and after a couple of turns later, he was on the street where he and Connie had lived together for so many years. He decided to stop at his house to check on things and grab another suit.

He pulled into his driveway and sat for several minutes, admiring the modest, two-story brick house. He could see the inside lights he had set up on timers so as to always make it appear someone was home. He got out of the car and grabbed his mail from the mailbox next to the front door. Placing the mail under his arm, he then unlocked the deadbolt and then the door. He walked in, disarmed his ADT system, and then headed for his kitchen. He had just popped open a can of La Croix from his fridge when his burner phone rang. It was Frank.

"You okay?" Frank inquired.

"Yeah. I'm just really mad, man. I wanted to karate kick that skinny guy in the throat."

"I don't blame you. Hey, the good news is that the audio we got was perfect. We have the entire conversation. And my guys were successful in placing the tracking device on their car. We should have some good intel by the time we meet tomorrow night at Swann. Hold on, Greg's calling in. I'm going to add him to our call."

Winston sat at his kitchen table, put his phone on speaker and laid it on the table, took a swallow of his drink, and began sorting through his mail.

"Winston, I've got Greg on the line," said Frank. "Okay, let's review what we now know about your midnight encounter. First of all, you showed excellent judgment in alerting us of their request to meet with you, but if there's ever a next time, please give us more than a few hours. And just so everyone knows how good our security detail is, they were all over the scene immediately. Five guys, plus Greg, were there and were closely monitoring your walk with infrared equipment. We had two snipers set up and ready if needed, and the tracker we set up on their car is active."

"Yeah, Frank," Greg acknowledged. "Our guys are good. As for me, I didn't have time to properly gear up. I should have gone home to get my down parka. Instead, I froze my ass off laying in that thorned thicket.

Winston, I was only twenty feet from where you took your stroll. Although, it was worth it to see when you walked away from them. They stood frozen for a minute, not knowing what to do."

"Dammit!" Frank snapped, sounding distracted over the line. "Not good. They must've detected our tracking device. They threw it out from the overpass as they drove over the beltway. Okay, we'll run the tag and see what we come up with. The bottom line is you're safe. We'll review the transcript and see what we can determine."

"Well, they both had Russian accents," recalled Winston. "And I saw that the fat guy had what possibly could have been a government-issue Sig Sauer."

"Strange. Hey, Greg, can you get us some photos of Russian- and Soviet-era handguns for us to review?" Frank requested.

"Will do," said Greg.

"Guys, thanks for backing me up out there," Winston said. "Greg, sorry it was so cold. It's late. Do we need to go over anything else tonight, or can it wait until we meet tomorrow?"

Frank responded. "Tomorrow's good. Winston and Greg, good work tonight. Good night and see you all tomorrow."

Winston disconnected the call and put his phone in his vest pocket, then walked to his bedroom closet, where he found the suit he wanted. Back in the living room, he gave a quick look around, felt melancholy, rearmed the security system, locked the door, and got back into his car.

Not even two miles from his house, he noticed in his rearview mirror a car with its high beams quickly approaching. Then he saw the telltale flashing blue light. Winston darted his eyes down to his speedometer. He was going forty-one in a thirty-five zone—hardly worth pulling someone over. He shook his head as he pulled off to the right and into a commuter parking lot.

From his rearview mirror, he squinted in the bright light and could see two silhouettes get out of the car. One of them walked up to Winston's driver-side window. Winston pushed the button and opened his window.

The officer shined his flashlight on Winston's face. "Driver's license and registration, please?"

Winston slowly reached for his wallet in his vest pocket and pulled it out, making certain it was fully visible to the officer. He opened his wallet and pulled out the license. "Officer, here's my driver's license. I need to open my glove box to get my registration." Winston very slowly leaned over and opened the glove box. His view was aided by the second officer on the passenger side of the car, who shone a flashlight through the window on the glove box.

Winston found the registration and handed it to the first officer.

The officer looked at the license, then at Winston. "Mr. Winston, are there any weapons or illegal narcotics in your vehicle?"

"No, officer," Winston answered respectfully. "No weapons, no drugs."

The officer then unholstered his gun and pointed it at Winston. "Sir, get out of the car."

Winston's pulse quickened as he opened the door and slowly got out. "Officer, what is this about?"

The officer ignored the question and told Winston, "Follow me."

Winston could now see the officer was dressed in black, not a patrol uniform. He thought he must be undercover.

Winston followed the officer, who led him to the rear of the police vehicle—which Winston could now plainly see was not a police vehicle. It was the Mercedes-Benz SUV that sped by him earlier at the WMAL Tower site. He also noticed the car had a diplomatic license plate that began with the letters "YR."

A Russian diplomatic vehicle.

Standing behind the Mercedes and waiting for Winston was the second officer. As Winston got closer, he could see the second individual also was not in a police officer uniform and was wearing all black. Their eyes met; they were all that was visible behind the black ski mask.

"Mr. Winston." The individual began to speak; it was a woman with a heavy Russian accent. "We are here to follow up on our comrades' message that was just delivered to you from that field." She flicked her hand as if to point. "This should be proof that we can get to you at anytime and anywhere we so choose. Am I making myself perfectly clear to you, Mr. Winston?"

"What the hell do you want?" demanded Winston.

The women continued, "We will be providing you with critical information to assist your investigation. This new information will include the empirical evidence you so need to prove who killed President Blake. I will be contacting you later this week with this information. You will take what I provide to your little posse. Then you and your group will meet with the FBI and US attorneys to provide them the material. You will present the information I provide to you as the results of your investigation. Understand, Mr. Winston, this is not a request. This is an order. Should you fail to follow our directions, the consequences will be dire."

She stepped closer to Winston and said, "Let us take Gwen, for example. Such a wonderful little daughter-in-law. We are all so happy for that great news you received today. We just hope Gwen will remain healthy and safe and can bring into the world that grandchild you're so excited about and have been waiting so long for."

Winston became enraged. He felt his fists clench, but before he knew it, with lightning speed, the woman punched him hard in the stomach. Winston instantly fell to his knees, bowing down in agony and gasping for breath. The woman knelt next to him and in a soft voice said into his ear, "Be sure and follow our instructions so you and your family will be safe." She stood and looked down at Winston who was still struggling to catch his breath. "Thank you, Mr. Winston. Until we meet again."

The man and woman got into their car and sped off, leaving Winston in a cloud of exhaust.

Winston struggled to stand. He staggered a bit, then regained his balance, holding his stomach as he walked back to the car and opened the door. Winston found that his driver's license and registration had been tossed on the seat. He grabbed the items and fell into his seat, closed his eyes, and thought hard. The pain in his stomach continued unabated.

Five minutes later, Winston parked at a Bethesda 7-Eleven. His stomach still hurt but not nearly as bad as it had in the beginning. He went inside and paid cash for a new burner phone. Once back in the car, he set up the phone, then using the Signal App, he entered a phone number he knew by heart. After three rings, there was an answer. "Sam Poundstone."

A close friend of Winston's, Sam was a former Navy SEAL who had spent twenty-two years in the Secret Service as the lead for the emergency response team. He then worked a half dozen years for Interpol until age fifty-five, when he retired from that position, moving on to undercover intelligence in Moscow and Istanbul. Sam then moved to the West Coast where, for the past several years, he'd been in Santa Monica running a very successful business providing security services to the rich and famous. Sam's older brother, Jack, was a former Army Ranger who had spent thirty-three years in the Secret Service. Long ago, Winston had saved Jack's life. After that, Sam had made it clear that his help was always just a phone call away.

Winston took a painful, deep breath. "Hey, Sam, it's me."

Sam's strong and steady voice came over the line. "Winston? You okay? You don't sound so good."

"I'll make it. I have a favor to ask."

"Must be important. It's after 2 a.m. out there. What do you need?"

"I've made some new Russian acquaintances that have threatened harm to Win and Gail," Winston told him.

"Are they still at 8330 Summit Way?"

"Yeah. How'd you remember that?"

"It's how I get the big bucks." Even when joking, the man sounded serious. "Okay, I've got assets nearby. They'll be in place by midnight our time, 3 a.m. your time. I'll cover their work location too. Win and Gail still working at UC San Diego Medical Center?"

"Yes. Oh, and Sam? Gail's pregnant."

"That's great news, Grandpa. Congrats! Don't worry about anything."

"Sam, thanks and I owe you."

"What are you talking about? You'll never owe me!"

Winston changed the subject. "How's your brother?"

"He's enjoying his senior years like you should be doing, my friend. Okay, let me get to work. Get some rest!"

Winston terminated the call, then, still using his 7-Eleven burner phone, texted Frank: *CXSMP1*. One of the codes that Frank had the team members memorize in case of a problem arose, it stood for: communications compromised switch media priority 1. Seconds later, Winston received a response: *Roger that.*

Winston started his car and headed to the White House. This time of morning, it would only take twenty-five minutes. He glanced at the time: 2:25 a.m. He hoped to be in bed by 3:00.

On his drive back to the White House, Winston's mind wandered: the sucker punch in the stomach that dropped him to all fours; struggling to gain his breath. The loss of control and feeling of weakness had made him realize how vulnerable he was. He missed Connie more every day. His thoughts drifted to Win and Gwen; they were all he had. Connie had been good about making time to visit family. Winston, not so much. He hated that they were so far away. Winston had never given much thought about age, but now, at seventy-five, he was starting to think about his remaining years and what he wanted to accomplish, especially while he still had his health. He had been fortunate in that area, had never really been sick—if one didn't count the occasional sore back now and then. Having a son that was a doctor was nice. Win was great about making sure his father got regular checkups; Win monitored his dad's routine lab work results far better than Winston did.

Winston pulled his car up to the south end of West Exec Avenue. A uniformed Secret Service officer walked out to meet him, while a K-9 officer walked around his car alongside a powerful-looking German shepherd. Winston held up his White House credential for the young officer to see. The officer commented, "Good morning, sir. Getting an early start?"

Winston smiled. "I'm not sure if it's an early start or a very late ending." Winston touched his ID to the reader and entered his PIN. The gate opened, and Winston drove to his assigned parking spot.

At 3:10 a.m., Winston turned off the light. He lay in his bed in the ushers basement suite and listened to all the sounds: the giant HVAC air handlers, various creaks and miscellaneous noises from the Secret Service patrols, midnight-shift engineers doing maintenance, and maybe even the noise of a lost ghost fumbling through the night. He couldn't seem to find a comfortable position that would alleviate the soreness in his stomach. He was too keyed up to sleep, his thoughts stuck on a memory.

The third year of the Carter White House, 1979. That was the year Mrs. Carter had reached out to Winston. Billy Carter, the president's controversial younger brother, best known for his attempt to capitalize on his sibling's position in the oval office by creating Billy Beer—a business venture that had turned out to be short-lived. Afterward, Billy became a registered foreign agent for the Libyan government and was trying to broker an oil deal. It was reported that he had been paid upwards of $2 million for his influence peddling. The situation had caused tremendous embarrassment for the president, who refused any contact with his brother after learning of the deal. Both the president and Mrs. Carter became concerned when intel reports suggested that Libyan terrorists had threatened to kidnap brother Billy and make demands on the US. President Carter, knowing US involvement would have only caused additional scrutiny and embarrassment for the first family, decided to work through some back channels to get his brother out of Libya before he could be taken captive.

The president and Mrs. Carter had supreme confidence in Winston's ability to handle things confidentially. Mrs. Carter had always involved herself in such sensitive matters during President Carter's term, and so had asked for Winston's advice and counsel.

Sam Poundstone's older brother, Jack, was an Army Ranger when he and Winston served together in

Vietnam from 1966 to 1969. Jack had been wounded during a firefight. Winston had been the nearest man in vicinity to Jack when he went down, so he had done the natural thing and carried Jack to safety. Jack recovered from his wounds, and the two became as close as brothers. After Vietnam, Jack joined the Secret Service in late 1969, just months before Winston joined the Nixon White House in 1970. Jack was an interesting character, strong and physical as you would expect from an Army Ranger, but Jack was also borderline genius. A voracious reader, he was fluent in four languages, including Arabic. He had scored a perfect 1600 on his SATs but refused to apply to any colleges. He ended up spending thirty-three years in the Secret Service before retiring as a captain and then moving to Western Pennsylvania, where his primary activities these days involved trying to become a published author while battling his alcohol addiction.

Winston fell asleep as he reminisced about the draft Jack had shared with him of his book—*Rescue from Tripoli*.

***

Winston awoke to the alarm from his iPhone. It was 6:30 a.m. He had managed to get a solid three hours of sleep. As his mind began to clear, he suddenly remembered his situation and he worried for the safety of his son and daughter-in-law.

Chapter 30
7:10 a.m., Sunday, March 8: The White House

Winston closed and locked the door to the basement usher's suite, then took the service elevator up the first-floor pantry. He moved gingerly as his stomach still hurt and poured a cup of coffee. Despite the soreness in his abdomen, he was still a bit hungry. He then stepped to the far end of the room and opened the door to the food warmer, where a number of golden-brown, heavenly scented croissants sat. He grabbed one, the familiar warmth in his hand giving him an immediate sense of comfort. Winston then headed to the ushers office, where Jim sat on duty.

"Good morning, Jim," greeted Winston. "Everything under control?"

"All's quiet." Jim grabbed a small package off the desk and handed it to Winston. "This package is for you. It was sitting on the desk when I got here at 5:55."

Winston took the small parcel, went up to his private office, and turned on CNN, which was broadcasting the week in review. He stared at the TV but was too busy thinking about what to do next to really pay attention to what was on the screen. He took a second bite of the croissant, washed it down with a big gulp of coffee, placed his coffee down next to the croissant, and then opened the package. It was a new phone, just as he had assumed. Winston turned it on, and he could see that a text message was waiting. He clicked on the Signal app and saw it was from Greg. His text message via the app read: *Here's your new phone. Frank said to keep the old one. Just toss it in a drawer.*

Winston texted him back: *Roger that, thanks.*

Winston decided to hold off sharing his early morning traffic stop and sucker punch with his team. He needed to give the entire incident more thought and had other things to focus on for now.

He left his office and headed for the ground floor, where he was warmly greeted by Officer Bill Wallace, who was working Post F1, next to the doctor's office.

"Bill, I need to get into the doctor's office. I can use my master key," Winston said.

"Of course, Winston," replied Wallace, who remained seated as Winston unlocked the door, walked in, and closed the door behind him. He flipped on the light and surveyed his surroundings. It was a two-room office separated by a small pantry area. The first room was where the nurse would be stationed; the second room was a combination examination room and doctor's office.

Winston walked into the small pantry; its walls were lined with cabinets, and a white countertop went all the way around the room. A clipboard on the counter contained a log of visits. Winston reviewed the log, noting that the most recent entry was from two days ago—a visit on Friday afternoon by Wendy Wolf. Prior to that, Wendy had visited a week earlier on Friday, February 27 at 12:30 p.m. Then-President Blake had visited the doctor that same day at 12:55, which matched the record in the usher log. Winston pulled out his phone and looked at the image he had taken of the log. There was no entry on the doctor's office log for President Blake's visit last Saturday at 12:05.

The next most recent entry was from February 25: Vice President Gentry at 5:05 p.m. All the prior entries were from months earlier. December 5, secretary of state; October 30, Mrs. Blake; July 3, President Blake. All the older entries appeared to be routine. The log did not provide any other details; the area for notes was blank. Winston took a snapshot of the log entries.

He then checked the mini-fridge in the corner. Two bottled waters and four small containers of insulin were inside. Winston walked into the office/examining room. Everything looked orderly, nothing out of place, no notes, and no computer. Winston wiggled the drawers to the doctor's desk. Finding them unlocked, he opened each drawer, revealing office stationery, a stethoscope, and a tin of Altoids. Nothing out of the ordinary. Winston peered in the trash can: a lone, empty M&M bag. He then took a pen and used it to slowly lift the lid to the hazardous waste container.

Inside were cotton swabs, wrappers, and at least two used hypodermic syringes. Winston removed the orange plastic waste bag from the container and placed it on the floor, closing the bag using its tie-strings. He found a fresh orange waste bag in the pantry, which he inserted into the container to replace the bag he had just removed. He then checked the trash containers in the pantry and in the nurse's area, which were all clean. Winston found a new white plastic trash bag, placed the bright orange, hazardous waste bag inside of it, and walked out of the medical office.

"Okay, Bill. Thanks. I found what was needed."

Bill, still seated right outside the doctor's office, never looked up from his crossword puzzle. He simply offered a half-wave and muttered, "Sure thing."

Winston got back to his private office and called Mary the housekeeper, who answered after two rings.

"Good morning, Mary. Remind me, what's the procedure regarding the hazardous wastebaskets in the doctor's office?" asked Winston.

"Oh, we never touch them. The military office has a special cleared contractor that picks up all the medical waste. The contractor handles each medical unit in the west wing, old executive office building, and new executive office building. They cover the entire White House complex. It used to be every other day, but their contract got cut, so now they only pick up the executive residence doctor's office on Monday mornings. But they often forget, so we're always having to call to remind them."

"Do you know if they came last Monday?" inquired Winston.

"Let me think…" Mary paused. "Oh, wait—no, they didn't. That was the day after the president died. Nobody was here. It was a national day of mourning."

"Yes, of course, it was."

"They should be here tomorrow," assured Mary. "I'll let you know if there is any problem."

"Perfect, thank you." Winston then texted Greg: *I've got the medical waste from Dr. Jenkin's office. How fast can we get it tested?*

Greg responded ninety seconds later: *I've got someone at GW that can do it this afternoon. Bring me what you have. Meet me at Swing's Coffee on G-street in forty-five minutes?*

Winston replied: *Swing's has too many members of the White House press corps. Plus, west wing staffers are there all the time. Meet me at the cigar shop on 15th and G.*

Greg responded: *See you there.*

***

Winston returned to the White House, got another cup of coffee from the pantry, and while on his way to his mezzanine office, stuck his head into the ushers office and asked Jim what was happening.

"It's been very quiet." Jim glanced up at the wall clock. "It's almost 9:15, and the president hasn't stirred. The admiral had coffee at six and breakfast at 6:30, but that's it."

Winston nodded. "Okay, thank you. I'll be in my office working on the budget."

From his office, Winston watched the Sunday morning news shows. They focused mostly on the assassination and funeral of President Blake, though there were a few minor mentions of Chef Sullivan. Frank's positive spin effort on Brent's image may have started showing results. Generally, the news reports didn't seem as critical of Brent. It had been days since any mention of Brent's so-called jihadist conversion, and there was no additional mention of his ex-wife's press conference. In fact, George Stephanopoulos on ABC's *This Week* mentioned Brent's advanced degree from Johns Hopkins and also referenced Brent's award for excellence in leadership from the ODNI.

But the story getting the most focus at the moment was the recent BBC report that President Blake had been building an allied coalition for possible military action to end the Russian occupation of Crimea and action to eliminate the Russian forces in Syria. While Russia had not issued any statement, Iran made it known that they would not tolerate the removal of Russian troops from Syria, and Saudi Arabia had stated that they endorsed the former president's efforts and were hoping that President Gentry followed through with the plan. Meanwhile, there had been no communication on anything relating to the Blake coalition from the new president.

Meet the Press and *Face the Nation* did, however, discuss Attorney Frank Osborne and his possible insider trading charges, which were currently being considered by the Securities and Exchange Commission and the attorney general. They talked about Frank's significant stock earnings, especially his holdings in Apple.

Winston waited until it was 9:30 a.m., 6:30 West Coast time. He knew Win would be up by 6:30. Winston used the Signal app on his new burner phone to text his son: *Good morning, Son. It's your dad. I'm using a temporary new phone. We're going through updated security protocols here at the White House. I just sent you an invite to start using an app called Signal for our texting. Also, for now, use this number when texting or calling me.*

Two minutes later, Win responded with: *Got it, Dad. Sounds very cloak and dagger ☺. I've been using Signal for a couple of years, so all good. BTW Gwen's starting to experience some morning sickness, so she was up early, but all's good. Love you!*

Winston checked the weather: partly sunny, light winds, forty-nine degrees with a high expected in the mid-fifties. Winston decided to take a couple of hours and get a bike ride in.

Chapter 31
8 p.m., Sunday, March 8: The Swann House, Northwest DC

Winston was the last to arrive and joined Frank, Greg, and Brent, who were already seated in the living room.

Winston decided to continue holding off on sharing any of the details regarding his 2:00 a.m. encounter with the Russians. He felt the less people that knew, the better. Plus, he couldn't be sure, but maybe the Russians were monitoring Swann House. He would not take any chances and worried that if anything happened to Win or Gwen he would be to blame.

"Gentlemen, sorry I'm late. Tonight, we drink scotch." Winston placed a twenty-four-year single malt on the coffee table.

"What the hell?" exclaimed Frank. "You know something we don't?"

"Well, after the WMAL tower experience last night, I realized that I've grown to appreciate you guys more than you know. Plus, Greg and I may have information that could change the focus of our investigation and possibly introduce a new suspect!"

"Yeah—but we already have our prime suspect: Sous Chef Patrick Sullivan," Frank pointed out.

Winston winked and smiled. "That's what they wanted you to think."

"I know! It's Wendy, isn't it?" Brent asked. "She was always so sweet, but I knew she wasn't what she seemed!"

"No, calm down. It's not Wendy," said Winston. "Look, regardless of everything, at least tonight, we're not just drinking beer!"

Winston poured four scotches, neat, and each man took a glass.

"Okay, let's get serious." Frank addressed the men. "Winston and Greg, I have fully briefed Brent on last night's events at the WMAL Tower site. Greg, anything new to report on that?" Greg shook his head. Frank continued. "Last night's other important event: Winston issued the emergency code because he had reason to believe our comms had been compromised. I received his message at 2:23 a.m. By 2:25 a.m., you should have received my text repeating the code so that you all knew not to use your phone. The new phones were in operation by 4 a.m. and delivered by 6 a.m. The old phones for now have been disabled. We will keep them and determine if they can be of any use in a possible misinformation campaign. I have also had Swann House, Greg's house, and our cars swept for any surveillance devices. None were found. Winston, we need to get your car swept. Based on Winston's suspicions, there may be a possibility that the ushers office or all the White House phones are bugged."

"Frank, on that, I've got the Secret Service technical security division doing a sweep of the ushers office right now. They'll let me know if they find anything," reported Greg.

"Excellent," Frank approved. "As I mentioned, Swann House was swept. It was completed right before I arrived. Nothing was found—all clean. Okay, let's move on to our reports. Winston, since you brought us scotch, you go first."

Winston gave a nod. "I have confirmation from a source that the FBI, and nearly everyone else for that matter, knows nothing about the White House usher log. We keep detailed diary entries for all the activities that take place in the White House that pertain to the principals, the president, the first lady, family members, and/or senior members of the administration. The log documents all of their movements within the mansion's 132 rooms and surrounding grounds. I decided to review the log from the day the president died, then took a look at the two days prior, and what I found deserves our focus."

Frank laughed. "Okay, I'm on the edge of my seat. Thank God for the scotch that's making all of this bearable. Oh, and Winston, if you're right on whatever it is you've figured out, the next bottle is on me!"

"Frank, let's focus." Winston was not joking around. "Gentlemen, I'm handing you the ushers log for the final three days of the Blake presidency. I found the number of visits the president's physician, Dr. Jenkins, had with the president quite curious. Now, I have worked for a few administrations—ten to be exact—and I have never seen a doctor with that much access since President Reagan was recovering from his assassination attempt. Also, I found it strange that the doctor visits were marked OTR, meaning off the record. Other than the usher log, no evidence of these meetings exists. No one, not even the Secret Service or the president's diarist, has a record of OTR visits."

Winston passed around the log, which they all read.

```
USHER LOG

Friday, February 27

     6:45 Breakfast for the President and First
Lady in Bedroom
     7:59 The President to the Oval Office
     12:05 Lunch for the First Lady
     12:40 The First Lady departs the White House
en route Beijing, China
     12:55 The President to the Doctors Office
     1:30 The President to the Second Floor
     2:00 The President to the Oval Office
     5:30 The President to the Second Floor
     5:32 (OTR) Dr. Jenkins to the Second Floor
5:50 down
     7:00 Dinner for the President
     7:45 (OTR) Dr. Jenkins to the Second Floor
7:50 down
     10:30 Retired
```

Saturday, February 28

```
    7:15 Breakfast for the President in Bedroom
    7:50 The President to the Doctors Office
    8:00 The President to the Oval Office
    12:05 The President to the Doctor's Office
    12:15 The President to the Second Floor
    12:45 Lunch for the President in the Solarium
    5:00 (OTR) Dr. Jenkins to the Second Floor
5:10 down
    7:30 Dinner for the President
    8:15 (OTR) Dr. Jenkins to the Second Floor
8:20 down
    11:30 Retired
```

Sunday, March 1

```
    7:04 Coffee for the President
    7:35 Breakfast for the President in the Family
Dining Room
    7:55 The President to the Oval Office
    9:03 The President to the Second Floor
    10:04 (OTR) Dr. Jenkins to the Second Floor
10:15 down
    1:35 Lunch for the President in the Family
Dining Room
    3:05 The President to the Oval Office
    3:45 The President to the Putting Green
    4:20 The President to the Second Floor
    7:30 Dinner for the President in the Family
Dining Room
    7:57 Emergency personnel to the Second Floor
    8:05 The Vice President to the Ushers office
    8:09 The President departs South Grounds en
route GW Hospital
```

Frank, last to read the log, handed it back to Winston. "When, typically, is OTR used?"

"It has been used in the past for visits involving sensitive relations. For example, a few years ago, the Chinese president had a ninety-minute meeting with the president in the private quarters, and the White House didn't want anyone knowing they were talking. Another time, former President Nixon visited President Reagan. I was told by the president's chief of staff to mark that meeting OTR. There have also been times when the chairman of the Federal Reserve visited the president. If word of such a visit got out, it would impact the markets. So, while OTR is not used often, it gets put into effect maybe two or three times a year at the most."

Frank asked, "Who knows about the usher log?"

"As I said earlier, very few," replied Winston. "The president usually doesn't learn about it until he's leaving office and we give it to him."

"So, who knew to tell the usher to mark Dr. Jenkins' visits as OTR?" wondered Frank.

"In talking to my assistants, Loretta and Jim, I learned the direction came from the president's chief of staff, Wendy Wolf," Winston said. "Except for Sunday, March 1st. Brent, can you fill us in?"

Brent nodded. "Yeah, I made the Sunday morning entry OTR at the request of Dr. Jenkins. He went up, then on his way back down, he stopped in the office and told me to mark his visit as OTR, so I did. Then I went down to the officer at Post F1 near the president's elevator and told him it was OTR. I then watched as he crossed out the recorded visit from Dr. Jenkins."

"Okay, Winston, so why do you think you know who murdered the president?" asked Frank.

"Greg and I met on this yesterday. Greg?" prompted Winston.

Greg nodded. "Our friends at NSA shared with me that they have a record of several calls between Wendy Wolf and Dr. Jenkins during the final three days of President Blake's life."

Frank frowned. "So, what does that prove?"

"By itself, not a lot," admitted Greg. "However, the NSA told me that during the past three months, there have been 142 calls and 566 text messages between Dr. Jenkins and VP Elizabeth Gentry. They believe that while she was vice president, she may have been having an affair with Dr. Jenkins."

Frank vigorously shook his head. "Hold on! Stop! Wait a minute! Let's go over what we know. In just this past week, we've learned that Elizabeth Gentry had an affair with the head of admissions at the Naval Academy, then murdered him. She almost had an affair with Brent while having an affair with Patrick Sullivan, who is now dead, and now we learn that she was also having an affair with the president's physician?"

Greg shrugged. "Yeah, well, she was good at covering all her bases."

"So, does this mean that everyone she's had sex with is dead? She's like a black widow spider!" Brent paused. "Does anyone know where Dr. Jenkins is?"

"Greg, check on that," instructed Frank. "But Brent, yeah, lucky for you that you kept your pants on! Greg, your NSA sources will never testify. We can't really reference any of their evidence, so we can't prove anything. What else we got?"

"I think I figured out the script for bipolar disorder and who's using it," offered Winston.

Frank lifted the bottle and started re-filling everyone's glasses. "Please share."

"Throughout the past seven days, I've witnessed extraordinary, unexplainable mood swings and superpowered activity with little or no sleep. I believe both the president and admiral are abusing narcotics," determined Winston.

"I looked into the prescriptions," added Greg. "Wendy had them filled, but Dr. Jenkins wrote the scripts. That's not all. I have a record of Jenkins' prescriptions. He's been writing them for Wendy for over two years, ever since Elizabeth Gentry became VP. I spoke to my Navy friends that manage the vice president's residence. At the Naval Observatory, they shared with me their logs that showed a two-year history of visits by Dr. Jenkins, and unlike the usher log, the Navy never marked his visits as OTR."

"Dr. Jenkins replaced the former White House physician when Blake became president," said Winston.

Greg added. "You may recall, the former physician left under some questions concerning his certifications, and rather than making it an issue, he left quietly. We now have evidence that the questions concerning his certs were fabricated by Wendy and Dr. Jenkins, and Jenkins benefited by being in the right place at the right time, and as such, became the president's new physician. We believe that Wendy, at the direction of Elizabeth Gentry, orchestrated the entire change of physicians,"

Frank shook his head. "Holy shit! Amazing. But again, guys, we have a lot of very revealing and alleged activities but nothing that's gonna keep Brent from frying."

"Whoa!" exclaimed Brent. "You said I would get a life term, not the chair!"

"Same difference! But seriously, men, we don't have any hard evidence."

"Be patient. We're working on the question of evidence." Greg picked a sheet of paper off the table. "Allow me to read you my one-pager on Jenkins." Greg began:

> **"Michael Jenkins**, fifty-nine. Received his undergrad degree from Towson University. Served two years in the Army as a combat medic specialist. Honorable discharge. Earned his MD from St. Lucia Health Sciences. Note, several states don't even recognize degrees from St. Lucia, but Washington, DC does. He did his internship and residency at the Saint James School of Medicine in Anguilla. In 1990, Jenkins became licensed to practice medicine in DC. In 1991, he was certified by the American Board of Internal Medicine as a specialist in internal medicine. Over the years, he worked at several community clinics throughout DC. He has been involved in six malpractice lawsuits of which three found no liability and the other three were settled."

Frank absorbed the information. "So, how did he get connected to President Blake?"

Greg responded. "Four years ago, while President Blake was still a senator, he got his nineteen-year-old nephew a prime internship working for the Senate Appropriations Committee. Blake's nephew became dependent on opioids. Dr. Jenkins was working at a community clinic on Capitol Hill when Blake's nephew was brought in for help. Jenkins spent a lot of time with the nephew, and after several months was able to get him clean. The nephew went on to complete his undergrad and is now getting his law degree from Harvard. Senator Blake, who later on became President Blake, always felt he owed Dr. Jenkins for saving his nephew's life."

"That's a touching story. So, now we know how Jenkins got on the inside, so to speak. But how can we tie Jenkins to anything?" Frank asked, sounding frustrated. "We don't have any evidence!"

"Until today," corrected Winston.

Frank looked at him. "What?"

"This morning, as part of my normal walk-through and inspection routine, I took a look at the doctor's office on the ground floor of the White House executive residence."

"And...?" prompted Frank.

"I found a log of visitors; the most recent entry occurred last Friday afternoon when Wendy was in the doctor's office. Before that, she had visited a week earlier on Friday, February 28th at 12:30 p.m. President Blake visited that same day at 12:55 p.m., which matched the usher log. However, there was no entry in the doctor's office log regarding President Blake's visit last Saturday, February 29th, at 12:05. The next most recent entry was from February 25th, which noted Vice President Gentry's visit at 5:05 p.m."

Brent frowned. "That makes no sense. I made the ushers log entry for Saturday, February 29th. The president absolutely was in the doctor's office because I was standing by on the ground floor with the elevator and saw him come out of the doctor's office and walk straight to the elevator. As the usher log states, he was in the doctor's office for ten minutes."

Frank waved at him. "Thanks, Brent, for the confirmation. Winston, please continue."

Winston obliged. "I then went into the next room, which is the examination room that also serves as Dr. Jenkins' office. I looked for a computer. There was none. Everything appeared orderly, put away. I looked in the trash can—there was nothing of significance. I then looked in the hazardous waste container and found cotton pads and syringes."

Frank's head jerked back a little. "Holy shit! Please tell me you took them!"

"Of course I did." Winston faced Greg. "And this afternoon, they were tested. Greg?"

"I have the results," Greg confirmed. "But before I get to them, you all know I looked into all the prescriptions that Dr. Jenkins has written over the past two years. There were over two dozen prescriptions written for Wendy, including the cariprazine Winston reported that he found in President Elizabeth Gentry's bathroom vanity. As we discussed at our meeting the other night, cariprazine is used in the treatment of schizophrenia, bipolar mania, and bipolar depression. Dr. Jenkins also prescribed Adzenys XR-ODT, a stimulant used to treat ADHD—attention deficit hyperactivity disorder. This was prescribed nine times, and again, it was written for Wendy. He also had seven prescriptions made out to Wendy for Nembutal, which is basically pentobarbital, used to treat tension, anxiety, insomnia. As for the prescriptions specifically written for President Blake, several were routine ones for his insulin, all in the same dosage, and there was a recent prescription added for 100 mcg of 6-dimethyl-benzimidazolyl cyanocobamide, commonly known as Vitamin B12, which is widely used for anemia. The supplement can be taken orally or, as was the case with Blake, as an injection."

"Wow, great work, guys." Frank shook his head. "I can't believe it. Drugs for bipolar depression and ADHD. Winston, I think we now know why you have witnessed such mood swings."

"Exactly!" agreed Winston.

Frank filled everyone's glass again before again addressing Winston. "So, do you have a theory?"

"I have a 'what if.' What if Dr. Jenkins was slowly poisoning the president?"

Frank looked thoughtful. "Those syringes are the key, but then we have to determine how long they were in the trash."

"Based on the east wing military office contract, the hazardous waste was last collected on Monday, February 24th. So, here's what we know: What I found got there between February 24th and today, March 8th," Winston added.

"Good, but we need more," Frank pressed. "I think we can all agree that President Gentry was driving all this and using Wendy, but how do we prove it? C'mon, Greg, share what you know."

Greg said, "I've only received partial results from the George Washington Lab. The full results will be available in the next few days. They should tell us everything we need to know."

"So, what did the partial results reveal?" Frank inquired.

"One of the syringes had been used for the Vitamin B12," Greg confirmed. "The other contained traces of onabotulinumtoxinA. In small, controlled quantities, this is commonly known as Botox.

Frank grinned. "Great, so that's why President Blake looked so young!"

"So, the two syringes that Winston retrieved from the hazardous waste container were likely used on President Blake Saturday, February 28th, and the second and final shot was administered Sunday morning, March 1st, eight hours before the president's death. My point is the type of botulinum toxin used. Type A is Botox, but what if we find out there was also type H? That's what we believe killed the president."

"Let's be reasonable here," Winston cut in. "Brent mentioned something earlier that I believe we need to emphasize. Elizabeth Gentry is a black widow. She has a track record of eliminating individuals to tidy up loose ends. The man she coerced to get her into the Naval Academy died in a mysterious drowning, so she eliminated the one person that could expose her. Then she eliminated Chef Patrick Sullivan, who not only was having an affair with her, but he knew her plan for killing the president. What Patrick didn't know was that he was actually the backup plan. So, like Brent asked, does anyone know where Dr. Jenkins is?"

"Maybe she doesn't feel there is a need to eliminate Jenkins because once Brent's convicted, she has no more worries," Frank suggested.

"But if we present all of our evidence and I'm freed? Then what?" asked Brent.

"First of all, even if the GW Lab results proved those syringes contained something sinister, or worse, a deadly poison, it can't be used as evidence because we didn't follow the chain of custody protocols. Our findings would never hold up in court," explained Frank. Everything we've done thus far has helped determine which direction our investigation has followed. In the future, though, if we find evidence, we need to involve the proper authorities to ensure that everything follows the appropriate chain of custody rules, and as such, can be used in court. But back to the point at hand. If indeed there is a so-called black-widow scenario at work here, then Brent, if you are freed, that would make you and Jenkins targets."

"But President Gentry is the one responsible for all this," Brent reminded them. "We need to nail her!"

"Brent, my job is to get you off," Frank clarified. "It'll be up to the FBI to 'nail' whomever."

Frank emptied the remainder of the scotch into everyone's glasses and proclaimed, "Gentlemen, sadly, we've killed Winston's scotch. I strongly recommend—actually, I insist—that no one drive and you all spend the night here at Swann House. What the hell." He shrugged. "I've rented the entire place. There are twelve luxurious bedrooms for you to pick from."

"I agree! And fellas, I'm well prepared. I actually studied the website. I hereby claim the Jennifer Green Suite," announced Winston.

Frank nodded. "Ah, that's one of the best!"

"Okay, okay, I'm in…" Greg opened the laptop he had brought with him and put it on the table. "Let me look at the website and pick a room before Brent does."

Brent smirked. "I already toured the place. I want the Lighthouse!"

Frank frowned. "But that's the smallest room."

"Yeah, but with the turret—it's one of the coolest," Brent remarked.

Greg's face was lit up by his laptop screen. His eyes quickly scanned down the page he was studying. "How about the Il Duomo? Looks like a honeymoon suite."

"Perfect, it's yours," said Frank. "I'll be in the Milano. I'm going to order us dinner, and I believe I know where to find another bottle of scotch!"

Frank called the Agora restaurant on 17th Street and requested a sampler of their highly rated menu items, ensuring that the men would eat in style that night.

"Frank, how are you handling this morning's reports on the news shows about your insider trading allegations?" Winston inquired.

"The SEC chairman lives two houses away from me. We had, uh, an 'OTR' lunch today. He explained that my situation was totally political and that my investigation wasn't official because it was not initiated by the SEC. It's not even through the US attorney's office. It's coming from the attorney general, who filed a complaint with the White House. The chairman then told me that this sort of thing had happened before during the Nixon White House. It had been quickly squelched, and that had been the end of it. He told me I should know more later this week. I told him it was all a guise meant to harass and distract me. He agreed."

Winston nodded. "That all sounds good. I hope you get it all resolved soon."

"Thanks. Okay, team, I'm done talking about work stuff. Guys, in about thirty minutes, you're gonna be eating the best Turkish food you've ever had!"

"Oh, one last thing," said Winston. "I cannot make our Tuesday night meeting. I'll be working the state dinner."

Frank nodded. "Got it. Oh, and I cannot make it tomorrow night. Okay, gents, no meeting Monday or Tuesday night. Now, let's relax!"

Winston went up one floor to his room, the Jennifer Green Suite, closed the door, and dialed a number on his burner phone. A familiar voice answered.

"Hey, Sam. How's it going out there?"

"Hi, Winston. All's great. No need to worry. No sign of any Ruskies anywhere in the area. I'll contact you if anything comes up."

"Perfect. Thanks!" Winston said as he hung up the phone. The reassurances from Sam were only somewhat comforting. Winston did not like the constant feeling of being threatened.

Chapter 32
11 p.m., Sunday, March 8: The Russia House, Northwest DC

Since 2003, Russia House Restaurant at the corner of Florida and Connecticut Avenues NW had been the go-to place for Russians in DC. The eatery had consistently earned good reviews, although this time of year, dining guests were sparse. Russian Foreign Services Agent Annika Antonov dressed in a comfortable heavy blue ski sweater and dark narrow jeans met with her superior, Roman Mirov. As she took her seat next to him on a leather barstool, she pulled her wool cap off, shaking out her short blond hair.

It was late; the two sat alone at the far end of the bar. The bartender placed two Mamont vodkas in front of them, then disappeared. Antonov and Mirov both took a drink.

Mirov, wearing a navy sportscoat with a gray turtleneck, spoke first. "Command is very pleased with how you have managed the project. I have been approved to inform you that you will be promoted in due course. Congratulations."

"This news makes me very happy," said Antonov. "I believe our efforts have been well worth it."

"Have you determined your remaining elimination targets?" asked Antonov's superior.

The bartender approached and told Roman Mirov that he was needed in the private room downstairs.

Mirov stood, downed the rest of his vodka, and placed his glass on the bar. He tugged on his jacket in a futile attempt to conceal his large gut, then looked at Antonov. "Get some food. I'll be back as soon as I can."

After Mirov had walked off, Antonov told the bartender, "I'll start with gravlax, and then the shashlik, and before you bring the food, I want a Beluga Gold, neat." The waiter nodded and left.

For the past several months, Annika Antonov and her comrades had been conducting surveillance on several of the White House staff. The key finding had come from Brent Williams. They knew his pattern well. When on dayshift, he would leave his condo at 1828 Riggs Place NW to head to the White House at 5:30 a.m. Still dark, he would walk out of the front door of his building, go left, and then left into the alley that led to the rear of his building, where he would toss one small bag of trash into the trash container and another bag of recyclables into the recycle bin. Then, he would walk to 17th Street and then directly to the White House. The group learned from Brent's waste. They knew his eating and drinking habits, and, most revealing, they learned that Brent, like President Blake, was a type 1 diabetic. This finding would end up being the critical component of their plan.

Antonov sipped her vodka and thought back to her last visit at the Russia house ten days earlier—the day of their group's regular monthly meeting. They had all sat in the lower-level dining area, which was dark and dank but made brighter by all nine of them enjoying the endless shots of elite Russian Vodka. They had told stories and had many laughs while enjoying their food. After the dinner dishes had been cleared, the door to their section was closed, providing privacy.

Roman Mirov began that February 26th meeting by saying, "Comrades, we have received approval to move forward. Our months and years of planning are about to pay off. Our action date of March 1st has been confirmed. Annika, thanks to your endless efforts and all the critical connections that you successfully cultivated on the inside, we expect this to go smoothly. Comrade Antonov, as the field lead, please provide status."

Annika spoke. "Let me start by thanking the team. The results of our surveillance have been better than expected. We have learned the habits and customs of Bartholomew Winston, Jim Allen, Brent Williams, Loretta Fitzgerald, and Patrick Sullivan. This intel has been critical to our success and has led to Command having confidence in our abilities, and as we've just learned, Command has given approval to go forward."

"Thank you, Comrade Antonov." Mirov nodded. "Please review your past and future eliminations."

"Yes, of course," Antonov said. "Number one: President Blake; number two: Patrick Sullivan; number three: Dr. Michael Jenkins; number 4: Loretta Fitzgerald."

Mirov asked, "Are you confident in your plan?"

"Yes, comrade. We will not fail."

"Very good. Thank you for your report." Mirov turned to face the group. "One last announcement, there will be a noontime flight Sunday, March 1st, which most of you will be on except for Comrade Antonov and some extra assets who will remain behind for cleanup activities. I will issue the final personnel assignments tomorrow. Thank you, comrades. Our meeting is done. Everyone, go home and get some rest. Annika, I need you to stay behind." The group dispersed, and Mirov closed the door as the last person departed. He then moved to a seat closer to Annika's.

"Good meeting," he said. "Is there anything you need from Command?"

"No, just be sure and get me out when it's time," requested Antonov.

"Of course, comrade. You are our priority, and soon, your name will be legendary to all future generations of Russia."

They both stood. Mirov kissed Antonov on both cheeks three times.

***

The bartender brought Annika another Beluga vodka and said her food would be right out. Annika took the last swallow of her drink, handed the glass to the waiter, and then picked up her fresh drink.

Halfway through her meal, Roman Mirov rejoined her. She asked while chewing, "Would you like to order something?"

"No, keep eating," he said. "I was able to eat while downstairs." He motioned to the bartender and then pointed to Antonov's glass, indicating that he'd have the same.

After the bartender had moved away, Mirov said, "The reason I was called downstairs is that I was informed by Command that your abductee, Dr. Michael Jenkins, has just claimed during our most recent persuasive interrogation session that he created a thumb drive containing all the specific details regarding his encounters with us, starting with your threat to expose his questionable prescriptions and his physical relationship with President Blake's nephew. He stated that you blackmailed him by threatening to release what you had to the press. He told us that he completed everything you had asked him to. He placed the bag you gave him into the ushers office with a note in his handwriting that said, 'For the President.' Jenkins revealed the location of his thumb drive—inside an Altoids container, in his unlocked desk in the White House doctor's office. This revelation has spared Dr. Jenkins his life for the moment. Command has instructed that your top priority is to retrieve the thumb drive at all costs."

Antonov stared straight ahead for a moment, then said, "I will take care of it."

"Get your plan to me, and I will ensure Command approves."

Antonov nodded. "You will have it within twelve hours."

"Excellent, comrade," Mirov approved. "We also received intel that the assistant director of the Office of the Director of National Intelligence, Jonathan Cartwright, is beginning to focus more on us. We need to expedite our cleanup plan and get out of here."

Mirov tipped his drink straight up and savored the final swallow, then put his glass down, looked across the room, and signaled to the bartender to bring him another. "Before I went downstairs, I asked you about your elimination list."

"Yes, of course. The only remaining one that's been approved is Loretta Fitzgerald, and I'm still deciding how best to accomplish this. I will report to you as soon as I figure it out."

"Excellent, comrade," Mirov approved. "Excellent."

"I do have a new concern that I have assessed as an emerging threat, and as such, I would like for you to seek approval for me to eliminate this one additional individual."

Mirov cocked his head. "I will certainly seek approval. Who is it?"

"Bartholomew Winston."

Chapter 33
5:30 a.m., Monday, March 9: The White House

Winston parked his car on West Executive Avenue between the west wing and the EOB. He entered the ground floor entrance to the west wing, said good morning to the Secret Service uniform officer, walked past the west mess dining area and down a hallway, and then took the steps up one level. He looked over his right shoulder and saw that the areas around the oval office were still dark. He waved to the uniformed Secret Service officer, then walked past the press office and press briefing room on his left, where he said good morning to another uniformed Secret Service officer.

Winston then walked out onto the colonnade and past the rose garden to his right, then entered the executive mansion via the palm room. Once he was on the ground floor hallway, he said good morning to the uniformed Secret Service officer at Post F1 across from the president's elevator. He then walked past the open elevator on his right and dashed up the stairs one level to the ushers office, where he dropped off his coat and bag before heading to the pantry to get coffee.

With coffee in hand, he sat down in the ushers office and reviewed the president's schedule, which appeared routine: oval office meetings from 8 to 11 a.m. A trip to the Willard Hotel for a speech. Congressional leadership lunch on Capitol Hill from 12:30 p.m. to 2:30 p.m. An Agence France interview in the green room at 4 p.m. Then in oval office from 4:30 to 6:00. Drinks in the west sitting hall at 6:30 with the Senate majority leader, then dinner with the admiral at 7:30.

Winston reviewed the schedule for the entire week and made some notes, then composed an email to the staff highlighting the week's scheduled events. The big event would be Tuesday's French state arrival and dinner.

At 6 a.m., Loretta arrived, wearing her typical dark-gray, mid-length skirt, matching jacket, and white blouse; as they exchanged greetings, Winston noticed something different: She was wearing makeup. He then noticed her gold earrings and very nice new pumps. He thought she was stepping it up a bit but didn't dare say anything with her being so shy. Winston stood to allow Loretta to sit at the desk, then excused himself, saying he would be working in his mezzanine office, but before he headed up the steps, he went to the pantry to get breakfast.

Thirty minutes later, Winston came back downstairs to the main office and was reading the newspaper when the door to the president's elevator auto-opened on the first floor. Winston told Loretta that he would handle the elevator for the president and quickly exited the office and caught the elevator just as its doors were closing. As the elevator arrived on the second floor, the agent who had been seated just outside the door by the staircase told Winston that the president had poked her head out and asked him to call the elevator.

Winston, per normal routine, propped open the doors to the private residence and stood by, awaiting the president. While he was standing there, the admiral walked from the Lincoln bedroom toward the west sitting hall, saw Winston, and came over with a big smile.

"Hey, Winston! When will that new bedroom be ready for me on the third floor?" Then in a half-whisper, he added, "You know, I love the Lincoln bedroom. If it were up to me, I would be most happy staying there."

The president's appearance interrupted their conversation. The admiral winked at Winston as the president entered the elevator. She offered a very cold good morning, trying her best not to look at Winston.

The elevator got to the ground floor, and the president exited and headed to the west wing, completely ignoring Winston.

***

It was late morning; Winston was seated in the ushers office reviewing the arrangements for the state dinner.

"Winston," began Loretta. "Would you be able to cover if I escaped at lunchtime to handle a couple of errands? I may need an hour from, say, 11:30 to 12:30. Might that work for you?"

"Uh, yes. Of course. That is fine." Winston's White House cell phone rang. He looked down at his phone. It was his son calling.

Winston answered, "Good morning, Win. How are you?"

"Hi, Dad. We're doing well, Gwen is feeling better. I don't have any early appointments, so I'm still at home. Had a couple of minutes and thought it would be a good time to call."

"That's great, and I'm so glad that Gwen is feeling well."

"Hey, Dad, with all the craziness you've had to endure the past ten days, we haven't had any time to talk about it. How are you holding up?"

Winston made no effort to prevent anyone from hearing the conversation. "It's been crazy. Fortunately for me, the new president has been wonderfully sympathetic and most supportive. She has such great energy and really knows how to bring people together. I believe she will be a phenomenal leader. I like her senior staff too. All good, hard-working folks."

"Wow, that's really great to hear," Win remarked. "But what about your staff? How are they doing with the allegations against your assistant usher?"

"It's been tough. No one could believe what happened. I admit, I myself did not believe it at first. I was in total shock and complete denial, but we now see that the evidence is overwhelming, and I now starting to realize the hard, hard truth. It's very sad, but we're moving on."

Win was quiet for a few seconds. "Dad, I worry about you. I hope you're getting enough rest and you're not under too much pressure."

"Win, you know how much I love my job, and I thrive on the pressures. It's all about being the best you can be, and the mission is very clear: Make the White House the best possible home to the president and family."

"Love you, Dad. You're always so consistent. Good luck with everything. I'm gonna hop in the shower. Gwen is blowing kisses to you. Take care and we'll talk soon."

"Hug her for me," requested Winston. "I love you too, son. Goodbye."

Winston then headed back to his private office and used his burner phone to text Win via the Signal app:

Excellent job, son. Thanks for all that. I'm sure once they review the transcript, I may notice things will be easier for me here. Not sure how much longer we'll need to communicate like this. Dad.

Win responded: *10-4 good luck XOX.*

***

Loretta walked out of the northwest gate, crossed Pennsylvania Avenue, and walked up Jackson Place, adjacent to Lafayette Park. She crossed H Street at the light and headed east, and at 16th Street she made a left, then entered the Hay Adams Hotel, walked through the lobby with her keycard in hand, and entered the elevator and pressed seven.

Chapter 34
3:00 p.m., Monday, March 9: The White House

The phone rang. Loretta answered, "Ushers office, Loretta Fitzgerald." After a few seconds she added, "One moment, please." Loretta put the call on hold and told Winston that Jonathan Cartwright was on line one.

When Winston heard the name, he became lost in thought for a brief moment; Jonathan Cartwright was Connie's old boss. Winston decided to take the call in his private office, so he dashed up the steps, closing the door behind him. He picked up the phone. "Jonathan! Nice to hear from you. How are you?"

"Winston, I'm great, man. I've been meaning to call to catch up for months, but as you know better than anyone, I continue to lose the battle with my schedule. But hey, I've got a meeting with the National Security Council at three in the west wing. Might you be available for a coffee afterward?"

"Absolutely. I'll swing by the National Security Council office, say, four o'clock, and see if you're free then."

"Perfect, see you then," said Jonathan.

Jonathan Cartwright had spent the past thirty years with the NSA, having worked his way up from an intelligence analyst to the unit director, and today, he was the assistant director for the ODNI. Prior to the NSA, Cartwright had spent ten years as an FBI special agent. He earned his undergrad, MS, JD, and PhD all from the University of Michigan and considered Ann Arbor to be his second home. Winston remembered that Connie really enjoyed working for him. She was one of his five direct reports. He was a good manager and exceptionally skilled in the type of work they did. Connie had Jonathan and his wife, Tina, over numerous times for dinner. Jonathan and Tina also had Connie and Winston over often and had invited them on their boat in Annapolis, where they would enjoy sailing the Chesapeake.

Jonathan was tall and thin with broad shoulders. A good-looking man, and at sixty-six, his neatly cut, medium-length hair was mostly gray and starting to thin at the top. He had always maintained excellent health, and like Winston, was an avid cyclist. The two of them had ridden a few centuries together. Winston liked the Cartwrights a lot; he always felt safe letting his guard down around them. He had only seen Jonathan once since the funeral; however, Jonathan and Tina called often to check in.

***

Winston arrived at the small waiting area outside of the National Security Council office in the west wing. The receptionist immediately recognized him, smiled, and asked him to have a seat.

At one minute past four, the door opened, and Jonathan was the first one out, walking directly to Winston with his arms extended. The two men hugged as the other meeting attendees exited the area. Jonathan, in a low voice so only Winston could hear, asked if there was a private place where they could talk. Winston suggested they head over to the executive residence and meet in the map room.

Winston used his master key to open the door to the map room. He led Jonathan into the room, then stepped out to use the phone near the Secret Service officer. He called the pantry and asked the butlers to bring a coffee service for two to the map room, reentered, then took a seat, recalling that just one week earlier, he had been in the very same room with close to a dozen FBI agents firing questions at him.

"Have you been in here before?" Winston asked his old friend.

"I think it was years ago. When you gave Tina and me a tour, we may have come in here."

"Oh, my, I vaguely remember. That was a long time ago. Let me refresh your memory. This was the White House situation room. It was here that FDR and Eisenhower began the plans for the Normandy invasion. Let me show you something." Winston stood up and led Jonathan to a large, framed print in the far corner of the room. "This was the final map used for the D-Day invasion, and it was updated by military aides throughout the day and night showing FDR the troop movements." Jonathan and Winston studied the map for several minutes. They then returned to their seats.

"Winston, I've missed ya, man," said Jonathan as he settled into his chair. "You finding time to ride at all?"

"Believe it or not, I do, but lately, nothing more than fifteen or so miles at a time. We should do another century when the weather warms up."

"I owe you an apology for disappearing off the face of the earth. Tina is always reminding me we have to have you over for dinner. How you are? How are things?" asked Jonathan.

"Jonathan, you never need to explain yourself. I remember from what Connie used to say that your schedule is beyond horrid. And hey, you and Tina have been wonderful with your calls and cards, but absolutely, let's have dinner soon. As for how things are, well, I'll be very honest with you—it's been a challenge. I think about Connie constantly. As for my job, well, the new president is overly demanding, her staff is inordinately inexperienced, and then, of course, I'm dealing with the investigation of my assistant usher, which is both troubling and upsetting."

Jonathan nodded. "That's why I wanted us to talk in person."

The men were interrupted by a knock at the door. Winston walked over and opened the door to a butler carrying a tray. Winston stepped back and said, "Thank you, Nathan." The butler placed the tray on a small table between the two men, then left. Winston closed the door behind him. The aroma of fresh coffee quickly filled the room.

Jonathan filled their cups from the silver pitcher, then put the pitcher down and admired the tray. "Oh, this is perfect. Those small pastries look wonderful."

Winston smiled. "Of course, only the best."

Jonathan got serious. "Winston, within hours of the president's death, the ODNI assigned me as the lead on the task force for the investigation of the assassination. I am heading up the group made up of NSA, FBI, and CIA personnel. An office will be ready for me tomorrow on the second floor of the west wing. I am speaking to you with the full knowledge of the task force, primarily because they know we are friends, and they know you can be trusted."

Winston nodded. Okay, thank you…I think."

"We're more aware of your efforts than you realize. And when I say 'your' efforts, I'm referring to your entire group that has been meeting at the Swann House. We're aware of your progress, and I also will share with you, we are all quite impressed."

"Well, I thought we were secure with our location and our communication."

"Yes, you all have done everything possible," said Jonathan. "But Winston, that's what we do. We have advanced methods and the most sophisticated tools in existence. We can monitor up to 95 percent of all verbal and digital communications in the world, and we do it 24/7, 365 days a year."

"What about the other 5 percent?" Winston asked.

Jonathan smiled. "Let's just say, we're working on it. We also have been successful in breaking every encryption. The only challenge we face on occasion is the speed by which we can break it, meaning the actual time it takes us can be anywhere from a nano-second to forty-eight or more hours, but in the end, we always figure it out."

Winston considered that. "Did Connie work on this sort of thing?"

"Connie's expertise was in forensics, and toward the end of her career, she was the best on staff when it came to digital forensics, so much of our capability today can be directly attributed to her work. Winston,

Connie was phenomenal, the best employee I ever had. I can't begin to tell you how much I miss her."

Winston said with a sigh, "You and me both, bud."

"First things first, everything I'm sharing with you is, of course, confidential. The autopsy and toxicology results revealed that the president died from botulinum toxin. It was administered through his insulin injection. He died immediately."

Winston gasped. "Oh, my god. So, the AP was right in their reporting?"

"Yes, someone leaked it to them, but there's more," explained Jonathan. "Brent's fingerprints were on the insulin container."

Winston was shocked. "What the hell? Does the AP know that part?"

"No, that information is top-secret, so we don't believe it's gotten out yet. But right now, it doesn't look good for Brent. We're far from done in our investigation, though."

Winston shook his head. "There has to be an explanation."

"We'll get to the bottom of it," Jonathan assured. "And Winston, we know what happened to you at 2 a.m. Sunday morning. We were monitoring the situation, but unfortunately, we were not in close enough proximity to get there in enough time to prevent what happened."

Winston cocked his head. "Oh, so you know about my being pulled over by Boris and Natasha?"

"Funny. It was actually Tom Stone, a Canadian freelance agent, and Annika Antonov with the Russian Foreign Intelligence Service, known as the KGB during the Cold War. As far as we can tell at this point, the Russians were not involved in President Blake's assassination, but I'm still investigating. And let's never forget they are indeed opportunistic and want to wreak havoc during the investigation in the hopes distracting us while they place resources inside the new administration."

"Wow." Winston sighed. "So, I am to expect from them information that I am to use to convince you and the FBI who the real killer of the president is."

"Correct. We're working to figure out how Antonov will deliver the 'information' to you."

"Well, I never even got a look at her. She was wearing a full-face ski mask. I don't know how I'm supposed to find her."

"Winston, don't worry. She'll find you."

"And I'm sure you don't want me to share any of what we've talked about with my friends at the Swann," Winston added.

Jonathan nodded. "Correct."

"Got it."

"Oh, Winston, there's something else," Jonathan added. "The Russians also have fairly decent surveillance techniques. They, like us, agree that Dr. Jenkins was responsible for the death of President Blake."

Winston looked thoughtful. "Well, I guess it's good to have agreement amongst all of us."

"What's more, the Russians, in their quest to subvert and ultimately control the outcome of the investigation, have kidnapped Jenkins, and while we have reason to believe he's still alive, we don't think he'll surface any time in the foreseeable future."

"Wow." Winston shifted in his chair, trying to regain his bearings. "So, what involvement does President Gentry or Wendy Wolf have in this?"

"I can tell you, both President Gentry and her chief of staff, Wendy Wolf, are involved in some questionable practices, and we are taking a hard look at them. But as far as we can discern at this point, they did not have any direct involvement in the assassination," said Jonathan.

"What about Brent?" Winston asked.

"We should soon be able to clear him."

"That's good news. How serious should I consider the threat from Antonov regarding my son and his wife?"

"We're taking that seriously and looking into it. You did the right thing by getting Sam Poundstone involved. We've used Sam on numerous occasions. He's stellar. And more importantly, congrats, Grandpa. That is great news!"

"Thanks, Jonathan, but I'm very much on edge. I would never be able to live with myself if anything were to happen to them."

"We're monitoring the situation, and I give you my word as a friend, I'm doing everything in my power to ensure their safety," reassured Jonathan.

Winston smiled a little. "Thank you. That does make me feel better."

Chapter 35
1:00 a.m., Tuesday, March 10: Northwest DC

Her plan approved by Command, Annika Antonov sat in the parked car in front of 2633 16th Street, Northwest DC, directly across the street from the Embassy of the Republic of Poland. Her past surveillance made her very familiar with the habits and customs of her target. She kept going over the plan.

***

At 1:27 a.m., a person in a long, dark coat exited the front of the embassy, made a right, and headed south along 16th Street, which was vacant at that early hour. It was only a two-minute walk to the Dorchester House Apartments at 2480 16th Street NW. Antonov waited for the right moment, flashed her headlights, then watched as the man leaped from behind the bushes at the intersection of Euclid and 16th streets. The man swiftly grabbed the pedestrian, pulling them back into the bushes. Antonov drove to the spot where she saw the man, and waited.

She looked up to see the two now-disabled cameras and was sure the only other cameras in the area were in front of the embassy, too far away to see anything. She saw the man approach her, carrying a large trash bag. She reached back and opened her rear door. The man placed the bag in the back while Antonov slid over to the passenger seat. The man got in the driver's side and handed Antonov a purse. She rifled through it until she found what she needed: the apartment keycard and the Polish embassy ID for the Polish Deputy Ambassador Anna Zielinski. She looked at the man, nodded, and then hopped out of the car and proceeded to her new apartment.

Chapter 36
5:00 a.m., Tuesday, March 10: The White House

Pre-dawn at the White House was typically quiet, and this morning was no exception. Winston sat at the ushers desk reading *The Washington Post*; he kept the TV off to enjoy the peace and tranquility. The double doors from the office looking out over the grand foyer were propped open. The only sound came from the occasional squelch of the radios belonging to the Secret Service uniform officers at their nearby post. The lights in the foyer were still set to their nighttime dimness. Winston savored his time alone; he knew that in just thirty minutes, the executive residence staff would begin to arrive, and their activities would bring the house to life.

Winston reviewed the president's schedule: 8 a.m. breakfast in the private residence with the national security advisor, 8:30 to 9:55 meetings in the oval office, 10 a.m. south grounds arrival of French President Jean-Claude Marchal, then meetings with President Marchal until noon, followed by lunch with her chief of staff and then a visit to Capitol Hill to brief the House leadership on priority items. Back at the White House by 4 p.m. for an interview taping in the library, then back to the private residence at 5 p.m. to prepare for cocktails with the French president, then the state dinner.

Winston turned on the TV and switched to the Weather Channel. Presently, it was thirty-five degrees. By 10 a.m., the time of the arrival ceremony on the south grounds, it would be in the mid-forties and partly cloudy with calm winds. Tonight would be colder with a chance of snow showers after eight. Winston thought, *that's about as good as it gets for DC in early March.* He switched to CNN, which was on a commercial break, so he left the TV on but muted the sound, then looked up to see his regular morning entourage waiting for any last-minute instructions.

Winston said good morning, stood, and waved in the group, which consisted of Bob, the man in charge of operations; Irv the executive groundkeeper; Mary the housekeeper; and Alfrado the maître'd.

"We've got a long day ahead of us," Winston began, "and we're all going to have to put in an extra effort to ensure President Gentry's first state arrival and dinner go well. Not a lot has changed since last week's planning meeting—except, Bob, Yo-Yo Ma will have his east room rehearsal at three, not two as originally planned, and new on the schedule is the president has an interview taping in the library at four. Irv, it'll be a bit cold but dry for the ten o'clock state arrival, but the forecast for tonight is snow showers, so please have your guys on standby in case we have to treat the east entrance area and the north and south porticos."

Irv nodded. "We'll be ready, and the refrigerated trucks with the cherry trees in full blossom will pull up to the north portico at seven. We should have them in place before the south grounds' arrival."

For the past several weeks, several dozen Japanese cherry trees had been housed in a special, temperature-controlled greenhouse at the National Arboretum in northeast DC. Irv and his team had monitored them very closely and methodically adjusted the temperature several times per day in order to bring the trees to full bloom a full six weeks ahead of schedule.

"Well done, Irv," congratulated Winston. "You again fooled mother nature! Our guests tonight will be so impressed."

"I think we did well," admitted Irv. "Not sure we'll ever outdo what we did with those peach trees several years ago."

Winston nodded in recollection. "That was amazing."

Irv looked above Winston and out the ushers office window. Winston glanced that way too. He could see that the truck with the trees was at the northwest gate. Irv said, "Ah, great. Love it when they're early. Winston, I'm going to excuse myself so I can deal with the delivery."

Winston waved him off. "By all means. Thanks, Irv. Okay, Alfrado, the final count for tonight's dinner is 128, and as planned, we'll use the thirteen six-foot rounds tables. Please tell the chef the final count and let the florist know the table count remains at thirteen."

"Yes, sir," acknowledged Alfrado. "Did President Gentry decide on which china to use?"

"Yes, sorry. I found out late Friday, we're using the Johnson china. And I already told the florist. We were lucky because it took so long for us to get an answer. The flower shop couldn't wait, so they took a chance by ordering flowers that matched best with the Johnson china!"

"And you wanted to know how many butlers we're bringing in from Ridgewells," Alfrado reminded Winston. "Same as our last state dinner: twenty-three."

For years, Ridgewells Catering had provided cleared part-time butlers for White House events. Winston, always cost-conscious, kept close tabs on the number of resources brought in for the events.

"Perfect, thanks." Winston turned to face the housekeeper. "Mary, as of now, the president and admiral have not invited any houseguests for tonight. Of course, that may change, and I will let you know if it does. We will need two of the housemen available for the coat check, and they need to be in place by 6 p.m."

"Got it, Winston," said Mary. "Thanks."

Winston stood and started to leave the office to get breakfast just as Loretta was arriving carrying a garment bag with her evening gown. They laughed as they danced around each other to avoid colliding. After a quick exchange of good mornings, Winston headed to the pantry.

A few minutes before 10 a.m., Winston had just completed his inspection of the set-up on the south grounds and walked into the diplomatic reception room. He propped open the double doors leading to the south grounds, then stood back a few steps just inside the room to be in the shadows so that the press members who set up on the south grounds facing the south portico to cover the arrival would not see him. As he was looking outside and admiring how nice the red carpet looked in the brisk, March sun, he suddenly felt an arm slip through his. It was President Gentry.

She gave him a warm smile. "Winston, I will be depending on you to get me through all of this today."

Winston was momentarily struck by how magnificent she looked, her eyes so vibrant, her smile so warm... She was très chic in her deep, red, full-length cashmere coat.

Winston smiled back. "Madam President, the sun has just come out. It's a glorious day for you and for the United States. And of course, I will be available for anything you need."

"Good. Stay close," Gentry requested, sounding a bit nervous. She withdrew her arm in order to face her chief of staff, Wendy, who had just walked up.

"Madam President," Wendy greeted. "The motorcade is less than four minutes out." She handed the president index cards held together with a rubber band and said, "This is the final revision of your remarks."

The admiral then arrived. He wore a black suit, no overcoat, but a stylish black fedora was perched atop his head. In a jovial tone, he asked, "Are we all ready for the big show?"

Winston nodded, then looked at the president and asked if she would like to briefly review the steps one more time. She nodded emphatically, looking to Winston for reassurance.

Winston began: "In about two minutes, the motorcade will arrive with the president of France's limousine stopping right here." Winston pointed to the end of the red carpet at the south portico. "The two of you will walk out and wait at the end of the canopy as the limo pulls up. The mil-aide will open the car door. After you shake hands with President Marchal and the French first lady, you introduce them to the admiral.

"Since you do not have a vice president, your next introductions will be to your cabinet members." Winston gestured toward the area where they were standing. "They will be over your left shoulder. You introduce them to President Marchal, then introduce Marchal to the joint chiefs." Winston indicated them with a wave. "You and President Marchal then proceed to the stage. The Marine Band performs the French national anthem, followed by the Presidential Salute Battery, when twenty-one cannon rounds will be fired. Then 'The Star-Spangled Banner' is played, after which you escort the French president off the stage and to the lawn in front of the stage and inspect the lined-up troops. This is just a casual stroll. Be sure and look at the troops as you walk by. They will salute. It's not mandatory that you return the salute—totally up to you.

"After your inspection, you then escort President Marchal back to the stage and watch the fife and drum corps conduct their pass-in-review. When they're finished, you go to the lectern and make your remarks. There is a translator, so allow time for your remarks to be repeated in French. President Marchal will then make his remarks. When done, you escort Marchal back in here. Then you and the admiral, with cabinet and joint chiefs, will all have coffee, and whenever you are ready, you invite President Marchal to the oval office for meetings. And you, Admiral, will then escort the French first lady on a tour of the ground and state floors. Don't worry, a member of the curator's office will accompany you. And that's it. Do you have any questions?"

Before the president could answer, the mil-aide announced it was time to get into position, and he motioned for the president and admiral to follow him.

President Gentry mouthed "Thank you" to Winston, and off they went.

Winston followed ten feet behind, then walked to the right to stay out of the press's view.

Chapter 37
5:00 p.m., Tuesday, March 10: The White House

The president finished her taping in the library on the ground floor and headed back to the oval office. As she passed Winston, who was standing in the hallway near the elevator, the president stopped to speak to him.

"Winston, this morning's arrival went very well. Thank you for guiding me in reviewing all the steps. I will call you after I'm dressed for tonight's dinner so you can review all the protocols."

Winston nodded. "Very well, Madam President. I'm happy to assist."

The president began moving away, then stopped and motioned to Winston to join her. "Walk with me."

Winston and the president headed toward the palm room, then onto the west colonnade along the rose garden toward the oval office. She continued, "I've got to take care of a few things in the office. When will the guests begin to come in, and what time does the French president arrive?"

"Guests begin to arrive on the state floor at 7 p.m. President Marchal and his wife arrive on the north portico at 7:40. You and the admiral should be in the grand foyer by 7:35."

They reached the outside door to the oval office. The agent opened the door for the president. She paused before entering and said to Winston, "Perfect, I'll call you before seven." And with that, she went into the oval office.

Winston turned around and headed back to the residence. He felt cold and looked out above the rose garden to the sky. It was cloudy, and it felt like snow.

Thirty minutes later, Winston had changed into his tux. He paused for one last look in the full-length mirror on the closet door in the ushers basement suite and admired his pointed-collar tux shirt. He felt it made him look more modern, more in style. He glanced at his shoes, hesitated for a second, then decided the pair could probably go at least two more wears before they would need to be polished.

Winston left the suite and rode the elevator to the ground floor, where he got out and began his pre-state dinner final inspection walk-through. He always savored the peace and tranquility that permeated the room moments prior to a state dinner. This was when the house was at its finest; shortly, it would be bustling with activity as the Marine Chamber Orchestra set up, military aides reviewed their assignments, and the Secret Service double-checked the event layout.

Winston headed west toward the palm room, and just prior to exiting the residence, he took the door on his right and entered the "back of the house," starting with the main kitchen where a dozen chefs and butlers were gathered around an easel that held an enlarged print-out of the menu:

First Course
Supreme of Smoked Trout
Mouse of Celeriac Sauce Verte
Fleuron's

Second course
Roasted Filet of Beef Bearnaise Sauce
Mushroom in Potato Bordure
Asparagus Polonaise & Buttered Carrots

Third Course
Endive Radicchio & Bibb Salad
Herbed Capri Cheese
French Bread

Dessert
Dried Pear Souffle
Caramel Sauce

Wines
Stag's Leap Wine Cellars White Riesling
2016

Clos Pegase Cabernet Sauvignon 2010 Scharffenberger Crémant

The assistant chefs, maître'd, butlers, and support staff listened intently as the executive chef, resembling a head coach before the big game, read the menu aloud, adding specific instructions pertaining to meal preparation and serving. Then the pastry chef gave an even more elaborate set of instructions about serving his dessert.

Winston glanced at his watch. It was 5:40. He needed to move on, so he nodded to the staff, cut through the kitchen, and walked out of the back and into the tradesman entrance, essentially the primary thoroughfare for the executive residence shops. He visited the grounds office, where Irv sat.

Irv looked up and smiled. "I'm watching the radar. Looks like the snow will arrive before seven. We've got our crews ready at the east gate where the guests arrive, and we have guys at the north driveway ready."

"Good. How much are they saying we'll get?"

"Depends. The European model says six inches or more. The US model says less than two inches," replied Irv.

Winston asked, "Did you check with the military office?"

"Yes, of course. They said the system is still forming, and with the temps expected to be low, there is potential for a significant snow event, but they won't commit to any accumulation estimates."

"And so goes the story of forecasting weather in Washington," concluded Winston.

They both laughed.

"Okay, Irv. Text me with any updates. I've got to complete my rounds."

Winston then took the main tradesmen hallway, walked the several hundred feet to the opposite end, and stuck his head into the flower shop, where several of the florists were relaxing. He waved to them, noticing they all looked a bit exhausted after having set up all flower arrangements for the event. They would remain on standby for the duration of the dinner. Winston then walked a bit further to the executive housekeeper's office, where Mary and a few housemen were seated.

Winston stood in the doorway: "How's the A-Team doing?"

Mary responded, "We've done everything and now are on standby for anything if needed."

"Excellent, thanks. I will call you if needed." With that, Winston saluted and left.

Winston took the small corridor past the curators office and opened the door that led him back to the "front of house" in the ground floor hallway directly across from the diplomatic reception room. There, he was surprised to see Loretta with Wendy Wolf.

Winston walked in. "Good evening, ladies. I'm surprised to see the two of you here."

Loretta wore an attractive, long, black gown. Winston thought, *She's really an attractive woman. Who knew?* Wendy was wearing a stylish gray gown. "The two of you look like you belong on the cover of a magazine," he commented. The ladies smiled.

Loretta explained, "I was just showing Wendy how we do our pre-event walk-throughs."

"Great," Winston replied. "I was just about to do mine, starting from the east entrance and then up to the state floor. You both are welcome to join me."

"Thanks, Winston," said Wendy, "but Loretta and I just did the entire route."

"I asked operations to get the coat-check rack into the family theater, but everything else looks great," Loretta mentioned.

Winston nodded. "Very well. Thank you both."

"Winston, the president is expecting us upstairs at five of seven," mentioned Wendy. "I'll come by the ushers office, and we can go up together."

"Perfect, see you then." He then left the room, leaving them behind.

Winston thought it a bit strange that Loretta had done the walk-through and stranger still that she had taken Wendy with her. He quickly dismissed the thought, attributing it to the circumstance. After all, this was the first formal event with Brent not present, and as such, Loretta was probably just trying to help wherever an extra hand was needed.

Chapter 38
6:50 p.m., Tuesday, March 10: The White House

Winston stood in the ushers office awaiting Wendy. He looked out the window to see the snow falling. The north driveway was already covered in a layer of white, and the grounds crew were beginning to treat the paved surfaces. He heard footsteps coming up the back stairs and went out to see who it was. He was surprised to see Jonathan Cartwright there, wearing his tux.

Before Jonathan even reached the top step, he called up to Winston, "We need to talk."

Winston nodded. "Let's go up to my office." He then realized his office might be bugged. "No, here, follow me." Winston led Jonathan down the back stairs and into the map room and unlocked the door. They stepped in. "Okay, we're secure here," assured Winston. "What have ya got?"

Jonathan began, "I received this info less than ten minutes ago. We have developing intel suggesting there is a possibility that Annika Antonov may be attending tonight's state dinner under an alias. I just forwarded to your burner phone a picture we have of her from several years ago."

Winston frowned. "Wait, how did you know about my 7-Eleven phone? Oh, geez, never mind!" Winston pulled out his phone and quickly looked at the full-length photo of a blonde woman from maybe fifteen feet away. The photo was taken at some sort of track event. The woman was a pole vaulter, the pole resting on her right shoulder as she looked straight ahead, no doubt concentrating on her attempt. Winston noticed the tight, red, scanty, two-piece track uniform, her mid-torso exposed to reveal a six-pack. The woman had muscular arms and nice legs. Her blonde hair was very short and her facial features rather ordinary—not what one would consider a beauty, but perhaps with age and makeup, she could be considered attractive. "This is the most recent photo you have?" Winston asked.

Jonathan shrugged. "This is the best we have. So, I've got resources observing the guests as they line up to enter the east wing. We will signal you if we make a positive ID, but you should be on the lookout as well.'

Winston shook his head. "Unbelievable. A Russian spy can just walk in like that?"

"Yep, the Russians have upped the stakes. There's more going on here than we know. Okay, I gotta run. I wanna be near the guest entrance when she comes in. Talk to you later. Good luck!"

The two men left the map room. Jonathan headed down the main ground-floor cross-hall and headed to the east wing guest entrance, and Winston jogged up the back stairs to wait for Wendy. Seconds later, he could hear someone with heels walking up the back stairs. Winston turned just in time to see Wendy reach the top step.

"All set?" he asked.

Wendy nodded. "Yes, she's in her dressing room."

As they stepped off the elevator and onto the second floor of the private quarters, the Navy strings could be heard warming up from their position just outside of the yellow oval room. Winston followed Wendy as they walked across the west sitting hall and into the president's bedroom. The door was open, and they walked in. Elizabeth Gentry was standing in front of a tall, portable, full-length mirror. One of the maids was assisting by tilting the mirror so that the president could see herself at different angles. President Gentry looked breathtaking in a dark green, stylish, off-the-shoulder velvet gown. Her hair was nicely styled on top of her head, and her makeup was perfect. Winston discretely admired her without saying a word.

Wendy broke the ice. "You look marvelous, and I love your shoes."

Winston finally gazed down far enough to notice the dark green pumps, and thought, *yes, they are nice*.

Gentry glanced down. "Oh, good. You like them? They're Christian Louboutin."

Wendy smiled. "I remember you mentioning that you wanted those. They're great. And that dress is Giorgio Armani?"

"Correct. Wendy, please make sure the press knows that this was off the rack. I did not use a designer."

Wendy nodded. "Will do."

Winston subtly cleared his throat. The president looked at him and smiled. "Winston, thank God you're here. Now tell me what I need to do in order not to look like an inexperienced idiot!"

"Madam President, you'll be fine," said Winston. "I can go over everything with you, and during the dinner, the maître'd will escort you to your seat. During dinner, George—the butler for your table—can answer any questions you might have."

"That's a relief to know. So, tell me about what I do before dinner," instructed Gentry.

"Absolutely. Right now, it is 7:07. The guests began to arrive at the state floor at 7:00 and are being guided by the military aides to the east room. At 7:20, members of the official party—consisting of the congressional leadership, the joint chiefs, a handful of Supreme Court justices, and a few of the higher-profile guests—will arrive at the north portico and will be escorted up here to the yellow oval room for cocktails.

317

You and the admiral are welcome to join them. At 7:35, the two of you will go to the state floor to await the president of France and his wife as they arrive at the north portico with full press coverage at 7:40. Once they arrive, you and the admiral will welcome them, then escort them inside and up the grand stairs to the yellow oval room. You okay so far?"

Gentry said, "Yes, go on."

"At 8 p.m., you and the admiral will escort President Marchal and his wife down the grand stairs, where you will stand at the base of the steps while the press's still photographers take pictures. After the photos, you will be announced and then form a receiving line in the main cross-hall in front of the blue room doors. After that, for the following twenty minutes, all the guests will go through the receiving line and then be seated in the state dining room. At 8:20, you and the admiral, along with the French president and his wife, will be seated in the state dining room. I shared with you who is seated at your table." The president nodded.

Winston continued, "The Marine Strolling Strings will then enter and spread throughout the state dining room and play for five minutes. Then dinner will be served at 8:30, and as you requested, we moved the toast until after the dinner. So, at approximately 10:15, you'll make your toast. This will be followed by President Marchal's toast. Then at 10:30, you and

President Marchal, along with your spouses, will wait in the blue room as the remaining guests are seated in the east room. At 10:40, the four of you will be announced and seated in the east room for the entertainment. After the entertainment, at approximately 11:35, you will be escorted to the north portico. Then you will bid farewell to the French president and his wife. After which, you are welcome to stay for dancing or retire for the evening."

Gentry smiled. "Winston, just so you know, I have been studying the protocol, and having you review it with me is most helpful. Thank you! Okay, where's my husband?"

A butler stepped in and told the president that the admiral had just joined the guests in the yellow oval room. The president laughed and said, "Good to know one of us is ready! I better go join him."

***

Winston stood unnoticed in a far corner of the east room, partially obscured by one of the blooming cherry trees. He watched as each of the guests was announced as they walked into the east room.

"Ladies and gentlemen, the Polish deputy ambassador, Anna Zielinski, and her guest, Baron Leopold Julian Kronenberg." Winston's heart jumped as he recognized the closest possible match to the photo. He adjusted his glasses to ensure he was seeing correctly. *Of course*, he thought, *this makes perfect sense*. The French and US had agreed it would be good to include all of the ambassadors and senior embassy attachés from each of the EU countries.

Ambassador Zielinski—or as he knew her, Annika Antonov—was tall with flat, blonde hair that fell to the top of her shoulders in no particular style. Winston thought her height gave her the appearance of being athletic. She wore a rather nondescript, long, light brown dress that simply fell around her, not revealing any hints as to her figure. Her guest, the baron, must have been in his late eighties. Hunched forward and moving with difficulty with a cane, he wore a formal, dark red military jacket covered with medals. Immediately upon entering the room, she grabbed a glass of white wine from a butler who was holding a tray for guests as they entered. The baron looked relieved as he sat in a chair that one of the mil-aides had provided for him.

Winston exited the east room from the north side, concealed by the line of blooming trees. He got back to the ushers office to find Jim at the desk, keeping the ushers log up to date. Winston looked out the window, watching the snow come down steadily. The north drive was becoming covered in white; the grounds crew had switched from spreading salt to now using shovels. Winston did not worry; he admired the beauty.

The uniformed Secret Service officer on duty leaned his head through the door of the ushers office and said that the French president's motorcade was coming in through the northwest gate. Winston looked out the window to the gate and could see the headlights; he then immediately used the ushers office door leading to the grand foyer. To his dismay, he did not find the president and admiral waiting there.

Winston rapidly walked to the base of the grand stairs and looked up. Not seeing anyone, he ran up, taking two steps at a time. He got to the second floor, paused to catch his breath, then forced himself to continue. Not finding the president, he dashed to the yellow oval room. Gentry was still nowhere to be found. Winston saw the admiral, who met him halfway with his arms half-outstretched.

"There was a wardrobe malfunction," explained the admiral. "She's in her dressing room with one of the maids. She told me to tell you to go ahead and greet the French president!"

Winston frowned. "Admiral, that's highly irregular. The French could take this as an insult."

The admiral, who obviously had had a few cocktails, said, "Okay, Winston, let's do it together!" The first husband then headed for the stairs, forcing Winston to half-jog to catch up to him.

Winston and the admiral rushed out to the north portico and were immediately blinded by the press lights and cameras flashing. As their eyes recovered, they could see the French president and Mrs. Marchal exiting the limo.

The admiral, acting overly gregarious, loudly announced, "President Marchal, welcome to the White House. Madam President had an urgent matter she needed to attend to, so she asked that I, along with Sir Winston, greet you."

Winston, thought, *Oh, God. Did he just refer to me as 'Sir Winston?' as in Churchill?* Winston hastily shook hands with President Marchal and his wife, who both reacted as if they recognized Winston from someplace. Winston made small talk about the weather while walking backward and motioning for all to enter the White House. Once inside, there stood President Gentry, who had come down and watched the arrival from the warmth of inside. After greeting the French president and his wife, she leaned close to Winston. "Thanks, hon. Told ya I needed you close!" She then escorted her guests up the grand stairs.

With one mini-crisis handled, Winston took the time to wonder how Annika Antonov would get him "the instructions."

As he walked toward the east room, he noticed in the green room Antonov huddled with someone in the corner. Winston quickly diverted to that room so he could get a closer look. He could see Antonov was animated and gesturing as if providing directions. *Odd*, he thought. Antonov was blocking Winston's view so he could not see who she was talking to. After a minute or so, Antonov left the room, and when she did, the person behind her became visible.

Loretta.

Winston approached her. "What was that about?"

Loretta looked surprised to see Winston and nervously replied, "She is the Polish deputy ambassador—"

"I know who she is," Winston interrupted tersely. "Why was she talking to you?"

Loretta had composed herself and calmly responded, "She's not happy because we didn't have a wheelchair for her guest, the baron. She asked me to get her one."

Winston noticed Loretta held a folded paper in her hand. "What's that?" he asked her.

Loretta looked down at the note. "Oh, she gave this to me and asked that I give it to the chief usher." She handed it to Winston.

Winston took the folded paper but didn't read it. "Have one of the mil-aides get a wheelchair from the east wing tour office. And when the ambassador and baron are ready to leave for the evening, tell the military aide to escort them with a member of the Secret Service. I emphasize: Make sure the mil-aide does it with a member of the Secret Service. Am I clear?"

Loretta nodded. Winston stared at her for a long second, then left. As he walked down the long, red-carpeted state floor cross-hall, he unfolded the paper to read the handwritten note: *Meet me in the vermeil room.*

Vermeil, mused Winston, meaning sterling-silver-plated with a layer of gold. The room named after that metal is located on the ground floor of the White House next to the china room. Formerly a staff bedroom, in 1902 it became a sitting room, and then after the 1948–1952 Truman renovation, it was known as the billiard room—until 1957 when mining heiress Margaret Thompson Biddle bequeathed over 1,500 pieces of vermeil silverware to the White House, the pieces of which are on display behind glass throughout the room.

Winston crossed the grand foyer and took the grand stairs to the ground floor, where he then walked straight across the hallway and into the vermeil room. There he found the ambassador, or rather, Russian agent Annika Antonov. Her back was to him as she admired the

Aaron Shikler portrait of Jacqueline Kennedy. Winston quietly walked up, stood next to her, and asked, "You're not going to sucker-punch me again, are you, Antonov?"

She turned to face him. "I am prepared to do whatever is required, but I hope additional violence won't be necessary. I need..." Antonov paused, waiting while a lady exited the ladies room and left the room. She then motioned for Winston to follow and led him into the bathroom, locking the door behind her.

Checking the bathroom to see that they were alone, Antonov continued, "Winston, I need you to listen carefully. We have Dr. Michael Jenkins in custody. We have his sworn video testimony. Dr. Jenkins has admitted that he is the lone assassin in the death of the president and has provided us with specific proof detailing how he substituted the president's insulin injection with the botulinum toxin that killed him. Jenkins provided specific detail on how he framed Sous Chef Patrick Sullivan. He also told us in specific detail how he murdered Patrick and made it look like a suicide. Winston, our investigation proves that Assistant Usher Brenton Williams did *not* kill the president."

Winston was losing his temper. "Why are you telling me this?" he demanded.

The doorknob to the bathroom turned, followed by a knock.

Antonov, in an improvised Hispanic accent, said, "This is housekeeping. We apologize for the inconvenience, but this restroom is out of order. You can go directly across the hall to the library and use the men's room." They listened as the person walked away. Antonov continued, "Winston, you must act immediately to convince your defense team *and* the Department of Justice that the findings I have just shared with you are the results of your investigation. Any failure in your ability to convince your team and the DOJ will result in permanent harm to you, your son, and your pregnant daughter-in-law."

Winston felt his blood pressure rising. Enraged, he lost his control and lunged for Antonov's throat, but before he could tighten his grip, she kneed him hard in the groin. He let out a gasp and fell to the floor.

Antonov went to one knee and leaned close to Winston's ear. "Do not make me have to hurt you again. We are in the process of taking measures to ensure you act in our best interests. We will be checking your progress shortly." Antonov stood and checked herself in the mirror. She casually removed lipstick from her purse and applied it, then unlocked the door and left the room. Still on the floor, Winston managed to pull out his phone and dial a number.

"Meet me in the map room," he managed to respond to the person who answered. He then hung up, slowly got to his feet, and left the vermeil room.

Chapter 39
5:10 p.m., Tuesday, March 10: San Diego, California

Sam Poundstone stood at the front of the control room, studying the large screen that displayed a live image of 8330 Summit Way. The only other light in the room came from the various laptops manned by two rows of staff seated at tables facing the large screen. Sam flipped his headset's microphone down from above his head to just an inch from his mouth.

"Ranger-1, this is Poundstone," said Sam. "We're all on. Go ahead."

"This is Ranger-1," said the voice being broadcast in the room. "We have activity—a black Mercedes SUV with Nevada tags just made its second drive-by of the protectees' residence. The first pass was at 20 mph, second at only 5. Drone thermal imaging detects five heat signatures: two in the front, three in back. Vehicle now slowing to a stop. Okay, it's now idling three doors away."

"Thanks, Ranger-1," responded Sam. "We have the image. Ranger-2, what are you observing?"

Another voice could now be heard. "Ranger-2 reporting. Protectees have just left UC Medical Center, traveling together in their blue BMW X3. Proceeding south on Front Street. Predicted destination is 8330

Summit Way, 4.8 miles. ETA: thirteen minutes. As of now, they are no longer in my view. Handing off to Mobile-1."

"Thanks, Ranger-2," said Sam. "Go ahead and relocate to Ranger-1's location and remain there for further instructions. Go ahead, Mobile-1."

"This is Mobile-1. I am now above the protectees, they're heading east on Lewis. Stand by, detecting possible pursuit activity. Circling back to get for a better view."

Sam gestured to the staff behind him and instructed, "Bring it up on a split-screen so we can see both." Instantly, the screen in the front of the room displayed the two live feeds: one above the house at 8330 Summit Way and the other above a highway zooming in to a closeup of a black Mercedes SUV.

"Black SUV, Nevada tags," reported Mobile-1. "Protectees have turned north onto Bachman. Stand by. Black SUV now turning north on Bachman and maintaining 167 feet of separation. Black SUV with two heat signatures, front seat. Protectees ETA 8330 Summit Way, 4.2 miles, nine minutes."

"Thanks, Mobile-1," said Sam. "We're watching your feed. Ground station, are we picking up any comms?"

"Ground station reporting. Negatory, no cellular activity. Stand by. We may have picked up some citizen band radio chatter. Stand by… Yes, we can confirm the two Mercedes SUVs are in contact with one another. Decoding message, stand by…"

"Go ahead, Ground station," Sam directed. "Hurry, go!"

"Hold…" The ground station operator went silent for an instant, then the voice returned over the line. "Okay, we have a partial transcript that reads, 'Cleared for go.' There is more but it is undecipherable, stand by. Language is Russian. Repeat, we confirm language is Russian!"

"Team, I'm implementing Operation Sleepy Cobra. Repeat, Sleepy Cobra. Everyone handle their assigned role!" Sam then darted toward a side door and threw it wide open, flooding the room with intense sunlight. He ran to his vehicle. "Mobile-1, I'm en route, ETA six minutes." Sam took a deep breath as he climbed into his SUV.

"Roger that," answered Mobile-1.

Sam was already driving. Only a moment later, he heard Mobile-1 deliver another report.

"Update. Heat sensors have detected a third individual inside the protectives' car. Rear seat, no motion, likely undetected by protectives."

Chapter 40
8:25 p.m., Tuesday, March 10: White House

Winston unlocked the map room door and stood outside. Not a minute later, Jonathan Cartwright walked up.

"I've just met with Antonov," announced Winston. The two men entered the room, and Winston locked the door behind him. Winston described the meeting and how he had lost his cool and Antonov had left him on the floor.

Jonathan glowered. "Bastards. When you and I talked yesterday, we had thought Dr. Jenkins was guilty, but with the Russians pushing it so hard, I'm now having my doubts. What are they up to? Beyond that, though, it sounds like they're going to make good on their threat to you."

Winston nodded. "Yes, that's why I called you immediately."

Jonathan's eyes, typically a bright blue that shined with curiosity and sharp intellect, now turned dark, almost gray. His angular jaw twitched which barely concealed anger at his friend's dilemma. "Have you called Sam Poundstone yet?"

"No, I was waiting for you."

"Let's get him on the phone," Jonathan recommended.

Winston pulled out his phone and punched Sam's number. It went immediately to voice mail. Winston left a message: "Hey, Sam, it's me. I'm with Jonathan Cartwright. We've got some intel we want to share with you. Please give me a call when you can." Winston disconnected the call. "Let's get back to the dinner. I'll ping you as soon as I hear from him."

Jonathan nodded. "Sounds good."

Winston put his phone in his pocket. "Better hurry it up. The dinner is scheduled to be served at 8:25. We're running a few minutes late, so you'll have time to be seated." The two men left the room.

Chapter 41
5:30 p.m., Tuesday, March 10: San Diego, California

Win turned left off Civita Boulevard and onto Via Alta. "Traffic seems light today. Oh, hey, I was able to move all my morning appointments for next Wednesday so I can take you to the ultrasound appointment."

"Aw, thanks for doing that," said Gwen. "I hated the thought of you not being there."

Win turned onto their street and immediately saw the red and blue flashing lights in his mirror. "What? I know I wasn't speeding." He pulled over to the right and lowered his window. He was shocked to see three police officers; two came over to his side and one moved to Gail's side.

One officer bent close to Win's window. "Sir, I need for the two of you to step out of the car, now."

Winston remained seated. "Officer, what is this about?"

"Sir, I need you to step out of the car. You too, ma'am. Now!"

Winston looked at Gail. "We better do as he says."

They got out of the car. The officer took Win by his arm and led him back several yards, where three police cars were waiting. To his left several feet away, Win could see Gail was also being hurriedly led in the same direction. As they reached the police cars, four men in black special ops uniforms seemed to emerge from the shadows just beyond the police vehicles. They sprinted right by Win and his wife, carrying rifles. Win and Gail both turned to watch as the men surrounded Win's car, pointed their rifles at the interior of it, and yelled for someone to get out.

Win and Gail watched in total disbelief as the rear door of their car sprung open, and a man slowly emerged holding his hands above his head. An officer instantly tackled the man to the ground, instructing him to lay flat with his arms spread wide apart. A gun was removed from the man's waist as two officers placed the man in handcuffs while a third placed shackles around his ankles. The officer who had escorted Win told him they had just thwarted their kidnapping. Suddenly, automatic weapon fire could be heard from just down the street. The officers yelled for Win and Gail to get down. The shooting continued for less than thirty seconds, then all was quiet. The officers told Win and Gwen to continue crouching.

A few moments later, a large man wearing all black with two full bandoliers crisscrossing his chest walked up. He cradled in his muscular arms a machine gun and said to the officer, "All clear! We've got five enemy

KIA. No one else hurt. There's a Mercedes SUV, Nevada tags, that will need to go to impound. Ambulances and tow trucks ETA less than ten minutes. The ambulances will serve as hearses. Once the bodies and vehicles are taken care of, I will need everyone out of here before the press arrives."

He pointed to the dark, bearded man in handcuffs. "We'll take him with us." The police officer nearest Win said, "We have a second SUV and two suspects in custody." He pointed to fifty yards behind where they were standing. Sam smiled when he saw Win and Gwen and stepped over to them. "I'm Sam Poundstone. I am a friend of your dad's, and I am so glad you are safe. You were the target of a foreign power's terrorist plot to kidnap you. My team has eliminated the immediate threat, but we will continue to monitor and provide protection for you all."

"Wait," Win blurted out. "I know you. You used to be in the Secret Service. Dad would talk about you all the time."

Sam and Win shook hands. "Yes, your dad and I have worked a lot of…let's call them situations, but I haven't seen you in a long time." He faced Gail. "And I've never had the pleasure of meeting your wife." Gail and Sam shook hands.

"I'm sure you have a lot of questions," Sam said. "You will be fully briefed later. Right now, the White

House is expecting my call. Your home is safe and undamaged. All the shooting occurred on your street a few doors away. The shots were all contained—my team doesn't miss. You are free to go, and I'm sure I don't have to mention this, but do not talk to the press, or anyone else for that matter."

Sam looked toward the police officers. "Gentlemen, as always, outstanding support. Thank you. I could not have done it without you." He waved at the officers and then jumped into the waiting SUV that had pulled up while he was talking. A second SUV identical to the first followed. Two black-uniformed men got out and collected the handcuffed man and loaded him in the back. The officer pointed to the other two, and they were brought over and loaded into the SUV.

Chapter 42
8:30 p.m., Tuesday, March 10: White House

Annika Antonov crossed the grand foyer and opened the double mahogany doors to the ushers office. She stepped in to see Loretta seated at the main desk, and a doorman was seated at the other desk. "Yes, hello," Annika said. "We met earlier. I am the Polish deputy ambassador, Anna Zielinski. Do you have anything for a migraine?"

The doorman looked at Loretta. "I can take the ambassador to the medical unit."

Loretta quickly stood up. "No, I'll do it." She turned to Antonov. "Madam Ambassador, follow me."

The two left the ushers office, walked down the back stairs, and headed to the ground floor, where they just missed Winston and Jonathan Cartwright, who had gotten on the elevator to head up to the state floor.

Loretta crossed the hallway and entered the doctor's office. She said hello to her friend, Nurse Jackson, the only person in the office. She explained that the ambassador needed something for a headache. Nurse Jackson stepped into the vestibule, opened a cabinet, and pulled out a bottle of Tylenol. In a swift motion, she picked up the ringing phone as she got back to her desk. After a quick exchange, Jackson grabbed her medical bag and handed the Tylenol to Loretta, explaining she was needed urgently in the main kitchen—one of the chefs had cut their hand. On her way out, she nodded to the ambassador and told Loretta, "You can grab a bottle of water from the fridge for the ambassador. I've gotta run. Please close the door when you leave. I'll check back with you later. Thanks, hon."

Antonov could clearly see Dr. Jenkins's desk, which was in the next room just beyond the vestibule.

Chapter 43
10:20 p.m., Tuesday, March 10: White House

Winston stood patiently at the doorway between the state dining room and the cross-hall. The dinner was over, and the guests were slowly departing the dining room to head to the east room for the entertainment. Winston met Jonathan's eyes just as he walked through the large doorway and motioned with his head for Jonathan to follow. They used the back stairs and went down to the map room.

"Okay," began Winston as he closed the door behind him. "I didn't interrupt your dinner because everything was handled. Sam called me an hour ago. He eliminated a major threat in San Diego. Win and Gwen are safe."

Jonathan held up his hand. "Yeah, I know. Right after he talked to you, he sent me a classified text. He handled it well, but we still need to understand what's behind the Russians. They lost a lot of resources in that endeavor. Sam's team and some of my resources are interrogating the three they have in custody. We should have something soon. For now, we need to keep a close watch on Antonov. She seems to be the one calling the shots."

Winston nodded. "The guests should be filling up the east room for the entertainment."

"Right, let's get back upstairs. I'll try to sit near her if I can."

"It's about to start. Let's go."

***

Jonathan took his seat in the east room. As was typical for White House state dinners, there were always an additional two dozen or so guests called "after-dinner guests," most of whom had already taken their seats. Jonathan, being one of the last to arrive, ended up in the far back corner in the second to last row. He careened his neck to get a better view as he scanned the seated individuals one by one, looking for Antonov. *Where was she?* The band played ruffles and flourishes, and then all stood as the president and admiral were announced, followed by the French president and his wife. *There she was!* Antonov sat a half-dozen rows from the front on the far side. The lights dimmed, and a spotlight illuminated the stage. Yo-Yo Ma entered to rousing applause, took a seat close to his pre-positioned cello, and began to play.

***

As Winston was about to enter the ushers office, Secret Service Uniformed Officer Wes Chandler, who was on his post next to the office, commented as Winston walked past him, "Hey, it's coming down at a rate of over three inches an hour!" Winston didn't respond as his gaze was fixed on the view outside the ushers office window. *Yes*, he thought. The snow was coming down harder than he had ever remembered seeing at the White House. He watched as the grounds crew on the north drive pushed snow with plows attached to tractors to keep the road clear. Winston grabbed the office phone receiver and punched the direct line to the White House military office. "We've got 180 guests that will be walking out of here in about forty-five minutes. What's the latest forecast?"

The voice answered, "Sir, we have over fourteen inches on the ground. There have been reports of thunder-snow in the area, which means totals may be higher in places. We can expect an additional four to six inches until it tapers off to flurries after midnight. Temperatures will remain in the mid-twenties."

"Okay, thank you." Winston then pressed the direct line to the grounds office. Irv answered.

"Irv, how are we doing?"

"We've got two plows on the north drive, three working East Executive Avenue. For now, we've abandoned the south drive," Irv responded.

Winston gazed out the window. "I'm looking at the north drive. The French president's motorcade is starting to form up. One plow should be able to maintain it. Move the other one to the east side to focus on that. We need it clear for the guests to be able to leave."

"Got it," replied Irv. "Will do."

Winston looked at his watch. It was 11:15. He had about fifteen minutes until the entertainment ended. He decided he better inspect the north portico, then walk through the east wing to check East Executive Avenue. He grabbed his hat and coat, told Loretta he would be back in fifteen minutes, and left the office.

***

Yo-Yo Ma completed a number. As the audience clapped enthusiastically, Cartwright watched in panic as Antonov stood and rapidly exited through the closest door that led to the green room. Just as Cartwright readied to stand, Yo-Yo Ma's deft fingers moved on the fingerboard, bow sweeping across the strings. Cartwright couldn't leave as the music floated over the room without causing and unbearably rude scene. He remained seated and glanced quickly over his left shoulder. His best bet, he determined, would be to go around the back and exit out the north door of the east room, which would take him to the top of the grand staircase. He faced front, anxiously awaiting the next round of applause to leave his seat.

***

Antonov briskly walked through the side connecting doors from the green to the blue room, hurried through the red room, and then exited from the main door, where she had a direct line of sight to the ushers office. She headed across the main hall and paused just outside of the president's elevator before falling to one knee as if disoriented. Uniformed Officer Wes Chandler rushed to her aid. She said something that he couldn't hear, so he leaned closer. Antonov thrust violently upward with the heel of her hand, catching Chandler just beneath his nose. He fell hard on his back.

Antonov was on him in a flash, wrapping her arms around his neck in a chokehold until he passed out. She then unsnapped his holster and removed the nine-millimeter sidearm. With the gun pointed straight in front of her, she rushed into the ushers office. Loretta was seated at the desk, alone save for the doorman in the guest chair who looked on in horror. Antonov pointed the gun at Loretta and ordered her to stand. After Loretta obliged, Antonov rushed over, locked an arm around her throat, and with her free hand pressed the gun against Loretta's temple. She then forced Loretta forward and pushed through the opposite door she had entered from. Together, they walked out and into the grand foyer.

Secret Service personnel and military aides who were standing by waiting for the entertainment to end froze and looked on in alarm. Antonov motioned to the door to the north portico and yelled to the Secret Service uniformed officer to open it or she would kill the usher. The uniform officer quickly opened the door and got out of the way. Antonov forced Loretta in front of her, and they walked outside. Several Secret Service agents who had been lining up the French president's motorcade were now jumping out of the vehicles with weapons drawn. Antonov yelled for everyone to stay back, or the usher would be shot. She held Loretta closely while pushing her along. They stepped off the north portico steps and onto the driveway, which was now snow-covered.

The grounds crew quickly abandoned their tractors when they saw what was happening. As Antonov and Loretta headed toward the northwest gate, Secret Service counterassault team members could be seen forming off to the side. The snow was coming down so hard, they could only see twenty or so feet ahead.

Jonathan exited the back of the east room. When he got out to the grand foyer, he saw the mass bedlam unfolding. Jonathan quickly closed the door behind him to suppress the noise. Several agents with automatic weapons were protecting the doors to the east room. Presidential protection detail agents were arguing with the French security detail, who were insisting on evacuating President Marchal. Jonathan displayed his badge. Seeing several of the Secret Service officers looking out the north portico door, he ran to the door to learn that a tall blond woman with a gun had taken

Loretta hostage, several officers pointed and yelled, "Northwest gate!"

Jonathan ran through the door to the outside and down the steps to the driveway. With the snow coming down so hard, he could not see how far Antonov and Loretta had gotten. He continued to hold up his badge for everyone to see and rushed to the northwest gate. As soon as he got on the driveway, his feet slipped out from under him, and he went flying and landed hard in a seated position. He quickly got back on his feet, realizing his dress shoes were useless on the icy surface. So, he maneuvered himself to the edge of the driveway and onto the lawn, where the deep snow gave him better traction.

Antonov approached the gate while holding her gun up in clear view of the Secret Service, then pressed the tip of the barrel to Loretta's head and yelled for them to open the gate. The large driveway gates began to slowly open. She pulled Loretta along, and the two of them squeezed through the opening. They approached a waiting Mercedes SUV, and Antonov opened the back door and flung Loretta in, then jumped in behind her and slammed the door. The driver floored it; the car spun wildly until it gained some traction, then it straightened out and sped west on Pennsylvania Avenue toward 17th Street.

By the time Jonathan got to the northwest gate, the gate had been fully opened. Cartwright ran through and hurried in the direction the uniformed officers hastily indicated. He could barely make out the taillights of the SUV.

In the meantime, Winston was on East Exec Avenue when he heard the Secret Service radio chatter. So, he ran up East Exec, made a left onto Pennsylvania Avenue, and then headed toward 17th Street. As he ran parallel to the White House on his left while within view of the northwest gate, a loud clap of thunder shook the ground, and the snow began coming down even harder.

Inside the SUV, Antonov gently caressed Loretta's arm. "I'm sorry, babe. I hope I wasn't too rough, but I had to make it look real. It worked, we made it out, and we'll be safe soon."

Loretta said, "I'm fine. We planned for everything—except for this snow! But, wow, you had me scared. You were so convincing back there. They'll never suspect me."

Antonov nodded. "True, and the snow is actually a blessing. No one in DC knows how to drive in this stuff."

The streets bordering the White House were gridlocked with cars stuck all over the place. The driver of their SUV flipped the red and blue flashing lights on, which had the expected effect. The cars in the intersection parted, allowing them to make a left on 17th. They maneuvered around several abandoned vehicles, at one point driving up on the sidewalk. Traffic was now at a standstill on 17th, so the driver made a hard right onto G Street, which hadn't been plowed. They inched ahead for a while, but the weather conditions soon proved too much for the SUV. They made it as far as Swings Coffee, then spun back and forth for a minute until they could go no farther. The driver announced, "Time to get out and go on foot."

Antonov reached in the back and grabbed two blankets. "Sorry we don't have coats, but this will work." She handed one of the blankets to Loretta, and the two women each wrapped themselves up. Just before exiting the vehicle, they looked at each other and kissed.

Antonov opened her door, and the falling snow blew in. Loretta got out on her side, only to see a man in front of her in a tuxedo crouch down and fire two shots. She quickly turned to see where the man was shooting but was abruptly engulfed in someone's arms and pulled to the ground. She didn't notice her cell phone slip out as they both landed in the snow.

Jonathan could be heard yelling, "I can't see a thing. I can't tell if I hit one of them. How's Loretta?"

Winston still lay on top of Loretta. He lifted off her and met her eyes. "Are you okay?"

Loretta rapidly blinked to rid her eyes of the snow falling into them. She recognized Winston after a few seconds and gave a slight nod. "Yes."

"Thank God," Winston said, and they slowly stood. He noticed something metallic in the snow and picked it up. Not sure where it had come from and too cold to worry about something that seemed relatively trivial in that moment, Winston instinctively handed the snow-covered cell phone he had just found to Jonathan and turned his focus to Loretta as he put his arm around her. He could feel her shivering.

Jonathan walked around to the front of the car and looked. "There's blood here, but I can't go any farther. I can't see, and I can no longer feel my fingers."

The three of them turned to head back toward the White House; Jonathan and Winston were on either side of Loretta. As Jonathan placed his gun back into his shoulder harness, he asked her if she was okay. Loretta, believing that Jonathan ruined the plan, and worse, may have just shot her love, sneered at him with a look of total hate and refused to answer. Emerging out of the blinding snow directly in front of them were four heavily armed Secret Service counter-assault team members.

Jonathan said, "Feel free to pursue the suspects, but we're heading back inside."

The counter-assault team lead responded with, "Our orders were to ensure your safety and bring you back. We're not to pursue the suspects."

The group then headed to the White House, vanishing from view in the driving snow.

***

Jonathan sat in his west wing office. It was after midnight, and he still hadn't completely warmed up. He looked at the wrapped gift sitting on his desk; it appeared to be a bottle, at least that was what he hoped it was. He read the card: "Welcome to your new office. Here's a little something for those late nights." It was signed by the director of national intelligence. *What about early mornings?* he thought. Jonathan removed the wrapping paper. Perfect! He smiled as he held the bottle and admired the Pierre Ferrand cognac. Jonathan looked around his office for a glass. As nothing handy presented itself, he decided that his coffee cup would have to do. He opened the bottle, pulled off the corked lid, poured two fingers, savored the aroma, and then took a drink. He was rewarded as all his senses came back to life. He said out loud to no one, "Wow did I need this!"

Jonathan kept thinking about the look of pure hate Loretta had given him right after he fired those two rounds at Antonov. *Such a strange reaction*, he thought. Jonathan held the iPhone in his hand, which

Winston had given him earlier. He took a closer look at it. Finally, he used his office phone and called Winston.

Winston answered immediately. "You still awake?"

Jonathan smiled. "That's what I was going to ask you! Get dressed and get over to my office, ASAP."

"I'm still dressed and was enjoying some wine."

"I've got something better!" Jonathan revealed. "Oh, and bring a coffee mug."

Not even three minutes later there was a knock. Jonathan opened the door. "You must've run!"

Winston walked in. "I would have been here sooner, but I couldn't find my damn coffee mug!"

Jonathan gestured toward a chair. "Sit down." Winston grinned as Jonathan poured him a cognac.

The two exhausted men sat there in their tuxes, ties hanging loose, drinking cognac from coffee mugs.

"Winston, for the record, I hereby read you into this Top Secret Sensitive Compartmented Information. Please sign this non-Disclosure."

Winston signed the document.

Jonathan reached under his desk and pulled out a hardened metal briefcase, placing it on his desk. "Hopefully, we'll be able to unlock this phone in a reasonable amount of time." He touched his index finger onto a reader; the case buzzed and unlocked. He opened it to reveal a sophisticated built-in console. He pulled out a bag of adaptors and sorted through them until he found the one he wanted. He took a yellow fiber cable and connected it to his Joint Worldwide Intelligence Communication System adaptor port on his desk. He then flipped open the screen and pulled out a keyboard from inside the briefcase. Using his White House ID card, which contained his Top Secret token, he authenticated to the top-secret intelligence network, brought up the mobile device forensic tool portal, and selected the tools to use for the iPhone, choosing the most current iOS. He then used a special adaptor and connected the iPhone, started the GrayKey application, and sat back. "Now, we wait."

"How long?" Winston inquired.

"The GrayKey software can crack a six-digit PIN in as little as a few minutes to several hours. If it's a seven or eight-digit PIN, it can take up to several days."

Winston sighed. "Let's hope it's quick."

"Oh, while we're waiting," Jonathan began, "let me share with you the latest from the assassination crime scene investigation. We believe we've figured out a likely scenario. Turns out, both Brent and President Blake use the same insulin brand, Lantus. We now believe our Russian friends lifted Brent's trash and used one of his old insulin containers, which obviously had his fingerprints on it. Then they filled it with the deadly toxin and somehow got it into the White House."

Winston considered that. "Sounds possible— except for the 'getting into the White House' part."

"Yeah, we're still trying to figure that out. We also now have evidence that the Russians may have been conducting surveillance on all the ushers, including you.

Winston shook his head. "Wow. Well, they wouldn't have gotten a lot from me. I haven't been at my house much in the past few months, and I can't even remember the last time I took my trash out. I'm curious… What led you to all this information?"

"Secret Service, working closely with the MPD, has reviewed hours of DC video footage. Let's just say, we've observed some interesting individuals rummaging through trash cans at Brent's, Loretta's, and Jim's houses, and we also have evidence the same occurred with Patrick Sullivan. As for you, we don't have video proof, but we assume, given who was being watched, that you very likely were as well."

The screen beeped, and Jonathan said, "Wow, great. Less than fifteen minutes!"

Once logged into the device, Jonathan confirmed that the phone belonged to Loretta. For the next twenty minutes, the two men reviewed current and deleted texts, images, and call logs.

Jonathan grabbed his desk phone and called the special hotline of the United States District Court for the District of Columbia. After two rings, there was an answer: "James Robinson, District Court Emergency Warrants. How can I help you?"

"Hi, Mr. Robinson. This is Jonathan Cartwright, ODNI assistant director. I am the lead investigator into the assassination of President Blake. I need an emergency warrant issued in order to take a prime suspect into custody for questioning."

"Yes, sir," replied Robinson. "Stand by while I connect you to Judge Raymond Clancy."

Judge Clancy answered the line a few moments later. "Jonathan, there better be a damn good reason you're interrupting me at 1:55 in the morning!"

"Ray, sorry to be calling so late, but you know I would never bother you unless I thought it was critical."

"You're about the only person in DC that I don't mind hearing from. Bring the order to my place. You know the address." The phone went dead.

Jonathan then called FBI headquarters and asked for the special agent in charge.

"This is Thompson," answered the man Jonathan was connected to.

"Hey, Dan. It's Jonathan Cartwright. I need an order drafted. I just emailed you the specifics. I'll come by and pick it up. Judge Clancy is waiting for me, and I'll need two of your agents to accompany me when we issue the warrant. I'll be there in six minutes. Thanks."

"Reading your email now," Thompson reported over the phone. "I'll have everything ready by the time you get up to the eleventh floor. See you then."

Jonathan hung up and addressed his friend. "C'mon, Winston. Let's go make America safe."

The FBI headquarters was located in the J. Edgar Hoover Building at 935 Pennsylvania Avenue, NW DC, less than a mile from the White House.

The two men exited the basement of the west wing onto West Exec. A few steps away they cleared the snow off Jonathan's large SUV, got in, and started the vehicle. Jonathan headed north on West Exec, now so cleared of snow that the only way one would have known the storm had occurred would be to look to their right at the north lawn of the White House, which looked peaceful under the heavy blanket of white. They stopped at the north end of West Exec Avenue and waited for the gate to open, then made a right on Pennsylvania Avenue.

Jonathan flipped on the rooftop blue strobe light and hit the gas; they sped past the White House, slowed to await the opening of the gate at 15th Street, made a right on 15th, sped the two blocks, and made a left on F Street, which was snow-covered but had little traffic. Jonathan floored it; Winston felt his head jerk back from the near G-force. They drove for six blocks, passing snow crews, made a hard right onto Ninth, spinning a bit in the snow. After two blocks, they pulled up to the Hoover FBI building garage, where Jonathan and Winston held up their White House IDs. An officer walked out and scanned the IDs. The gate soon opened, and Jonathan pulled into the garage, found a spot near the elevator, and parked.

The two men got off the elevator on the eleventh floor, walked a long hallway, and made what seemed like several turns. Jonathan commented to Winston, "I hate this building. It's a maze of hallways. I swear J. Edgar designed it so any intruder would get lost and die of starvation before reaching their intended destination!"

They entered through a door with a sign that read: "FBI Division Director's Office."

Dan Thompson was waiting for them in the lobby. "It's printing out now. We'll bring it to you in two minutes. I also have three special agents that will meet you at the address once you inform me that the judge has signed."

A staffer walked out with the document and handed it to Thompson, who quickly reviewed it and then handed it to Jonathan. Jonathan spent a few minutes reading it carefully, then frowned. "Sorry to take so long, gents. This needs to be perfect. Otherwise, Judge Clancy will make an example of me for the world to see as he is known to embarrass agents who make mistakes!"

A moment later, after the document had been adjusted and re-reviewed, Jonathan said, "Okay, Dan, we're good. We're heading to Clancy's house in Georgetown and will call you once I have his signature. I appreciate your help."

Thompson nodded. "Of course. Good luck."

Chapter 44
2:50 a.m., Wednesday, March 11: Northwest DC

Jonathan knocked on the door of the 1870s-era, detached, two-story, brick, federal-style house at 3129 N Street NW in Georgetown. After a moment, the foyer light turned on, and the door opened. There stood Judge Raymond Clancy, a distinguished man in his late sixties. He wore a blue bathrobe and cradled a glass of brandy in his hand, his white, curly hair completely disheveled. He gave his guests a once-over, and a wry smile came over his face. Clancy's speech was slightly slurred as he said, "My, my, the two of you are very nicely dressed to be serving warrants. C'mon in."

Jonathan led the conversation. "Hi, Ray. I'd like you to meet Bartholomew Winston, chief usher of the White House."

Judge Clancy struggled a bit with his balance as he moved to make room for the two men to enter. "Winston and I are old friends. Jonathan, you seem to forget, I have been to the White House many times in the past."

Winston nodded. "Nice to see you again, Your Honor."

"Oh, Winston, don't be ridiculous. Call me Ray. Can I offer you gentlemen a spot of brandy?"

"Maybe later," Jonathan suggested. "Right now, we need to handle business."

Clancy held out his hand. "Of course. Let me see it."

Jonathan handed the order to the judge, who swapped the document for his brandy, handing his glass to Jonathan. Clancy then spun around to a small table in the hallway, pulled opened a drawer, and rummaged through it until he found a pen. "There we go." In one swift motion, he signed the document without even reading it, turned, and handed it back to Jonathan, who handed back the glass.

"Thank you, Ray," said Jonathan. "I really appreciate this."

"Anytime, but next time you needn't dress so formerly."

Jonathan opened the door to leave, and both he and Winston thanked the judge and bid him farewell.

Back in the car, Jonathan called FBI headquarters and got Special Agent in Charge Thompson on the line. "Dan, the judge signed off. We're headed to 1725 New Hampshire Avenue, NW. We'll meet your guys out front. Our ETA: nine minutes."

***

It was 3:15 a.m. Jonathan and Winston sat in the car in front of 1725 New Hampshire Avenue. A large, black SUV pulled up next to them. Winston pressed the button to roll down his window, and Jonathan reached across to show his gold law enforcement badge. The driver of the SUV nodded, then pulled up and parked directly in front of them.

Jonathan looked at Winston and said, "Game time." The two men got out of the car, stepping in the deep snow, and walked up to the SUV. Four heavily armed special agents got out, three men and a woman, all were wearing black with "FBI" in big white letters printed on their fronts and backs.

Jonathan looked surprised. "Four of you?"

"Mr. Cartwright, I'm Lanny Bronk, the lead agent." The two shook hands. Lanny continued. "Yeah, I know you requested three, but headquarters insisted on four."

Jonathan responded, 'Excellent."

"This place does not have a twenty-four-hour concierge." Bronk said. "So, headquarters contacted the emergency maintenance company. They're sending someone to let us in the front door. That person will also have the key to unit 406 if needed."

Jonathan nodded. "Good. Okay, everyone. Gather around. Lanny, here's how I need you to place your team. One agent will wait at the front door, one inside at the base of the steps, and two will accompany Winston and me to room 406." Lanny pointed to each member of his team, assigning them per Jonathan's instructions. Jonathan went on. "Agents, we're apprehending Loretta Fitzgerald. She is an employee of the White House and reports to Winston here." Jonathan pointed to Winston. "Ms. Fitzgerald is a forty-seven-year-old white female, dark hair, five feet, six inches tall, 125 pounds. She will not be armed."

Jonathan paused as he did a quick visual survey to see where their vehicles were in relation to the front door of the building, then continued. "Okay, let's review weapons protocol. Everyone will leave their rifle locked in the vehicle. Keep your sidearms, however. I do not want anyone's weapon unholstered. You will not be using your weapon unless there is a matter of life or death. When Fitzgerald opens her door, Winston and I will be the only ones to enter. The two agents accompanying us will wait in the hallway out of sight, and when we leave, the two agents on the fourth floor will take the stairs, not ride in the elevator with us. And while we expect Ms. Fitzgerald may be emotional, we expect her to come with us peacefully. Is everyone clear?" Jonathan looked around to each agent as they nodded yes. "We will wait to handcuff her once we're outside and next to the vehicle. She will be riding in the car with Winston and me."

A small pickup truck pulled up and struggled a bit to park on a pile of snow in front of the FBI SUV. The truck's door opened, and a young man wearing a medium blue jacket with the service company insignia got out and walked up to the group, the large key ring on his belt with dozens of keys attached to it jingling with each of his steps. When he got close, he introduced himself as Rashon from the building management company.

Jonathan looked at the man. "Rashon, thanks for coming out at this time in the morning. I'm Jonathan Cartwright, assistant director of the office of national intelligence." They shook hands. "We need you to let us in the building, then stay out of the way. Understand, there is no danger. Nothing for you to worry about. I just don't want you in harm's way. We do not expect this to last more than ten minutes, so once we're gone, you are free to leave. Do you know if the residents in the building have peepholes on their doors or chains?"

Rashon thought for a second. "I think there are a handful of doors with peepholes and quite a few with chains."

Jonathan looked at Winston. "Winston, this is where you come in. I need you to be the closest to Loretta's door."

Jonathan looked around at the group. "Everyone ready?" The agents gave the affirmative. "Okay, let's go. Rashon, you can now let us in the building."

The group entered the building, and Jonathan said to Rashon, "Thank you. You can wait in the lobby." He looked at the agent posted at the door. "Keep the door open."

Lanny pointed to the base of the steps and motioned for the assigned agent to take his post. Lanny and the female agent followed Winston and Jonathan onto the elevator, and Jonathan pressed the four.

Unit 406 was on the southeast side of the building. The hallway was dimly lit; as they approached the door, they could see there wasn't a peephole. Jonathan felt for the warrant in his vest pocket and then instinctively checked that his gun was secure in his holster, quickly realizing how ridiculous it was for him to even feel for his gun. He rapidly knocked four times, waited, then knocked again. He motioned for Winston to step forward, and once near the door, Jonathan said in a near whisper, "If she asks who it is, I want you to answer." Winston nodded.

Jonathan knocked again. Now, a light could be seen emerging beneath the door. A small, scratchy voice, barely audible, squeaked out, "Who is it?"

Jonathan pointed to Winston, who quickly responded, "Loretta, it's Winston. Please open the door." The sound of the door chain being removed could be heard, and the door slowly opened. Loretta stood in her pale blue flannel pajamas, looking very confused as she tried to assess the situation. Winston asked if they could enter, and she moved out of the way, backing into her condo. Winston entered, followed by Jonathan. The three of them stood in the entry foyer near the open doorway to the kitchen.

Jonathan began with, "Loretta, we are sorry to be here so late, but we need to ask you some questions." Loretta looked at Winston and then pointed to Jonathan, shook her head, and gritted her teeth before asking, "Why is he here?"

Winston offered his most soothing voice, "Loretta, Jonathan is the assistant director for the ODNI, and he's the lead for the investigation into the assassination of the President. We just have some questions we need you to answer. It would be most helpful to the investigation."

Loretta was now fully awake. "You're freaking me out. I mean, I can understand helping by answering a few questions, but Jesus, you coming out here to my home in the middle of the night makes it seem as if you must have more than just a few questions! What if I don't want to answer them?"

Jonathan frowned. "We need for you to come with us."

Anger was building on Loretta's face. She ignored Jonathan and looked directly at Winston. "Winston, this is fucking bullshit. I'm not going anywhere. If you have questions, I can answer them…" She glanced at her stove clock. "…in a few hours when I'm in the office! Jesus! All the time I'm at the White House, you guys couldn't talk to me, and then you come out here now? This is bullshit!"

Winston could not believe what he was hearing. Loretta had, to his knowledge, never uttered a curse word throughout the entire time he had known her. Now he watched the veins start to bulge on her forehead.

Jonathan tried again. "Loretta, let me make this very clear to you. You don't have a choice. You need to come with us. It's a matter of national security."

Loretta looked hard at Jonathan. "Look, you bastard, I don't answer to you. You can leave now, or I will call the police."

Jonathan added, "Loretta, we can do this nicely or we can force you to come with us."

"Is that a threat? I feel harassed. Do I need to call an attorney?"

Jonathan responded with, "Would you like to get dressed before we go?"

"You are a shit for brains, you total fucking asshole! Tell me, am I under arrest?"

Jonathan sighed and said to no one in particular, "We don't have time for this." He stepped back and opened the door to the outside, then motioned for the two agents to come in. He faced Loretta, pulled the warrant out of his vest pocket, and held it up for her to see. "Loretta Fitzgerald, this is a warrant for your arrest. You have the right to remain silent. Anything you say can be used against you in court. You have the right to talk to an attorney for advice before we ask you any questions. You have the right to have an attorney with you during questioning. If you cannot afford an attorney, one will be appointed for you before any questioning if you wish. If you decide to answer questions now without an attorney present, you have the right to stop answering at any time. Do you understand your rights?"

Loretta stared blankly at him, then snarled out, "Eat shit!"

Jonathan looked to the two agents and pointed to Lanny. "Agent Bronk, cuff her and let's get out of here."

***

Alexi Smirinov was well hidden behind the hedge in front of the Rwandan Embassy at 1714 New Hampshire Avenue. A mere 155 feet away, the image through his Zeiss V6 9-30x 50 scope was uninterrupted and he had a perfect view of the entrance of the apartment building across the street. The excellent light-gathering capability of the German optic lens made the target area appear to almost be in daylight.

His target, Loretta, appeared between two FBI agents who stood head and shoulders above her.

It was only twenty-five feet from the entrance lobby to the waiting SUV, but that gave Alexi plenty of time to set the crosshairs on the center of Loretta's head, which was bent forward. This position was optimal for Alexi, who knew the bullet would enter the top of her skull and hit the medulla oblongata, rendering her instantly obliterated.

His finely manicured finger took up the first stage of the trigger, and he smoothly exhaled to ensure no bodily movement apart from the gentle squeeze of the trigger's second stage.

The .338 Lapua Magnum, 250-grain partition bullet fired from his ORSIS T-5000 .338 sniper rifle made nothing more than the usual supersonic crack. The Wolverine PBS-1 Sound Moderator adapted to fit the T 5000 and ensured that 90 percent of the report was absorbed by its ultra-efficient sound baffles, which gave the shooter the advantage as the group across the street would have great difficulty pointing out the direction from which the shot came.

At precisely the same instant that Alexi fired, Agent Lanny Bronk reached forward to open the SUV door. This brought his head in a direct line of sight with Alexi's rifle, blocking Loretta's head.

The back of Lanny's head literally exploded, showering the surrounding area in a three-foot diameter blood mist.

Alexi, believing he had completed his mission, withdrew from his position and followed his carefully planned exit route.

The instant Jonathan heard the shot, he yelled for everyone to get down as he lay on top of Loretta, who was already on the ground. Winston, on one knee, frantically looked around, trying to determine where the shot had come from. He heard, then watched as a motorcycle down the street fishtailed wildly through the snow, speeding away in the opposite direction. Loretta was screaming hysterically. She was covered with blood, only it wasn't her blood. Agent Lanny Bronk was on his back in a growing pool of blood; a bullet hole could be seen in his left temple.

Chapter 45
4:50 a.m., Wednesday, March 11: Interrogation Facility, Undisclosed Location

Loretta, wearing an orange prison jumpsuit, sat at a metal table, her hands in cuffs, her legs in shackles. A black hood was pulled down over her face, preventing her from seeing anything.

The heavy metal door to the room opened, the loud sound causing Loretta to sit up straight. The door then closed, and the room went silent. Loretta couldn't be sure if someone had entered or not; she could not see any light through her hood. The next sound she heard came from directly above her.

"Loretta Fitzgerald, we have a series of questions for you to answer. Please nod if you understand." Loretta remained motionless.

"Loretta Fitzgerald, did you know Annika Antonov?"

No response.

"Did you have a relationship with Annika Antonov?"

No response.

"Did you frequent the Russia House restaurant where you met with Russian businessmen?"

No response.

"Are you a member of the Communist Party?"

No response.

"Did you assist in any way in the assassination of President Blake?"

No response.

The questioning continued for ninety minutes. Loretta never so much as shifted in her seat.

Down a long corridor from the interview room, in what was a rather plush conference room that also served as the facility cafeteria, Jonathan met with a half dozen members of his staff. "We're getting nowhere. I need you to introduce her iPhone evidence." Jonathan glanced at his friend. "Winston, thanks for being here. Any insights you have would be helpful."

Winston was impressed with what he had observed. This was a larger complex than he had imagined, other than the dungeon-like integration room. Everything was modern, clean, and brightly lit. He said, "I'm just amazed at the operation here. Was this where Brent was held?"

Jonathan nodded. "Yes, but he was in a different room. I wasn't in charge then. I feel badly about that. I was not pleased with how they treated Brent. We're treating Loretta much more humanely. In fact, her court-appointed lawyer is here, but we're not finished getting him cleared yet."

"Well, that's good to know. I'm happy to be here," said Winston. "Thanks for including me. The past several hours have actually made me feel closer to Connie." Smiling, he added as he held up his coffee mug, "And I've gotta admit, you all have amazingly good coffee."

"Winston, you're gonna think I'm crazy," said Jonathan, "but sometimes, I feel like Connie is here watching."

Winston smiled.

***

After an hour's break, the questioning resumed.

"Ms. Fitzgerald, can we provide you with a drink or something to eat?"

Loretta paused, then responded, "Yes." Her voice was shaky.

Loretta was startled by the sound of the heavy door opening again. She could hear the footsteps. Someone was approaching her. She then felt her hood taken off her head and squeezed her eyes shut. Slowly, she reopened them, trying to regain focus and take in her surroundings.

Her hands were unfastened by a person dressed in black and wearing a ski mask and sunglasses. Another masked individual came into the room and placed a tray containing breakfast pancakes and coffee before her. Loretta ravenously attacked her food. A moment later, an individual entered the room escorting a small man in a light brown suit. "Ms. Fitzgerald, this is your court-appointed attorney, Nelson Fenwick."

Loretta, mouth full of food, managed to get out, "I don't need an attorney."

A voice from the speaker above her head said, "Ms. Fitzgerald, your appointed attorney will remain in the room, and should you have any questions, they are here for you."

After she finished her breakfast and began to drink her coffee, the voice from above asked if she needed a bathroom break. She looked up to see a speaker in the rafters far above her and nodded.

After she was escorted back to her chair, her legs were re-chained, though her hands were left free, and the hood was not placed back on her head. Her court-appointed attorney sat alone a few feet away. A voice from above announced that the questioning was about to resume.

The interrogator continued, "Ms. Fitzgerald, we have completed our review of your iPhone. With help from your carrier, AT&T, and expert analysis from NSA, FBI, and ODNI, we now have evidentiary proof that you and Annika Antonov have been in direct contact with one another for over eight months, or more precisely, thirty-seven weeks, or 259 days. During this period of time, the two of you have exchanged 1,088 text messages, 172 phone calls, and 231 emails. We have all your conversations and your photos. We also discovered exchanges between you and other Russian officials, some of which are on the US Government Watch List."

Loretta appeared tense as she shifted in her seat.

The interrogator continued. "We are providing you with a written copy of what we're about to read to you."

The large door to the side of the room opened, and Loretta watched as the person in black walked in, placed several pages in front of her, provided a copy to the attorney, then left the room.

From the speaker above her head, she listened…

"TEXT DATED DECEMBER 25TH. 10:17 A.M., LORETTA TO ANNIKA: 'I've only been gone from you for fifteen minutes, and I already miss you terribly. The FF will be at Camp David until after New Year's Day. I need the following from the ID you are using: full name, DOB, and SSN. I will clear you for 6 p.m. Heart emojis.'" The interrogator clarified. "And for the record the FF refers to First Family."

"TEXT MESSAGE DATED DECEMBER 25TH. 10:22 A.M., ANNIKA TO LORETTA: 'Babe, I miss you so much too. I wish I didn't have to work today but am counting the min. until we're together tonight. We will spend a very romantic Xmas together, our first of many. Please use: Jennifer Bartlett, 6-15-89, 577-66-8990.'"

Loretta blinked her eyes as tears formed.

"TEXT MESSAGE DATED DECEMBER 25TH, 10:29 A.M., LORETTA TO ANNIKA: 'All set, 6 p.m., come to NW gate, and I will come get you.'"

"TEXT MESSAGE DATED DECEMBER 25TH, 5:53 P.M., ANNIKA TO LORETTA: 'Walking across Lafayette Park now. I'll be at the gate in two min! XOXOXO.'"

"TEXT MESSAGE DATED DECEMBER 25TH, 5:53 P.M., LORETTA TO ANNIKA: 'Looking out the window. Can't wait! Heart emojis.'"

"TEXT MESSAGE DATED DECEMBER 26TH, 1:31 P.M., ANNIKA TO LORETTA: 'Babe, that was so special of you to have me come to the White House and spend Christmas night with you. I loved seeing the second floor. I loved even more our time in the giant Queens bathtub!'"

"TEXT MESSAGE DATED DECEMBER 26: 1:33 P.M., LORETTA TO ANNIKA: 'Let's meet tonight. Heart emojis.'"

Loretta broke down sobbing. *"Stop! Please, no more!"*

The interrogator announced, "Ms. Fitzgerald, we have fifty-one more pages of texts we can review with you. Shall we proceed?"

Loretta with her hands covering her face, sobbing: "*No*! Stop. I'll talk to you, but not like this! Please stop! I'll cooperate, fully. Just stop this. Please, I need help. Please!"

Chapter 46
8 p.m., Wednesday, March 11: The Swann House, Northwest DC

The freak snowstorm had left the city under eighteen to twenty inches of snow. With temps now in the upper fifties, the streets in Washington were being cleared in record time. Winston and Jonathan were surprised by how well-plowed 16th Street was as they arrived at the Swann House with little trouble.

Winston punched the code on the door, then held it open for Jonathan. They walked into the Swann House's living room, where Frank, Greg, and Brent were already seated and waiting. Winston nodded. "Gentlemen, I would like for all of you to meet Jonathan Cartwright, the assistant director of the ODNI and the lead investigator for the Blake assassination."

The men stood, and everyone shook hands.

Jonathan, taking the seat farthest away from the others, said, "Thanks for allowing me to join you tonight. Winston already knows this, but I will share with you also: We in the intelligence community have been very impressed with the work you all have done, and tonight, Winston and I will be sharing the latest developments from the past twenty-four hours."

Frank nodded. "Great! Before we start, Jonathan, we sorta have a tradition at these meetings: to have really good beer or really expensive scotch, and tonight is Brent's turn. Tell us what you got."

Brent opened the cooler, where twelve Two Hearted Ale bottles were on ice. "This is a great beer outta Kalamazoo, Michigan. I think you all will like it."

Greg stared at the cooler. "Well, I hope we don't like it too much. There's only twelve of 'em!"

Brent handed a bottle to each of them, then grabbed one for himself.

Jonathan smiled. "Nice. I'm sorry I missed the other meetings!"

Winston gestured at his friend. "Jonathan, please bring the group up to date."

"Absolutely. We had a very eventful state dinner last night. We have been monitoring Russian Foreign Agent Annika Antonov, who, by the way, was involved in the WMAL Towers caper the other night. She went on to make specific threats against Winston's family, and thanks to Sam Poundstone, her attempt to kidnap Winston's son and daughter-in-law was thwarted.

"Last night, Antonov attended the state dinner as Polish Deputy Ambassador Anna Zielinski. We had planned to apprehend her, but before I could be in a position to do so, she disabled a member of the Secret

Service, took his gun, then at gunpoint kidnapped Assistant Usher Loretta Fitzgerald…"

For the next thirty minutes, Jonathan and Winston provided the full recap of the prior evening's events. Greg, Frank, and Brent fired off questions, practically interrupting each other.

"Wow!" Greg finally exclaimed. "I had heard only fragments of the details from the guys I work with but not the entire story. Did you get Wes Chandler's service gun back? How is he? This is unbelievable!"

"Is Loretta okay?" asked Brent.

"Any clues as to Antonov? And her driver, they got away? And what was President Gentry's reaction?" Frank asked.

"So, was Scott Saras the watch commander?" asked Greg.

"Guys, slow down!" implored Winston. "We'll get to all of your questions. Please allow us to continue."

"Gentlemen, let us get through our brief," Jonathan seconded. "Then we'll take time and answer everything, and more." He paused and looked to each person for their nod of approval, then continued, "It was sometime after midnight, and I was in my west wing office. It took me a while to thaw out—I can't believe I didn't have frostbite. And guys, I have to admit, I relied on a taste or two of my Pierre Ferrand cognac."

"Oh, man. I love that stuff!" piped in Frank.

Frank, Greg, and Brent were motionless, staring at Jonathan, waiting for him to continue. Once the room went silent, he began. "Shortly before four this morning, we took Loretta into custody for questioning. Our initial interrogation was going nowhere. We then presented the evidence from Loretta's cell phone and suggested that the NSA and AT&T had provided additional details. Faced with this overwhelming evidence, Loretta finally cracked. She was very upset and lost control. After some time, she calmed down. Actually, she became stoic, almost trancelike, and began telling us all sorts of information.

"She admitted that she and Annika Antonov had been in a romantic relationship for the past eight months. At first, she had not known of any possible connection between the president's insulin and any deadly toxin. It wasn't until rumors of the toxin were released by the Associated Press that she began to speculate. Then last night, when, at 8 p.m., the White House released the detailed autopsy results, the media broke the story, and Loretta realized her greatest fear: that she may have somehow facilitated the toxin getting into the White House.

"She recalled finding two small bags on the ushers office desk and a note from the duty nurse saying it was for the president. Loretta wasn't sure if both bags were to go upstairs, so she looked inside. One contained a bottle of Mylanta, the other Lantus insulin, the brand the president used, so she was then certain and took both bags up to the private residence. The president was in the oval office and the first lady was doing an interview in the red room, so Loretta, as she had done in the past, placed the insulin in the small fridge in the president's bathroom and the other bag on the table where all envelopes for the president and first lady are placed.

"The more she thought about it, the more worried she became. Therefore, after the media broke the story, she remained at her desk the remainder of the evening, too fearful to venture away from the office. She told us that she and Antonov had come up with last night's plan to escape the White House, where Antonov used Loretta as a hostage to get away. Loretta told us their plan was to live together in Russia.

"We presented Loretta with the evidence that Annika and Patrick Sullivan had a brief affair and that Annika had used Patrick to get the gift of Polish sausage into the White House. Winston has since retrieved the sausage, and it's being tested. If tests reveal a toxin, then Patrick was likely the backup plan. Loretta said she has no idea why Patrick would have committed suicide, but she felt horribly guilty for breaking up with him the day he died, although she also admitted that she never believed that she and Patrick would ever have a serious relationship.

"We then shared our evidence that Annika had murdered Patrick and made it appear as a suicide. This, of course, upset Loretta even more, so we took a break while grief counselors worked with her. After we resumed, Loretta revealed that Annika had tried to lure assistant usher Jim Allen but failed. Loretta wasn't sure how, but she believed that Dr. Jenkins may have been involved, although she didn't know the details.

"Loretta now admits that during her relationship with Annika that she very likely may have unwittingly provided information that helped in the assassination, and as such, she admits that she was an accomplice and hopes that her now cooperating with us will lessen her sentence. By the way, the analysis of her phone communications revealed several instances during which she shared details about the first family's schedules as well as some descriptions of the physical attributes of the executive residence, which indeed make her an accomplice to the crime.

"We're still working to validate her statements. We have questions on certain things she said, and we need to fully comprehend all of her motives. But, men, this is essentially where we are at this point."

"Wait!" yelled Brent. "What about what they said about me? My laptop? And what about the vials that were in my pocket?"

Jonathan answered, "Brent, per Loretta, at Antonov's instruction, Loretta used your laptop to search the dark web in order to leave a digital footprint, and she admitted she placed the two vials that Antonov had given her into your suit jacket. Loretta had no idea what the vials were. She only did it to gain favor with Antonov."

Frank frowned. "Are you telling us that President Gentry and Wendy Wolf are clean in all this?"

Jonathan shook his head. "I don't know that I would go so far as to say 'clean.' We have a lot more to investigate, but as of this moment, I've shared with you what we know."

"So, what's your theory on motive?" asked Greg.

"At this point, we only know what Loretta has told us, and she seemed sincere in her claim that her inspiration and motivation were attributed to her love and dedication to Annika Antonov. She has asked to be exiled to Russia, where she expects Annika is waiting for her. I should note, we've reached out to our assets, and the Russians are aware of last night's events but thus far have not shared any communication on the matter. Our psychologist believes Antonov successfully exploited Loretta's need for companionship and intimacy and that Loretta knew Patrick would never seriously be interested in any type of long-term commitment. We also believe that Antonov, to prevent any possibilities of Patrick talking, killed him and made it look like a suicide."

Winston shook his head. "Personally, I have a hard time buying that Loretta did this all for Antonov. I can't help but think there's more to this than we know."

"I'm with you, Winston," Frank seconded. "I also think we need to understand Dr. Jenkins' role."

"So, Patrick and Loretta were in a relationship," Greg summarized, "while Loretta and Antonov were in a relationship, while Patrick and Antonov were in a relationship. Didn't we uncover that President Gentry had a relationship with Patrick and that President Gentry likely had something going with Dr. Jenkins? Okay, I need a whiteboard to try to diagram all this!"

Jonathan looked up from his iPhone. "Gentlemen, throughout the past ten days, the four of you have done outstanding detective work, which has been very helpful. And Brent, Winston, and I had hoped to meet with you earlier this afternoon, but we were taking naps." The men laughed. Jonathan continued, "So, Brent, we wanted to tell you, we have concrete evidence that there was an usher involved in President Blake's assassination—but the good news is that it's not you! Tomorrow morning, this group will have achieved its primary goal. I have just received confirmation that the attorney general has scheduled a press conference for 9 a.m., where he will announce all charges against Brent have been dropped."

Brent jumped up, pumped his fists in the air, and yelled "*Yes!*" while Winston, Frank, and Greg applauded.

Chapter 47
5 a.m., Thursday, March 12: The White House

Winston sat alone in the ushers office, slowly shaking his head. On his lap was the latest edition of *The Washington Post*, the front page of which offered the screaming headline:

"ASSISTANT USHER LORETTA FITZGERALD CHARGED AS ACCOMPLICE IN THE ASSASSINATION OF PRESIDENT BLAKE."

On the office TV, CNN was reporting nonstop on that very same story, including the details of the White House assistant to the chief usher's romantic liaison with a Russian foreign intelligence service agent, and that together they had planned and executed the murder of the president and Sous Chef Patrick Sullivan and the disappearance of Dr. Michael Jenkins. The CNN anchor also announced that later that morning, the attorney general planned to make the statement that Brenton Williams had been cleared of all charges. Meanwhile, Antonov remained at large while the FBI and intelligence community continued to work to apprehend her.

Epilogue
Eight months later

Jonathan Cartwright

Jonathan retired with honors. However, his retirement was staged; he is presently serving as the chief for the Department of Justice National Security Division's Office of Intelligence. From a remote, secure location, he leads a highly classified intelligence-gathering mission investigating the numerous touchpoints between President Gentry and Russian leadership. More and more the evidence has pointed to the leading theory that Elizabeth Gentry and Wendy Wolf began a relationship with the Russians while Gentry was a Navy pilot and involved in some of the design aspects for the F-35a Stealth fighter, which in probability led to how the Russians obtained key classified components to the design plans of the aircraft. As a quid pro quo, the Russians had likely committed to doing everything possible to get Gentry elected to office. Once she was elected to Congress, Gentry's meteoric rise in politics could be mostly attributed to her ability to persuade and attract voters.

Jonathan and his team obtained evidence that ties Russian oligarch Roman Mirov to Elizabeth Gentry; this relationship was with the Kremlin's backing. Cartwright and his team have diagramed the money trail starting from Gentry's days in the Navy and Mirov having recently contributed to President Gentry's reelection PAC.

Then-Senator Blake due to his well-publicized disdain of Russia and Communism, was seen by Russian leadership as the biggest threat to their plans for world domination. While the Russians for years had Blake in their crosshairs, their plans were accelerated by two significant developments: 1) Once Gentry became vice president, the Russians realized their good fortune since if Gentry were to become president, they would have significant influence and control of the White House; and 2) With the leak of the Blake coalition plan to liberate Crimea and Syria, the Russians felt they had no choice but to move forward using their foreign service agents, who successfully infiltrated the Blake White House and were able to take advantage of their relationship with Gentry. As a result of this, the Russian strategy to eliminate Blake was realized.

Loretta Fitzgerald

Three months after the results of the investigation were released to the public, and after a government-sanctioned psychiatric review, Loretta Fitzgerald was found not fit to stand trial, and due to the danger of self-harm she was committed to the criminally insane ward at Washington, DC's St. Elizabeth's hospital, where she now resides in confinement. Her legal team has started the process to file for an early release.

Annika Antonov

Annika Antonov remains at large; possibilities exist that Jonathan Cartwright mortally wounded her while she was trying to flee during the snowstorm, although no proof can be found. The consensus belief is that she is back in Russia.

President Elizabeth Gentry

President Gentry's popularity continues to soar, while she and her chief of staff Wendy Wolf work secretly on their "enemies list" to wreak havoc on any and all who oppose Gentry's efforts. Since becoming president, Gentry has effectively implemented a series of executive orders and modifications to various regulations that have resulted in a soaring stock market while achieving her clandestine goal of trade policy changes that have resulted in significant benefit to the Russians. Meanwhile some conspiracy theorists have started to push the idea of Gentry having ties to the Russians, but these so-called theorists have been derided as crackpots by mainstream media.

Admiral Curtis

The admiral was sent on an extended trip to the Mideast to help broker a peace deal.

Dr. Michael Jenkins

Dr. Michael Jenkins was never seen again and is feared dead.

Brent Williams

Given all the publicity surrounding the assassination, while being completely exonerated of any wrongdoing, former Assistant Usher Brent Williams would never again return to the White House. He is currently attending the University of Maryland, where he is working to earn a PhD in cybersecurity.

Frank Osborne

Attorney Frank Osborne jumped at the opportunity to take a few months off and successfully completed his second trans-Atlantic sailing tip. He is now working undercover with Jonathan Cartwright on the investigation into President Gentry.

Greg Leidner

Greg Leidner resigned from the Secret Service and is now on the West Coast serving as Sam Poundstone's right-hand man.

Bartholomew Winston

On his seventy-sixth birthday, August 1, Winston retired from the White House after fifty-one years of service. He sold his house in Bethesda and bought a condo in San Diego, not far from Win, Gwen, and their new twins. When he's not spending time with the grandkids, he's biking, writing his memoirs, drinking fine wines, and occasionally helping out with Jonathan Cartwright's investigation. Winston and former First Lady Beverly Blake have become close. She often visits, and they have plans to travel together.

The End